Serenity In The Storm

599

ENDURING FAITH SERIES

7

Serenity In The Storm

SUSAN FELDHAKE

ZondervanPublishingHouse

Grand Rapids, Michigan

A Division of HarperCollinsPublishers

Serenity in the Storm
Copyright © 1996 by Susan Feldhake

Requests for information should be addressed to:

ZondervanPublishingHouse
Grand Rapids, Michigan 49530

Library of Congress Cataloging-in-Publication Data

Feldhake, Susan C.
   Serenity in the storm / Susan Feldhake.
      p. cm. — (Enduring faith series; bk. 7)
   ISBN: 0-310-20261-2 (pbk.)
   1. Title. 2. Series: Feldhake, Susan C.. I. Enduring faith series; bk. 7.
PS3556.E4575S46 1996
813'.54—dc 20   95-52881
                                                  CIP

Edited by Robin Schmitt

Printed in the United States of America

96 97 98 99 00 01 02 /❖ DH/ 10 9 8 7 6 5 4 3 2 1

Serenity In The Storm

chapter
1

Watson, Illinois

LEMONT GARTNER LEANED on the gate after he'd closed up the chicken yard behind himself. He set the small wire bucket of eggs on the ground at his feet, then leaned on the fence and watched what was left of Lizzie Mathews' chickens glean kernels of golden corn from the gray, hard-packed, clay dirt.

Evening was falling, and one by one Lizzie's chickens, left in his care just as her children had been, gave up the search for choice morsels and hurried into the henhouse, fluffing their feathers as they went through the little swinging door that allowed them the freedom to come and go at will.

There was something comforting about being able to lock the hinged gate every twilight and know that the chickens would be safe until the coming dawn, when he'd unlatch the gate, prop it open, and let them have free run of the nearby environs.

The flock had diminished, as had the number of Lizzie's own children who'd remained under the roof after Lem came to live as guardian and caretaker of the brood. Without Lizzie around, they hadn't set any hens on a nest full of eggs, and what fowl remained in the flock were aging creatures but still good producers.

Too good for their present needs, Lemont thought, bending over to retrieve the bucket of eggs still warm from the nests.

His own appetite wasn't what it used to be, and nowadays eggs stacked up so that he had plenty to sell to neighbors for a bit of cash to squirrel away in a jar to present to Lizzie someday or to trade against supplies at the mercantile in Watson.

The strutting old rooster stood stock-still, glanced around his fenced-in domain, seemed to assure himself that no hens lollygagged in the enclosure. Then, with regal bearing, he slowly strutted into the henhouse, his tail feathers seeming to give a satisfied flourish as he ducked his crowned head to slip through the flap opening.

"Lucky feller," Lemont sighed. "You know where them you're in charge of be at."

Although it was a beautiful spring night, lightly scented with the wafting aroma of lilac blooms hanging heavy from Lizzie's prize bushes that clustered close around the cabin, Lemont's heart was burdened. He had never thought he'd see the day when he found himself envying a cocky old rooster. But he did.

As a bachelor, he hadn't known what it was to be responsible for others. After readily volunteering to move in with Lizzie's brood when she and Brad moved to Minnesota—they were following after Harmony and Lester Childers, two of Lizzie's children from a previous marriage, who'd decided to relocate to the northland—Lem had discovered what it was like to be a ma and pa to young'uns.

It wasn't an easy task.

One time, he'd heard Lizzie ruefully say, "Once a woman bears a young'un, she's a mama 'til the undertaker's replacin' blood with embalming fluid."

Lem couldn't help wryly smiling now at the memory. Lizzie had a way of cutting right to the chase, she did. And she laid everything out, flat as gravy on a platter. She never backed away from the truth, awful as it sometimes was. He'd considered the blood-to-embalming-fluid remark a grim way of phrasing it.

But as he'd learned what it was to eye the grandfather clock, doze in the chair past midnight, and wait for young Thad to return home from his scalawagging, Lem had realized what Lizzie meant.

The cabin had always seemed a rollicking place, so full of life, harmony, happiness, and activity when Brad and Lizzie and their combined youngsters had lived beneath its roof. Sheltered by towering old trees, it seemed lonely as a tomb tonight.

How the old neighborhood had changed, Lemont thought, suddenly feeling very, very old. But then, he wasn't a young man anymore, he reckoned. In fact, truth be told, he was way past his prime. Too old, likely, to be losing sleep over what the young'uns would choose to do with their lives.

But he'd promised Lizzie he would watch out for her children.

And he had.

Brad's girls had been easy to mind. They were good girls, smart, industrious, and ambitious. Brad's eldest, Miss Rosalie, had up and wed a nice young man in Effingham, a fine bloke from a good Christian family, and now she was efficiently keeping house in the county seat.

Misses Jayne and Linda had traveled off a bit farther, together, and had obtained employment as house girls, helping wealthy families in their dwellings in the Chicago area. It had been reassuring to learn from their letters that they saw each other frequently, had found a church where they fit well into the congregation, and were behaving themselves.

Miss Patricia had long seemed to cotton to the idea of schoolmarming, just as Miss Rosalie had done before she married and moved off, hoping to form the minds and behaviors of her own children. When Miss Rosalie had wed, the community was in need of a teacher—and Miss Patricia had exactingly filled the bill.

Lemont hadn't realized how accustomed he'd grown to having Lizzie's children around until Miss Rosalie married, Misses Linda and Jayne moved out not long afterward, and then—almost before Lem had adjusted to their absence—Miss Patricia went to live in the teacherage.

That had left Lem with only Thad Childers to tend.

"Oh, Thad ... Thad ... Thad," Lemont sighed in a weary whisper as he trudged through the darkening gloom to the cozy cabin. "Where are you? And what on earth are you up to?"

In recent weeks, he had learned not to wait up until Thad arrived home safe and sound. Lemont had spent entirely too many nights in the rocking chair near the hearth and then awakened with a start to find that it was dawn, and the rheumatiz in his back complained horribly throughout the new day.

Too many nights, Thad had failed to come home a'tall, and Lemont came to realize that the fact that he waited up for Lizzie's youngest son and hoped that he would hie on home was no guarantee that the boy would comply.

"My, how the boy's changed," Lemont sighed miserably as he let himself into the cabin. The screen door banged shut behind him, the sound seeming to echo off cavernous walls, making the dwelling seem even larger and more lonely than ever before.

He set the bucket of eggs on the countertop, then found the matches and lit the coal oil lamp in the middle of the dining room table and quickly touched the flame to another kerosene lamp resting in an ornate bracket high on the wall.

The light was cozy and comforting, chasing away the

gloomy darkness that had overshadowed the world outside the cabin walls. Through the open window came a cool evening breeze and the plaintive cry of a whippoorwill.

From force of habit, Lemont took down the Good Book from the mantel and seated himself to read, bent over the dining-room table, but as had happened in recent weeks, his thoughts wandered horribly. Unable to concentrate fully on Scripture, he found his mind consumed with worry.

He knew he wasn't the only one.

But he felt the most responsible. After all, it had been he who'd given his word to Lizzie and Brad Mathews that he'd watch their children and oversee their needs and behaviors as zealously as the couple themselves could. Perhaps, being a bachelor, he'd been a little naive about knowing what he'd bit off to chew, and deep down he didn't think Lizzie would blame him or hold the situation against him.

But Lemont Gartner was helpless not to blame himself.

Had he missed telling signs?

Could the situation have been stopped if he'd been more aware?

Might things have worked out differently if he'd understood early on the direction in which things were progressing and asked a younger man, like Seth Wyatt or Rory Preston, to intervene and have a talk with Thad, speak some sense into him?

"Maybe," Lemont thought, giving up and replacing his marker in the text of his worn, black Bible. "But that boy's a hardheaded 'un. Doubt he'd have listened to anyone. Mayhap not even his ma."

When Lemont had volunteered to serve as a guardian to Brad and Lizzie's children, he hadn't thought off into the distant future. The neighborhood young'uns had always been such good children, upright, obedient, ethical, God loving, that he'd never dreamed problems could arise, never anticipated a moment's trouble.

And generally that's what he'd been blessed with—serenity and harmony—until Thad reached his majority.

"I should've seen it comin'," Lemont whispered wretchedly. "Oh God, how could I have been so blind? The handwritin', it was on the wall since Thaddie was a young whippersnapper. Iffen I'd just looked. But there ain't none so blind as those who won't see."

Lem had known the entire family as they'd grown up. Quiet, decent, hardworking Maylon, the Childers' adopted son, so obedient and honest. He'd died young, a victim of smallpox. And Lester. There was a youth to be proud to know. Had the selfsame traits that made Maylon Childers such a joy to know—but had more of a zesty outlook, so he was easier to converse with and get to know than Maylon, who kept his own counsel except when he chose to confide in Lizzie.

Ah, but Thad. He'd always been a wild one. Hobbling around with sprains from some daredevil escapade, sporting bandages from close encounters with barbed wire fences and bramble bushes as he scrabbled through life. Stuck with his nose in the corner in disgrace more times than Lemont had really remained conscious of. And always trying to convince the older children to abandon their choring and escape with him into fun and games, be it playing out imaginative rough riding from the wild and rowdy West or pretending to be pirates on the high seas.

Lemont, like no doubt everyone else who'd watched Thad grow up, had figured he'd mature beyond such visions of wanderlust and a desire to seek out adventurous living. But that hadn't been the case.

A good-looking lad—too handsome for his own health,

Lemont had idly concluded recently—Thad was a hard-laboring if uninspired worker during the daytime hours, but his evenings and weekends, he played the dandy. And played the part entirely too well to suit Lemont. And eventually Seth—and even Rory, who'd had his own walk on the wild side, so he hadn't felt he had much room to talk until Thad seemed to get totally out of hand—spoke to him.

By then it was too late.

Instead of listening to Seth and his Uncle Rory, considering what they had to say and giving thought that maybe his new behaviors needed mending, Thad had been defiant. Angry. Emboldened with his newfound and well-funded independence, he had left home.

Lizzie had done nothing if not instill thrift in her children, and before the unsettling change in Thad, he'd worked hard, banked his funds, and been prospering.

Now Lemont shuddered when he considered how fast Thad could run through the income that he'd earned by the sweat of his brow and that he was likely frittering away in the dens of iniquity in Effingham, wasting small fortunes on good times, girls, and—unless Lemont missed his sorry guess—whiskey.

What, oh what, was he going to do? Lemont fretted.

Seth had sadly told him there wasn't much he could do, just pray, wait, and entrust Thad to the Lord.

Rory had sighed and offered basically the same suggestion, quietly admitting that nothing, and no one, could've stopped him when he temporarily abandoned the way of his raising to sample worldly delights and wanton ways.

"Some of us have to learn the difficult way, you know," Rory admitted. "Sometimes it ain't pretty, and folks harm themselves and do injury to others. But look at me! I have a wonderful Christian wife, lovely children, and a good life—because the Lord knew he had a plan for me even if I had some pretty recalcitrant notions of my own there for a while."

"Well . . . I worry," Lemont admitted.

"We all do," Rory agreed. "All we can do is pray. And remember that as much as we love 'n care about Thad, the Lord cares and loves him way, way more."

That had comforted Lemont for a few days.

His heart had almost been at ease when Thad had returned home. So relieved was Lemont to have him safely under the roof, going to work regularly, that he hoped that perhaps Thad's wild episodes were behind them. And so tense was the elderly bachelor that he didn't raise the issue of where Thad had been or what he'd been doing to occupy his time. Too great had been his fear that it would shatter the uneasy serenity, and the situation would go from bad to worse.

Too late Lemont realized that his efforts to be genial and gracious, hoping for good, had been a futile endeavor.

Lemont hated to consult the calendar that mocked him from the place where it was tacked to the kitchen wall, for Thad Childers had now been gone for five days. No one had seen nary hide nor hair of him, and no word had arrived—good, bad, or indifferent.

As Lemont sat at the table, nursing a cooling cup of coffee, ruminating, his eyes fell on the plump envelope that leaned against the base of the coal oil lamp centered on the checkered oilcloth that protected Lizzie's round oak table.

He'd taken the missive with him to church services the preceding Sunday, and those who'd known Brad and Lizzie passed the letter around to read about their new life in Minnesota and learn how Harmony was doing and Lester and his new bride, a young woman called Joy.

Lizzie was a good and loyal correspondent, and Lemont was aware that he himself had been considered pretty handy with pen, ink, and foolscap, too. It had always made him feel good to write to Lizzie and Brad, to send off newsy and detailed correspondence to them and anticipate the arrival of their response.

Now he couldn't bring himself to even write to Lizzie and Brad, although he knew that he couldn't postpone the action much longer. It had been difficult to write when he'd last taken pen in hand.

For months now it had been easy to pass along the news, as he was aware of it, of all the people in the community that he knew Lizzie and Brad would expect to hear about, and it was pleasant enough to share what he'd heard from Misses Rosalie, Jayne, Linda, and Patricia.

In the past, he'd always included plenty about how Thad was doing and what he was up to. Sometimes, even Thad would take a moment before he retired in the evening and scrawl a few lines to his mother and stepfather.

But it seemed like months since that had been the case, although surely, Lemont consoled himself, it hadn't been that long. Or had it?

All Lemont knew was that he felt terrible keeping from Lizzie what the reality was. He sometimes felt that a half-truth was worse than an outright lie. And the last time he'd penned a missive to Lizzie and Brad, he'd chronicled the goings-on of their other children. Knowing that he couldn't trouble Lizzie with the difficult situation, with her so far away and all, he'd settled for simply writing a rather innocuous line regarding Thad: "And Thad's just Thad. Same as always."

He'd at least managed to mention him in the letter. But Lemont had refrained from adding, "And worse than ever," for fear that Lizzie would know things weren't going well. Weren't going well at all.

With a gesture of grim determination, Lemont drained the coffee from his cup, arose to get himself a steaming hot mug, then located the foolscap, pen, ink, and he sat down to force himself to write to the new manager of the Grant Hotel in Minnesota, who'd been like a daughter to him, and her young'uns like the grandchildren he'd never had.

Dear Brad and Lizzie, Lemont wrote in a neat but somewhat archaic hand. *I hope that this finds you well. Your lilacs are a treasure for the eye to behold, and a pleasure for the nose as well....*

On and on Lemont wrote until he had a decently long letter, brimming with news. He stared at the pages, then quickly folded them, sealed them in an envelope, affixed a stamp from the little glass whatnot container in the cabinet, took a lantern, and walked the letter to the mailbox, which was a skip and a hop from the dinner bell's location at the end of a short lane.

He wanted to post it before he could lose heart or give in and share the alarming truth: that Thad was away—and no one had any idea where he'd gone!

Lemont hoped for the best and felt that the letter, while perhaps a bit deceitful on his part, was merely buying him time. He prayed that Thad would return. And if and when the young man did—Lemont was going to marshal forces with Seth and Rory and they were going to exhort him good and proper.

In the meantime, Lemont hoped that when Lizzie read the letter that he had just dispatched on the journey to its faraway destination, she would be so inundated with news of kith and kin that she would fail to even notice that there'd been not one mention of Thad.

Maybe it was for the best to do it that way, Lemont comforted himself. After all, he'd grown up with his own mama cautioning him, "If you can't say something nice—then don't say anything at all!"

And lately there seemed nothing good to say about Thad.

Williams, Minnesota

Lizzie's heart was so heavy with burdensome yet unidentifiable concerns that she felt as if she were going to jump plumb out of her skin.

She couldn't remember ever feeling quite like she had in the past days—weeks, actually—and with the unfamiliarity of the emotions and thoughts that sometimes overwhelmed her, she wondered if now that she was heading into her middle years, all that was the matter with her was what she'd heard her mother and other matrons whisper about: *a woman's change.*

That had to be it, she comforted herself, because everything was well in her world, and there was no plausible explanation for the dark, frightening, premonitory feelings she had of desperation and disaster ahead.

Lizzie was startled when tears leaped to her eyes—hot, copious, and totally beyond her control.

She chewed her lip—hard—and tried to concentrate on that pain so that she could gain control of her thoughts and emotions. The harder she tried not to cry, the faster her tears ran as she silently wept while her strong hands rhythmically kneaded the bread dough destined to be hot dinner rolls for the evening's diners at the Grant Hotel.

She'd been so immersed in her thoughts—so engrossed in the instinctive actions of years baking breads and rolls—she hadn't been aware of Brad's entrance.

She didn't even know he was in the kitchen, until he was

right beside her, had reached out to touch her shoulder, and had quietly inquired, "Liz darlin', what's *wrong*? Why're you—"

At his touch, Lizzie recoiled as if she'd been jabbed by a hot stove poker. Her pulse galloped to an unpleasant gait, and she let out a helpless, shrill squawk of alarm.

"Brad Mathews, you scared the livin' starch out o' me!" Lizzie cried. "Don't you ever, ever, ever, ever, *ever* do that to me again!"

"Oh my heavens. . . ." A startled Brad Mathews regarded his ordinarily serene and even-tempered wife. "What on earth is goin' on? Lizzie, talk to me! What is it? Tell me!"

"I don't know what to say!" she bawled.

"Whatever's riling you, Liz, I want to help you deal with it. Now, tell me what's wrong."

"Nothing," she sniffed and tried to turn back to her labor. Brad refused to let her do so.

"Nothing?!" he said, his tone softly mocking. His gesture took in the tears' ravagement. "You're tellin' me that *nothing* is wrong?"

"Nothing's wrong," Lizzie whimpered, unable to meet his eyes. "Oh drat, mayhap *everything's* wrong."

"Everything?" Brad gently chided, drawing his wife into his arms, affectionately kissing the crown of her hair, giving her an amused little squeeze. He knew his wife's penchant for spirited exaggerations.

"All right . . . not everything."

"But something?" Brad coaxed.

"Oh, Brad," Lizzie whimpered, clinging to him. "*Something*. I don't know *what,* but I have this horrible, prickly-like, dark-o'-the-night sensation that something's goshawful *wrong*. And I don't know what it *is* so's I can do somethin' about it."

Brad regarded his logic-oriented, horse-sense-solid wife.

"It's not like you to take on like this."

"I know it," Lizzie said, gently extricating herself from his embrace, dabbing at her reddened eyes with a corner of her apron. "I know it ain't. Maybe it's that I'm . . . well . . . gettin' to be an . . . older woman."

"Well . . . maybe," Brad said carefully, instantly understanding the circumstances toward which she hinted. "But . . ."

There was doubt in his tone.

And tension in the silence that enveloped them.

Brad finally cleared his throat when it was clear Lizzie was going to say no more unless he pried it out of her.

"I know you, Liz, and you don't take on so over no reason. There's *something* that's upset you. And I want you to tell me what it is."

Lizzie faced him and then stared at him a long moment.

"You ain't even noticed, have you? You truly ain't even *noticed!*"

"Noticed *what?*" Brad asked, a hint of frustration mingled with fear entering his voice as his mind clawed back over recent weeks. He tried to consider what possibly could've been upsetting his wife, that he'd been so oblivious to that he hadn't even noticed what was clearly too evident to his keen-eyed, sharp-minded wife.

"The change in Lemont's letters," Lizzie sighed, the horrible truth leaving her feeling totally deflated as the words seemed to oppressively hang in the very air.

"I . . . uh . . . can't say that I have," Brad admitted. "I know that they've been newsy. Perhaps a bit more infrequent in arrivin'. But he's pro'bly kept a mite busier with Rosalie married and livin' in Effingham, Jayne and Linda in Chicago, and Patty off at the teacherage. With just him 'n Thad to see to the place—"

"That's what's been plaguin' me," Lizzie said.

"They can handle it. Lem's a steady worker, even iffen he's agin' like we all are. But Thad's a young gent, a hard worker, 'n—"

Lizzie was scrambling through a cubbyhole in a cabinet where she kept Lemont's letters so that they were handy to share with Lester, Harmony, and Alton Wheeler's adult daughters, Marissa and Molly, who also hungered for news of the folks from their old home area.

"Thad used to write a few lines every now 'n again. Brad, it's been *months* since the boy took time to pick up a pen and scribble even a few words to his fam'bly up here. And Lemont—he used to write a lot about Thad's comin's and goin's. Kept us filled in—real proud-like of how Thaddie was doin'."

"Yeah . . . I know that," Brad said.

"It's *stopped!*" Lizzie pointed out, her voice suddenly becoming a tear-choked bawl. "About the same time these horrible, crawly sensations of impending no-good began to plague me. Lo 'n behold iffen it don't exactingly coincide with when I looked back over some o' Lem's letters and saw a pattern developing."

"You're right, Liz. I'm sorry I didn't notice. You must've been beside yourself, aware and keepin' it all to yourself."

"I didn't want to worry y'all," Lizzie mumbled. "It was bad enough worryin' as I have been myself—and I hope 'n pray that it's *needlessly*—'thout havin' the rest of you rackin' your wits over what might be goin' on a thousand miles away, too!"

"Oh, Liz," Brad whispered, sudden worry tingeing his tone.

"Just look at this last letter," Lizzie said, tearing the

22

foolscap, so hasty was she in unsheathing a letter from its envelope and finding the passage. "'Thad's just Thad. Same as always.' Unquote." Lizzie's eyes sought and searched Brad's. "I don't like that. Cain't even tell you exactly why—but I don't."

"We're about due to hear from Lemont any day now," Brad said. "Maybe we'll get a letter brimmin' with news from Lemont and, Lord willin', even a bit written by Thad himself."

"Maybe we'll hear—maybe we won't," Lizzie said in a helpless, grim tone. "Look at how Lem's letters have gotten to be spaced out." Lizzie shuffled through the thick stack of letters, calling out smudgy postmark dates, proof perfect that Lemont had ceased writing as regular as clockwork. "Oh, Brad, what're we going to do?" Lizzie lamented.

"I don't know," Brad said. "Iffen it'll make you feel better, we could telegraph Illinois and make inquiries."

"No!" Lizzie quickly countered. "Th—that's plumb silly and expensive. And if there ain't nothin' wrong, it'll rile and upset the folks to get a telegram askin' what's goin' on. Lem's doin' the best he can, I know that. Far be it from me to make an elderly gent who's volunteered to take on the load he has think he ain't performin' to our satisfaction." Lizzie drew in a deep breath, squared her shoulders, and her chin grew resolute.

"We'll just wait."

"And pray," Brad reminded. He drew Lizzie into his arms, and she sagged against him, drawing strength from him, awash in weakness moments before she required all of her strength to put on a dinner hour like the fine folks in Williams had come to expect.

"Mayhap tomorrow there'll be mail," Lizzie said. "Train's due then."

"Likely there will be," Brad agreed.

"'Course there will," Lizzie said, as if trying to convince herself of the fact. "Instead of raggin' about others' lack o' letters, what I really need to do is sit down tonight and jot off a few letters o' my own. Mayhap iffen I write one 'specially to Thad, it'll encourage him to pick up a pen 'n write his ol' ma."

"Reckon he can still lift a pen," Brad teased. "Lem ain't mentioned him havin' a broken arm, after all." But the light thought quickly became a frown when he realized exactly what he'd said.

Despair visited Lizzie anew.

"I'd be plumb happy with a broken arm," she sighed under her breath. "Better that than him traipsing off and discoverin' what it is to have a broken life."

chapter
2

Effingham, Illinois

THAD CHILDERS FELT lighthearted, like a young man on holiday, he supposed, although his own financially limited farming family had never taken a vacation or holiday away from the land in all the years that he could remember. The church basket socials and local fairs they'd attended for a day's respite from their labors really didn't count—enjoyable as those occasions had been.

Over the years, Thad had known good times around the Effingham area, but nothing he'd experienced previously could compare with the heady elation he felt as he climbed aboard the railroad coach, his pockets lined with funds he'd saved from his job with Seth Wyatt's lumbering concern, and fully realized that he was free and unencumbered and poised to explore the world that he knew was out there, but had never seen for himself.

He felt a strange mix of thrilling trepidation as he boarded the train. He was gripped with a hollow, lonely terror at the idea of perhaps never seeing his kinfolk again and at the knowledge that he was leaving behind all that was familiar, quite comfortable, but oh so boring.

Simultaneously Thad experienced eagerness to more fully savor the freedoms that he'd already tasted. His determination to escape kith and kin, although fleetingly overshadowed by concern for the future, was a resolve quickly renewed by anger, frustration, and the realization that no one ever seemed to understand him or care about how *he* felt.

To a one, they all seemed to think that they knew exactly what he should do in life. Lately it seemed they'd seldom tired of yammering at him, even on occasion shaking the Good Book in his face for emphasis. But how could they know so well what Thad Childers should do—when Thad himself had no orderly ideas? When he possessed only this burning longing deep within him to do something different from what he'd always known?

Having reached his majority several months earlier, Thad was aware he needed no one's formal permission to pull up stakes. His ma and Brad had struck out to begin a new life in Minnesota in their middle years. Harmony had a career as a nurse. And Lester had given up logging to turn his hand at something he found more fulfilling—and gained a lovely wife in the process. So why shouldn't Thad, as a man with his prime visible upon the horizon, be extended the same choice to seek change?

At the thought of his ma, Brad, and his siblings, Thad felt a sudden lump of nostalgic homesickness sweep over him. A moment later he considered that perhaps in his travels he'd just hie on up to Minnesota and pay a call on his kinfolk.

Almost as soon as the idea occurred to him, he discarded it, for he concluded that very likely Lemont or Seth's wife, Katie, or *someone* would have already written a tattletale letter to his ma. And while he knew that she'd probably always await him with open arms, her welcoming hugs might be accompanied by hard words or exhortation.

Of course, there was still Harmony . . . and Lester. . . .

"All aboooooooard!" the conductor bellowed, interrupting Thad's poignant thoughts.

A tingle rippled through him when, with a roar, huff, and a bellow of its whistle, the train gave a jolt. The steel wheels clashed against the rails, grating, screeching, and then the conveyance began to roll forward—heading west—destination St. Louis, Missouri, the Gateway City, through which thousands upon thousands had passed as they abandoned the eastern states and sought to find their fortunes in the open and untamed West.

At that instant, Thad fully realized it was the first time that he'd progressed beyond the Effingham county line, and momentarily he felt unnerved, almost like a small boy suddenly wanting to cling to his ma's skirts for safety. He drew himself up short at that idea and vowed that he would face the world as the man that his very age declared him to be. He knew he had a good brain, decent schooling, a strong body, looks handsome enough that he'd turned the girls' heads on the streets of Watson, and even in much bigger Effingham.

"I'll do all right in this ol' world!" he vowed under his breath. "Ma says that you can learn a lot by people watchin' 'n can pick up good manners by seein' how other folkses do things."

He shied away from the memory that his ma had also pointed out that you could learn a lot about how *not* to behave by watching those in the world, too.

A few miles west of Effingham, Thad realized how tense he'd been when he felt his spine sag against the plush maroon seats of the coach. Already he'd adjusted to the rocking of the train on the rails, a comforting, lilting motion that he thought was probably how a babe in its mother's arms felt as an old oaken rocker creaked near the hearth.

His nameless fears fled and promise filled his heart as he

saw how landmarks that had been familiar from overland trails looked so different from a worldview of the rail bed that cut through the townships on a cross-country route.

There would be a lot of sights to see between the central-Illinois county seat and the bright lights of the big city that spread out along the banks of the mighty Mississippi River and invaded the land miles to the west. He'd never been to St. Louis, which was one of the biggest cities in the nation, but already he knew a little bit of what to expect. It was a bustling, busy, business-oriented area where barges, river-boats, and paddle wheelers plied the murky, fast-moving water that made a natural route from northern Minnesota to the Gulf of Mexico.

The late Alton Wheeler, who'd been the same as a grandpa to Thad and his siblings, had known the place well as a young man and had occasionally spoken of those times even long after he made the Salt Creek area in Watson his permanent home.

Alton had said that in St. Louis, where there was a desire, there was a way to fulfill it. If a man wanted to work, he could find a job. If a man didn't especially feel inclined to laboring, he could still find a way to make an easy, soft living by being such as a doorman in a fancy-Dan hotel or signing on to drive around the city a carriage that rich folks could hire to take them home when they tired of walking. No doubt, there were so many easy jobs that a man intent on choosing what would be the best, most fun, and highest paying to turn his hand at could feel like a child in a candy store.

Thad looked at the hard calluses on his tanned hands. Heavens, the days he'd spent broiling beneath the sun, the humid air pressing in around him like warm, wet wool until there seemed no escaping its sultry presence! He'd had enough of *that*. And knowing what it was to go to bed with a backache that didn't ease, even with the application of burning, tingling linament, resigned that you were destined to wake up with the same grinding ache in your spine come morning.

He wanted better for himself. And the best in life was what he vowed he'd have.

Before Thad had spent enough time on the noisy, sooty train to take him halfway to St. Louis, he knew that certain things were in order as soon as he arrived. New clothes!

He was mortifyingly aware, when he saw wealthy folks board the train en route at Vandalia—which had been the state capital until that honor was transferred north to Springfield—that his garments immediately labeled him for what he was: an unsophisticated, country-bumpkin hayseed!

Thad studied the fine frocks that the young misses and matrons wore, and then eyed the raiments of the gentlemen who accompanied them. He'd know what to look for as soon as he could locate a good haberdashery! And he felt smug knowing that he'd cut as fine a figure in the luxurious clothing as any of these menfolk.

Lizzie's children had grown up hearing their ma quote, "A fool and his money are soon parted." Even though he had a sizable wad of cash secreted away, Thad wasn't going to waste a cent of it. His inborn and long-trained sense of thrift would no doubt stand him in good stead in the city. If he watched his money, he wouldn't have to look for a job immediately. He could even be choosy about when and where he went to work and hold out for the best and most interesting—and easiest—position to be found.

It was very late, and Thad was extremely tired, when the train ground into Union Station in downtown St. Louis. The locomotive had clattered and chugged across the railroad bridge that spanned the Mississippi River, causing Thad to momentarily hold his breath in alarm at how elevated they were above the wide waterway, which rippled with deep, powerful currents.

He had no possessions with him except for the clothes on his back and the money on his person. He hadn't taken time to pick through any mementos from home. He hadn't wanted to be burdened, and he'd felt that those who were prone to poking their noses into his business might be quicker to set out in search of him and bring him to bay like a truant schoolboy if they had as evidence the fact that his Bible and a few other highly personal items were missing.

Easing the kinks from his back as he arose from the plush seat and let womenfolk exit the conveyance ahead of him, Thad followed the throng of people out into the mayhem in the station.

He looked around, got his bearings, knew that Union Station was no haven and that he'd have to find lodging for the night or perhaps longer, and so made his way to the street.

The first friendly face he saw, Thad politely asked directions to a hotel that was clean and affordable. Three blocks away from the train station, he entered the lobby of a massive structure that made the Benwood Hotel in Effingham look like a country lean-to by comparison.

Within minutes, he'd tendered money for one night, accepted possession of the key, and then made his way up several flights of plush, durably carpeted stairs to a clean room with nearby lavatory facilities.

"This is livin'!" Thad said, after taking a warm bath and returning to his room and the comfortable bed.

Outside his window, gas lamps gave the streets a glow almost bright as daytime. In Watson—even Effingham— people "went to bed with the chickens," his ma had said.

Thad realized that in St. Louis, if you looked in the right places, there were things to do, places to go, and people to meet at all hours of the night and day.

Well, with the coming dawn, he was going to go right out and look the place over and keep an eye out for aspects that'd be to his personal liking.

As Thad leaned up to blow out the lamp beside his cozy bed, he saw a black Gideon Bible, which looked pristine and untouched. He was tempted to reach for it. Reaching for the Good Book at home had over the months become an infrequent action instead of a nightly habit. He'd left his own Bible behind. And for that night, he was too tired to borrow a communal book of Scripture left there for the convenience of whatever transient types might inhabit the room.

"Maybe tomorrow," he sighed as he rolled over and got comfortable.

In the morning as he was dressing and bringing order to his quarters so that the hotel maid wouldn't have to work overly much, on impulse he stashed the Gideon Bible in the chunky little drawer of the nightstand. With it out of sight, it was better out of mind.

After taking a look at himself in the fine beveled mirror on the solid-oak bureau, Thad slicked his burnished brown hair one last time, then, liking what he saw, he impulsively winked at himself, grinned, left the pleasant hotel room with quick strides, and eagerly set out to conquer new worlds.

Williams, Minnesota

Beads of sweat collected to form rivulets and run downward, trickling into the corners of Billy LeFave's eyes as he carefully repaired the chinking of the little log church in Williams.

Already his eyes had been stinging, not from the sweat but

from the scarcely pent tears of joy that had threatened to spill from his eyes when he considered the myriad twists and turns in his life, and the course of events that had taken him right to where he was at this moment in time.

A moment in time that he knew in his heart had been ordained for him by the Lord when he'd laid the very foundations of the universe.

Nowadays, with his gunshot wounds healed, Billy lived in quarters at the Grant Hotel, which was being managed by Lizzie and Brad Mathews in the absence of the actual owner, Rose Grant Ames, who'd wed her childhood sweetheart, Homer—now a middle-aged banker—when she'd been widowed midwinter past.

No one had known where Mr. Grant disappeared to.

His comings and goings had been of little interest to the townspeople, actually, for they'd been as leery of him as they were warmly welcoming of Rose, upon whom the entire boomtown lumbering village doted.

The mystery was solved when, following a blizzard, his remains had been unceremoniously plowed from their resting place by the cowcatcher apparatus of a slowly chugging train engine as it eased into town, conquering drifts laid down beneath the force of a fierce northern winter blizzard. Her drunken, ne'er-do-well husband had fallen unconscious and had frozen to death on the tracks of the Canadian National Railroad.

Homer Ames, her new husband, had taken her off to Fargo, North Dakota, with him. But Rose had promised that they would return!

"You've got a 'far go' ahead of you," Lizzie had teased Rose as the two women exchanged good-byes at the train station. "But you'll always be near to our hearts and close as our regular prayer remembrances."

"Home is where the heart is — and even though my beloved is spiriting me away from these parts, it'll always be home to me, for so much of my heart'll remain with y'all."

Home. . . .

Privately, Billy LeFave thought of the church building upon which he worked in the summer heat as his "home away from home." He loved laboring around the church grounds and spent random spare moments there, doing chores or, if nothing remained to be attended to, just sitting beneath the cool, pungent boughs of a pine tree, meditating.

At the church building, he always felt a sense of serenity and the assurance of belonging that he'd never entertained anywhere else on God's green earth.

And he'd known more than just the northern Minnesota area of the Midwest. He'd been with his folks, whom he scarcely remembered, as they went across Iowa and into the Dakota region. After that, life was a blur of cruel realities, and the harsh existence of having been rescued from death by two swarthy, filthy trappers who'd found his slain folks bloating in the sun, massacred by a band of Sioux.

Taken along with the trappers, used as a beast of burden and an article of pleasure, the young boy, scarcely more than a tot, found himself envying his parents their solitude in death, for he despised what had become his life.

But that was then. This was *now*—and William LeFave, whose coloring bespoke his French heritage, considered himself the happiest of men. The Lord had redeemed him—and Harmony Childers loved him!

Billy's stomach rumbled, causing him to realize just how famished he was. When he'd arisen at dawn to begin his day, butterflies had batted around in his stomach each time he considered what plans lay ahead, Lord willing, until he felt almost plumb gaggy with the nervous excitement and much too keyed up to eat.

Ordinarily a hearty eater, one who'd appreciated Rose Ames' vittles and did justice to Lizzie Mathews' culinary talents, Billy's inability to eat had piqued the concern of Harmony's mother.

Lizzie had exited the kitchen, patting her ginger brown hair, which was shot through with strands of silver, away from her face, flushed from the kitchen's heat.

"What's the matter with you this mornin', son?" she'd inquired, gesturing toward his nearly untouched plate and a mug of coffee that was filled to the brim and cooled to the point where no steam wafted upward. "Ain't ya feelin' quite pert today? Tell me what's wrong—and I'll see iffen I ain't got a nostrum to put a little spark in your spirit and zip in your veins. Or iffen I can't, surely Dr. Marc can. He was askin' after you, by the way."

Billy had glanced up and given a quick smile. "I'm fine. Just fine," he'd said, perhaps a bit too rapidly to suit Lizzie.

She'd given him an assessing stare, and without so much as a by-your-leave and as if he were a small boy instead of an adult man, she'd laid a flour-smudged hand across his brow, seeking a fever.

"Pardon me, Will, for makin' the observation, but you don't look fine, though you ain't feverish. You just look sort of . . . sort of . . ."—Lizzie, ordinarily never at a loss for words, had seemed to be picking through her country-girl vocabulary for tactful words—"well . . . perhaps a mite bit . . . flighty . . . on edge . . . like a long-tailed tabby cat in a parlor full of solid-walnut rockin' chairs."

Billy hadn't been able to keep from chuckling. That was

Lizzie. Direct and always to the point. Harmony, so much like her ma, wasn't quite so brusque.

Lizzie hadn't joined him in his laughter.

"You'd best be tellin' me, William LeFave, or I'll worm it out of you one way or t'other. Is something wrong?" Lizzie had demanded to know.

Wrong?! Billy thought. *Hardly!*

If anything, his life had become so very right that at times he could scarcely stand it. It almost frightened him, this perfection that had come so quickly. Suddenly there'd been the right combination of people and events to add up to the sum total of his new existence—found by claiming the Lord as his Savior and Redeemer.

What scared him was the spectre that as quickly as his horror-story life had become a heady dream come true, it might just as rapidly evolve to become a nightmare again.

A few times Billy, feeling oddly overcome with emotions, had dared to voice his fears to someone in his new church family. Even as he'd spoken, there was a prideful part of him that wished he could keep his mouth shut and not bare his deepest concerns—but he'd found himself doing it and had known relief in the confidant's understanding and counsel.

The menfolk he'd talked to—Lester and Brad—had nodded thoughtfully, then spoken in tones taciturn and direct.

"Nothin's going to happen that the Lord don't know about."

"If somethin' bad takes place, Billy, know that God's allowin' it—and for your eventual betterment and to serve a solid purpose in his plan."

"Read the Book of Job. That may help ya to understand."

"And then, you've gotta keep in mind that some things is

meant to be a secret unto the Lord. Not for our understanding in this lifetime."

"Life's an ongoin' lesson," Lizzie, who'd approached the knot of menfolk, had chimed in. "Guess it's the stubbornness of human nature, but all too often it seems we're more prone to learning from a harsh lesson than we are a happy one."

Billy realized that the men he'd come to know well seemed to understand whereof he spoke. And from Lizzie's remarks, he sensed that the womenfolk did, too. They understood.

But, he wondered as another wheel of butterflies flitted around in his innards, had there been any man—ever—who at the selfsame time had felt so happily hopeful yet also so helplessly despairing at the prospect of asking the woman he loved to be his bride?!

Billy paused his labors, eased a kink from the small of his back, and glanced at the sun that had beat down until he'd been forced to abandon his shirt in order to better capture the summer day's cooling breeze.

Sweat gave his coppery tan skin a sleek sheen that was marred only by the still-pink scars remaining from the wounds suffered in an altercation at the Black Diamond, Williams' saloon. That night, instead of being left to die in the sawdust outside the saloon entrance, he had been carried by lumberjacks to the town's brand-new infirmary building and placed into the care of Dr. Marc Wellingham and his pretty nurse, Harmony.

Dr. Wellingham saw to it that he lived.

Harmony, without realizing it, had taught him how to love. . . .

Harmony!

At the mere thought of her name, quickly followed by the memory of her fluffy blond hair, her sweet, creamy-skinned face, and her lithe but pleasingly voluptuous figure, Billy's pulse escalated to a melodious beat that almost reduced the strong man to a weak-kneed state.

In the months that he'd been in Williams, after he was well enough to be out and about, Billy had quickly discovered that the pretty, gentle nurse who'd captured his heart was the adored darling of the entire town's populace.

Why, Harmony Childers could have her pick of local gents from eight to eighty! But she seemed drawn to *him*. He could scarcely dare to believe—even as he knew it for fact—that when the beautiful young nurse had free time, she opted to spend it with Billy LeFave.

Harmony was kept so busy with her nursing duties and church activities, as well as sometimes helping her ma at the hotel, that Billy realized her time was at a premium. He couldn't help entertaining a bit of masculine pride that she obviously enjoyed his company enough to arrange to spend whatever leisure time she had available with him.

Billy returned to his chinking repairs, and his thoughts spun back to when he'd been released from Dr. Wellingham's care. His mind dwelled on the days of hard but satisfying physical labor. Working off his debts had given him a sense of honesty and personal worth. He considered the many new, decent, and godly people he'd met, and realized that they were friends strong and true.

A smile came unbidden to his features when his musings played back over the idle hours spent at socials, work bees, Sunday afternoon parlor gatherings, and impromptu sporting events in the burgeoning little lumber town. Those times, though Harmony could've spent her time with others, she had favored him with her attentions and had seemed to treasure his companionship, making efforts such as were ladylike and not too forward to allow them additional occasions to be together.

The first time she'd slipped her dainty forearm through the crook of his elbow, Billy LeFave had thought he'd died and gone on to glory. He'd felt dizzy from her nearness, almost intoxicated by her very presence.

Another such pleasant interlude was probably now only an hour or two away, he realized, gauging the time by the steadily lifting sun that had blazed away the early morning mist and soared high into the sky as it traveled toward being directly overhead.

Billy had been working all week to repair and beautify the church grounds. And each day, Harmony had taken time off from her occupational responsibilities to go to the hotel, fetch a lunch, and come to the church, bearing a hamper from the dining room. Then, idling away time and relishing a repast prepared by Lizzie, the two were able to spend a quiet luncheon together, enjoying each other's company along with their meal.

Food prepared by Lizzie was always delectable, but at times Billy hardly noticed the taste, due to his enjoyment of the deliciousness of Harmony's sweet-tempered, amusing company.

Goose bumps rippled over Billy's skin at the remembrance of her tinkling laugh, sparkling blue eyes, tender sighs, and the sincere compliments that she had expressed regarding the nature of the upkeep work he'd done at the church property.

He also treasured the knowledge that Harmony considered him a very dear friend—and claimed him as such before everyone in the community.

Billy realized that a lot of the people accepted him quickly because Harmony Childers had done so first and foremost. Billy knew that he cherished Harmony's friendship more than he had ever valued material possessions, and he'd known more than a few impressive assets, whether accumulated through good means or bad. Nowadays he drew comfort that the bulk of his past earnings—squandered, stolen from him, or buried in locations hidden too well, for they were now not only lost to others but to himself as well—had been earned through trapping and other honest labor.

Compared to the gold, silver, and copper he'd sometimes buried in remote caches—using natural markings to help him relocate the site, should he later choose to or remember to— he'd have traded it all to be able to place a gold band on sweet Harmony Childer's left hand.

Already he knew what it was to experience the warm, joyous glow that seemed to radiate from Harmony and consume him from head to toe when he was fixed in one of her tender smiles. He felt almost weak with delight when she touched his forearm, gazed up at him, her eyes so accepting and luminous, and he was aware that he was her trusted friend.

At those moments, he ached to hold her close, to promise to protect her forever and ever. To—

With a soft, anguished groan, Billy would let his thoughts travel no farther. But they had galloped off again to the realm of reality, where with every fiber of his being, he knew that he wanted Harmony Childers as more than just a friend . . . he desired her as his wife.

For several days, Billy had entertained the idea of proposing marriage to Harmony. His emotions had seesawed wildly between euphoria at the idea that she would give a soft, serene "Yes!"—and utter despair that her eyes might widen with startlement at the suggestion and it would cause her to gasp a horrified "No!"

After tossing and turning for much of the night, with the

dawn Billy resolved that not another day would pass before he managed to muster the courage and confidence required to ask Harmony Childers to be his bride.

Determined that he was going to carry out his plans as soon as possible, he vowed that he'd pose the most important question he'd ever murmured in his life just as soon as Harmony—and opportunity—appeared.

As Billy smoothed chinking material into crevices between the timbers, pressed it snugly into place, and shaped it with his calloused fingertips, he kept stealing glances in the direction of the Grant Hotel, hoping to catch the day's first glimpse of his beloved.

Finally, when Billy thought that he could endure the excruciating anticipation not a moment longer, he was rewarded by the sight of movement on the front veranda of the hotel. His heart leaped with the thought of Harmony's arrival—then, just as quickly, his soaring hopes were dashed when he saw that instead it was Lizzie approaching, a picnic hamper hung over her forearm.

As glad as Billy was to see the sweet, middle-aged, devoutly Christian woman who'd quickly become a mother to him—the only ma that Billy LeFave had ever really had—he could have wept with disappointment that it was Harmony's mother, not Harmony, who made her way toward him.

chapter
3

BY THE TIME Lizzie hove into easy sight, her gait rolling as she counterbalanced the weight of the wicker basket, Billy had recovered from the shock of his disappointment.

Wiping his hands on a damp rag, hastily tossing on his shirt, Billy went to greet Lizzie Mathews. Deftly he slipped the heavy luncheon hamper, which was covered with a white linen, from her arm to his own.

"Afternoon, Miss Lizzie," Billy greeted her, producing a sunny smile that neatly camouflaged his chagrin.

"Afternoon yourself, William," Lizzie replied. She surveyed the church grounds. "Land sake's alive, but you've been workin' miracles by your hand. I know the Lord's house ain't never looked better than it does on this lovely day o' his makin'."

Billy gave a pleased grin but then shuffled self-consciously, as if few heartfelt compliments had ever come his way but rather plenty of disapproving cuffs.

"I'm doing my best. The Lord and my friends deserve no less."

Lizzie patted his shoulder. "Well, you're doing a fine job, son," she assured as she began to efficiently lay out the foodstuffs she'd prepared for his repast. "Everyone's talkin' and clamorin' about the wonderful job you're a-doin'."

"They are?"

Lizzie shot him a quick glance when she detected the

shocked, almost disbelieving pleasure he drew from her words.

"Heavens, yes!" she affirmed. "And my Harmony couldn't be any more pleased and proud about the situation than if she was doin' the work herself."

With that information, Billy's heart burgeoned with joy.

"Then, Miss Harmony's satisfied with my efforts?"

"Why, I'd reckon to say the girl sure is!" Lizzie gave a delighted crow of laughter. "Several times this week, when folks has happened to comment to my Harmony about what a whiz-bang of a job you've been doing, she's been retorting, 'Isn't he, though? Billy LeFave is a regular workin' fool.'"

Billy, who had begun to feel a buoyancy that was lifting him from his letdown, found his emotions plummeting with Lizzie's admission.

Fool? The woman who'd captured his heart considered him a *FOOL?!* A fool for working as hard as he had, out of a feeling of joy and gratitude for all that God had given him even when Billy LeFave had been among the worst of sinners and considered himself most undeserving?

"Sh—she—Harmony thinks that I'm a . . ."—Billy seemed to strangle over the word—"fool?"

Lizzie shot Billy a quick, sharp glance, correctly assessing his confused, hurt state of mind.

"Land o' Goshen, *no!* Will, Harmony don't think you're a fool. Leastways not like you're concludin' she does, by thinking her words was commentin' on moronic or idiotic behaviors."

"It sounded like it to my ears," Billy said quietly, hating the fact that as tall as he was, and strong, there was a wavering in his tone that made him sound like a little boy about to cry. And he hadn't wept since he was five years old, although

Lord knew there were situations enough over the years to have been good cause to shed tears of grief.

"Oh, Billy," Lizzie cried, softly rushing to him with a hug when she detected the depths of his intense hurt, not just from her innocent words but from the scars of rejection that had been laid down, veneered one on top of another, until they had formed a hard shell around Billy LeFave's true feelings. "Mayhap it sounded like that to you—but you're hearin' all wrong, regardless of what the actual words' definitions might've seemed to mean."

"What do you—"

"Folks in these parts, Billy, in case you haven't noticed, well, they talk different from how us folks from downstate Illinois who've moved up here do. Not just in our accents, mind you, Will, but even in the turns o' phrase we sometimes use."

"Well . . . yes . . .," Billy agreed, but his reluctant tone conveyed that he wasn't wholly convinced.

"Down where we were originally from, Will, the phrase, 'He's a workin' fool' is purty common to hear. And instead of it bein' an insult, to be called 'a workin' fool' is actually a real compliment. It's the kind of assessment given to the work behaviors of a person who is considered salt of the earth, diligent in his labors, by folks who ain't exactly pikers in their own performances."

Billy felt flickerings of relief. "That's what she meant?"

Lizzie gave Billy another quick, sound hug before she released him and turned back to laying out his lunch. She gave a brusque nod.

"Just as sure as God made li'l green apples."

"That's a relief," Billy sighed, gratefully accepting a plate of food from Lizzie.

He bowed his head and offered words of thanksgiving,

then lifted his gaze to hers. He tried to smile, took a bite of food, then managed a faint grin.

"Good!" he complimented, seeming to wanly try to change the subject.

"Maybe it'll strengthen your relief to know from me, her ma, that rather than viewing you as a silly ol' fool, my girl's come to admire you with a capacity she's previously reserved for an exceptional few—her kin and special friends o' the fam'bly."

"That's heartening to learn," Billy murmured.

"Know beyond doubt, William LeFave, that my Harmony thinks the sun rises and sets on you. I must admit—'tis been somethin' of a surprise to those of us who've known her since forever, so to speak. As a wee girl, she always had her nose in a book. She was such a good and serious girl, not a lass anyone would consider flighty or flirty. By nature, Harmony's conduct has been such that over the years at times, we've teased her about endin' up a scrawny ol' spinster lady, no more attention than she ever paid to the fellers, 'ceptin' her brothers. Other gals, why, they wanted a good man and a fam'bly, and sometimes was a bit shameless in chasin' after the young menfolk in the neighborhood. But not Harmony! She always pined for a career, it seemed. The way she loved to read, she sort of cottoned to the idea of bein' a librarian one day. Or a school teacher. She'd also dreamed of mayhap bein' a nurse. Though at the time, she reckoned she didn't see how that would ever happen. As it turns out, though, the Lord provided the means for that fondest dream to become her reality."

Billy had continued to fork food into his mouth as he listened to Lizzie Mathews accurately and intimately assess the merits and mind-set of the girl he'd grown to adore. He paused for a moment to comment, "It seems to suit her and make her plumb happy to serve as a nurse, doesn't it?"

"Yessirree. Like we say down home, she's as happy as a pig in mud, just bein' a nurse."

Billy nodded silently. The fact that he was still alive, living and breathing to serve the Lord, offered unimpeachable testimony to the thoroughness of Harmony Childers' nursing abilities. She went above and beyond tasks asked of her, and he knew that a true love of medicine and satisfaction in healing was the source of such unstinting stamina and unconditional devotion. Had she given herself so fully to healing Christian love for others that a more personal, romantically centered love was impossible for her to know? Compared to the world of medicine . . . could any other path in life even hold appeal for a girl like Harmony?

"I've heard Lester and Miss Joy, as well as others, tease Miss Harmony about being married to her work," Billy said, his tone cautious as he sought to segue into a topic about which Lizzie's input could either cause a dream to come true—or utter despair to settle in forevermore.

"Right you are, Will—for I've been among that joshin' number myself."

"Do you suppose she'll ever marry?" Billy found himself asking, hoping that he sounded casual. He had to ask—had to know—even as he wasn't fully sure he could bear to hear Lizzie's informed opinion on the matter.

"Well, I sure do hope so," Lizzie said, patting a few stray wisps of graying hair into place after finishing a cookie from the hamper's generous supply. "She's never been boy-crazy, not a whit, so it'll take a really special man to turn the head of my serious and serene-minded career girl. Yep! A man among men to cause my girl's heart to quicken with romantic notions . . ."

"I'd assumed as much myself," Billy admitted, "no better than I know Harmony." Although he liked to think that he knew and understood her better than most.

He'd never been able to fathom Harmony's attentions to him, although he'd certainly appreciated her focus. He'd assumed that when—*if*—Harmony Childers ever married, it'd be to a man much like Dr. Wellingham, Luke Masterson, or even a fellow like Lester. Someone who would be accomplished, educated, even cultured, someone without a past as depraved and debauched as his own. A gentleman who had the capacities necessary to win the heart and hand of a woman like Harmony.

"I'm certainly not that special man," Billy mused aloud, and when a heartbeat later he realized he'd actually *spoken* his private thoughts, his face flushed hot with mortification, and he'd have given everything he'd ever earned in life if only to be able to buy back the thoughtlessly whispered words.

Lizzie frowned, then her eyes widened as if suddenly she were seeing with clarity something that had been previously foggy and indistinct, if even noticed at all.

"Mayhap you *are!*" Lizzie blurted, proof that she *had* overheard his anguished private admission. "Why, now that I give it some thought, it's purty clear that you've turned her head the way no bloke has ever managed to interest her in all o' her lifelong years. It's obvious to me how special you are to her, Will. What time Harmony and I get to spend together, it's a litany of 'Billy this' and 'Billy that.' You're special to her in a way no other man has ever affected her. And you're special to me too, son. I'm sure you've noticed I tend to call you Will, even as others call you Billy or Bill. There's a reason for that—my papa's name was Will. You'd have loved him. And it gives me special pleasure in callin' you Will out of my affection for my pa, and my belief that you're goin' to be fillin' a major spot in my heart, as my own dear pa did."

Billy didn't know what to say. Potential hurt had just evolved, miraculously, to become happiness unlike anything he'd known before that moment in time.

"Special enough, you think, that she might even . . . uh . . . one day . . . agree to . . . marry me?"

At that a shadow of doubt passed across Lizzie's smiling features. A sigh passed her lips, and as she bought time to organize her thoughts and frame her words, long seconds seemed to tick off in eternities to Billy.

"Now that, Mr. LeFave, is a question that you'll have to properly pose to Miss Harmony herself. I can't begin to know her mind 'n heart. I know that some o' Paul's writin's on the unmarried life seem to have found favor with her . . . and . . . well—iffen you're wonderin' if Harmony's the marryin'-up type, you'll have to ask her yourself—for I dunno!"

Another flush crept up Billy's cheeks. "I was set on doing that, Miss Lizzie, fully expecting to be asking her right now. Except you're here . . . and for some reason . . . she ain't."

"Oh, Will!" Lizzie said, her tone sympathetic as she realized the inner disappointment and prolonged anguish he was suffering at her appearance on behalf of her daughter, so that the tension was postponed and prolonged. "That's true enough. She was plannin' on being here, like she's managed every day this week, but then somethin' came up. A lumberjack brought his wife to Doc Wellingham's infirmary. The poor girl's been travailin' almost two days, 'n the babe is her first. 'Tis in breech . . . so they're havin' a time of it. Harmony's sore needed elsewhere."

"I'm sorry to hear that," Billy said, expressing honest compassion for the suffering woman who'd sought the small hospital building as a haven from her womanly miseries.

"It seems I hardly see Harmony myself these days," Lizzie remarked, trying to frame the comment so the words didn't seem like a complaint lodged. "In fact, I'd reckon you see more of her than her fam'bly has. Les was sayin' just the other day that no more than he'd seen of Harmony, a feller would be hard-pressed to know they lived in the same town 'n weren't still parted by a couple o' states instead."

"I'm grateful she's made time for me. That fact has given me hope. . . ." Billy's voice trailed off, and a companionable silence fell between them.

"By the way, Harmony ain't happened to mention getting mail from Illinois, from her brother Thad, in particular, has she?" Lizzie asked, finally breaking the silence that had enveloped them.

"Well . . . no. But that doesn't mean she hasn't. She could've and just didn't happen to mention it to me. And if she has, it could've slipped her mind to bring a letter along to share with the rest of you."

Lizzie gave a heavy sigh. "I doubt that she's heard from Thad . . . either. Would've been a newsworthy occasion iffen she had. I don't think she'd have forgotten to speak of it."

Billy cocked his head. "I hear the train coming. It'll pull in at the platform before much longer. Perhaps you'll have mail then."

"Lord, how I hope so," Lizzie sighed, then forced a bright smile so Billy wouldn't have his joy burdened with an awareness that she was worried. And worried sick . . .

"Well, sir, I'd better pack up what's left of these vittles and hie on back to the hotel. Think I'll loiter at the train depot afore I return to my duties, though, just in case. We'll see you at dinner tonight, Will."

"I'll be there."

"And don't you worry overmuch about what's burdening your heart, you hear?" Lizzie ordered. "I know you love Harmony," she acknowledged and laid her hand comforting-ly over Billy's tanned grip. "Indeed, the whole town's aware that ya outright adore the girl. It's my belief as her ma, Will, that mayhap Harmony loves you, too. Not just as she'd love a brother in Christ . . . but the way a woman'd feel in all ways toward a man chosen for her by God. As her ma, I know my girl well, but not so's I can predict her responses 'n answers. I know fondness when I see it, though. So there's reasonable hope."

Billy's sigh was laden with relief. "That's nice to know."

Lizzie's face briefly shadowed with a dark realization that caused a frown to flit across her features before she willed it away.

"There's somethin' else you really need to know, Will, if you're goin' to ask her to be your bride and take her as your beloved wife. I believe with all my heart that Harmony loves you, as you do her. But I also have an awareness that she loves medicine and performin' her healin' arts, doin' her best to assist the Lord in restorin' folks to good health. Because of that, Will, because o' that commitment, you need to realize, son, that there's always goin' to be a part of Harmony that you'll never be able to possess, because it's already been given to God 'n all humanity. You'll never have that part of her, Will, for it simply ain't there for her to give ya. If you ask my gal to be your wife and she agrees to go to you as your bride . . . then know and *accept* ahead o' time that there'll be some inconveniences when she'll answer the call to serve others, and it mayhap seem at the expense of her husband 'n fam'bly. But that ain't really so—for she's just doin' the labors the Lord's called her to perform. See?"

"I . . . think so," Billy replied, his tone reflective.

"I know how you feel in your heart, Will. But you'd best think this through real thorough in your head as well. Think hard about it, for it'll make such a difference to your overall happiness. Be sure before you do your proposin' that you'll be willing to accept Harmony the way she is—and the way she has to be—and not just expect her to be like any other man's wife."

"Oh, I won't, Miss Lizzie, I won't! Harmony's so special!"

Lizzie grinned. "Good!" She gave Billy's arm a tender pat of understanding and reassurance. "You're someone else who sees Harmony in as special a way as she's seen through her own ma's prejudiced gaze!"

"Harmony *is* a special woman. And if only she'll accept me as her husband—I'll marry Harmony on any terms—and consider myself a fellow blessed among men."

"She's plannin' on dining with us at the hotel tonight," Lizzie said, passing on Harmony's intentions. "You'll be there, of course?"

Billy's grin was like the first bright rays of sunshine cleaving the morning sky with glowing promise.

"I wouldn't miss it for the world, Lord willing."

"I expect you won't," Lizzie teased, chuckling. "But perchance life gets in the way o' livin' and she has to cancel out, then know, William LeFave, that it can't be helped and that when the Lord ordains it, you'll get your perfect chance, iffen you're meant to, and just the right words to pose that heady and heartfelt question you're just dyin' to ask as you're on tenterhooks wonderin' what the outcome will be."

St. Louis, Missouri

Thad was startled when he finally awakened the next morning and discovered by his pocket watch that the hour was just minutes before twelve o'clock noon! He didn't recall ever having lain abed that long, except when he had been seriously ill and his ma made him take his ease. But on a regular day, his ma'd have shaken the attic ladder apart over a son who stayed between the sheets until the sun was high in the sky!

"Time to be up and at 'em," Thad cajoled himself as he arose, dashed water from the basin over his face, through his hair, and toweled off.

He took care of his personal needs as best he could without toiletry articles, and he made a mental note to pick up the necessary items at a mercantile or pharmacy.

Thad squinted against the sun when he stepped out into the bustling thoroughfare. How exciting it was to arise from bed and minutes later be surrounded by folks who crowded the streets!

He'd bided a moment of time with the desk clerk, inquired about the location of good haberdasheries, and been directed to a street several blocks away from the modest hotel where he was lodging.

He made his way onto the fashionable avenue only a few blocks from the waterfront. His eyes widened when he saw the elaborate creations in windows of fine shops serving matrons, and he discovered, here and there, various small haberdasheries tucked in among the assortment of retail outlets.

He practically had his nose pressed to a haberdasher's window, like a child hungering for sweet treats behind the window of a candy shop, when he heard an almost rude chuckle from right behind him.

He turned around and looked into the grin of a fellow who appeared to be a few years younger than he but who was dressed so foppishly that Thad immediately concluded the young gent must've been born with a silver spoon in his mouth.

And the raven-haired beauty at the young man's side, with a figure so pert and trim, she as fashionably dressed as her escort, made Thad's heart stop when he peered deep into her violet eyes. Eyes that offered the most absorbing, exciting, challenging gaze he'd ever seen!

"Rich man's tastes and a poor boy's income?" the blond fellow in the waggish suit chided.

Thad felt a sense of umbrage. "What if I am?" he inquired, almost hotly. "We've all got to start someplace—don't we?"

The young man leaned close. "Then, let me tell you a secret. That's *not* the place to go. If you don't mind donning a pair of trousers or a cravat that's been worn by another . . . and purchasing the same for a trifle . . . then I've got the shop for you. I'll take you there for two bits. Elseways, you're on your own!"

"Do tell!" Thad retorted, fishing in his pocket, realizing that if the young gent was telling the truth, he'd save that amount many times over.

"Come along," the younger man commanded, with such a sense of urbane sophistication that Thad found himself envying the bloke his sense of confidence, and he made a note to pay attention to the fellow's flawless manners and worldly ways so he could emulate them himself.

"Where are we going?" Thad asked, gawking around, trying to keep his bearings so he wouldn't eventually find himself hopelessly lost, with no sense of direction to take him back to the hotel.

"We'll have to hike a piece," the young fellow said. "Are you up to it, Sis?" he inquired of the beautiful young woman.

"Of course," she demurely replied.

"Sis looks like a china doll," the youth said, "but don't let it fool you. She's tough as a hank of rawhide—and I 'spect if I was to put her up against an Indian fighter, arming each of them with a knife, Nanette could split her opponent's throat twixt one heartbeat and another. And when it comes to talents as a shill, pickpocket, or what-have-you, she's second to none! She fancies that she'd like a career as a singer someday, but so far I've convinced her starvation is a poor alternative to simply stringing folks along."

"You're just jealous!" Nanette flared. "You can't carry a tune in a bucket with a lid!"

"Nor have I any desire!" Nick retorted.

"Interesting," Thad said when he considered all that there was so neatly packaged in the petite Nanette. He was suddenly aware that he was as proud of Harmony as Nanette's brother was of his sister—but for very differing values. "What kind of shop are we going to, if not a haberdashery?"

"A pawnshop. A hockshop, you know? Where folks go with items for surety so they can get a loan of funds to tide them over until more funds are forthcoming."

"Oh . . . well . . ."

Thad had heard tell of such enterprises, but he'd never been into one. He wasn't sure what to expect.

"This one pawnshop, they have a clothing room attached, and it's run a bit differently. That's where wealthy folks send their house servants with armfuls of cast-off clothing. Garments that are too good to throw away but can be removed and bring some financial recompense, too. Why, some's hardly been worn at all. And when someone brings in the wardrobe of a deceased gentleman, you can outfit yourself head to toe if you're 'bout the same size—and don't

mind living it up in clothes that recently belonged to someone dead and moldering down in the ground."

"I don't . . . mind," Thad said quietly.

"Didn't figure you would!" the yellow-haired youth said
and tossed the quarter Thad had given him into the air. It
spun around, sparkling in the sunlight, and he deftly caught it
with his other hand and jammed it into his pocket.

"I heard you refer to your sister as Miss Nanette," Thad
said. "You have a name?"

"Oh, sure! Forgot my high-tone manners there for a
moment. Nick it is. Short for Nicholas. And my sister, of
course, as you already know, is Nanette. To look at us, you
wouldn't know it—but we're twins."

"I wouldn't have known," Thad said. "My name's Thad.
Short for Thaddeus Childers. I came to St. Louis last night
from Watson, a tiny burg in central Illinois, south of
Effingham."

"Pleased to meet you, Thaddeus," Nick said, quickly
extending his hand, as did Nanette.

"Nick and I don't tell just anyone that we're brother and
sister," Nanette said, falling in step between her brother and
Thad, linking a slim arm through the looped elbow of each
escort. "It's easier that way."

"More profitable, too," Nick said, winking, as he pulled
out a cheroot and lit up.

"I see," Thad said, although he actually didn't see at all.

Nick soon made it clear, however, as he told Thad about
leaving an upriver town just south of Hannibal, where they'd
lived in poverty with an alcoholic father and a mother who'd
worked herself to death taking in laundry when the twins
were ten years old and their older brother twelve.

"It wasn't easy living with Pa," Nanette said. "But we did our best, poor man, rest his wretched soul."

"Don't let her josh you, Thad. She hated his guts, same as I."

"Now, Nick!"

"We may have had no inheritance from our parents to squabble over, but one thing they bequeathed us, even if 'twas unknowing, is that they left us with good looks and quick minds."

"Fortunate," Thad said, unable to fully compare his own life with the sorry existence they sketched in.

"We had few funds when we landed in St. Louis a few months ago. But if a bloke's street-smart and has the savvy to ask in the right places, he can soon learn the ropes of getting by. So that's what we did. Working together as we do, occasionally pulling scams when need be, we're cautious about who we let know we're consanguine kin. If they knew—it could work against us."

"Here we are," Nanette interrupted Nick's magnanimous monologue as they approached a pawnshop.

Thad gave Nanette a hand up into the establishment as Nick held the door.

Thad wrinkled his nose as he stepped into the dusty, dimly lit pawnshop. The store owner hailed Nick and Nanette with an enthusiastic smile, and such warm greetings caused Thad to realize that the portly man was well acquainted with these two.

"We're here to outfit a gent newly arrived to town," Nick said. He assessed Thad. "I think something sporty and devil-may-care, but first-class, my man, first-class. The latest styles possible, too."

"I think we have just the things," the pawnbroker said, exiting into the adjoining space.

The paunchy merchant rushed around and soon broke a sweat as he piled garments on a stack for Thad to look through.

"If something doesn't quite fit but could be made service-able with a bit of tailoring, we can arrange that on the cheap."

"Good to know that, sir," Thad said.

Nick was riffling through the garments, tossing some aside with a ruthless gesture and allowing his touch to linger over some others, which he handled with what seemed almost rev-erence. "Here, Thaddeus, my man, try on these!" he ordered.

Thad glanced around.

"This way, sir," the pawnbroker said. "Our changing rooms."

A moment later he was in the closetlike space, shrugging out of the shirt his ma had made and the trousers from the mercantile in Effingham. His fingers felt clumsy as he worked at the fine buttons, prissy dress shirt, sleeve garters, and other fancy items that Nicholas had picked out and laid together.

Thad couldn't believe the transformation when he stepped out and caught sight of himself in a full-length mirror.

He no longer looked like a rawboned country boy! Why, just like Nick and Nanette, he—Thaddeus Childers—looked as if he'd been to the manor born!

When Thad glanced from the looking glass toward his companions and the establishment's owner, mirrored in their eyes was the same sincere approval he'd seen in his own.

"He's head-turning handsome!" Nanette cried and rushed forward to give Thad a buss on the cheek. "Oh, do get this out-fit, Thad. And maybe between Nick and the owner, they can put together another outfit so you'll have a change of clothes."

"Might even be that the good man would have a used car-petbag in the pawnshop that you could tote your new wardrobe around in."

"Remember, Nick, that you're lookin' at a poor boy with a rich man's tastes."

Nick gave the pawnbroker a friendly cuff on the upper arm. "Keep that in mind, you old rascal, as you're ciphering up the total figure. This un's different than some."

"Very well, my good man," the pawnbroker agreed with a nod.

Thirty minutes later Thad stood by the cash register as the pawnbroker neatly folded an armload of men's clothing and stacked it into a shiny leather valise that had seen little wear. There'd been a few ratty carpetbags, to be had for a pittance, but Thad had fallen in love with the leather valise and knew that he had to have it.

"A grand total of fifteen dollars," the pawnbroker said. "It'd have cost you five times that or more in one of the fine haberdasheries uptown, where most of these garments were originally purchased."

Thad reached for his ready cash, having known enough from his ma's upbringing not to keep all of his funds together, in case he collided—literally—with a pickpocket.

He counted off the money with seeming reluctance, as if the money were more precious to him than it actually was. He noticed that Nick—and Nanette—seemed to observe his reluctance.

"There you are. Fifteen dollars even. And it's been a pleasure doin' business with you, sir," Thad said.

"Same here, same here," the pawnbroker replied.

Thad turned toward the door. Nanette looped her arm through his. "Oh . . . I'm so proud to be seen with a gentleman as handsome as you, Thad. Clothes certainly do make the man. Or the woman," she added with a coquettish wink.

"Aren't you forgetting something, Mister?" Thad heard Nick quietly say to the pawnbroker.

"Going for it right now!" the man said. He reached into his pocket and spun a silver dollar through the air. Nick caught it, but his hand shot right back out. The pawnbroker dug deeper, and a half-dollar joined it, as did complaining words that he'd charged Thad less than he would've someone else, because of Nick's warning.

"This gent's a friend—you can make up for it on the other suckers I snag in front of the haberdasheries and bring your way!"

Nanette realized that Thad was taking it all in.

"We do this at least once a day. It earns us meal money, if nothing else. And we do meet interesting people this way." She gave a lighthearted sniff. "It has its dangers, though, for it seems some of the haberdashers realize that Nicky is pur-loining their potential paying customers. Last week, we were chased off by an irate store owner wielding a broom."

Thad laughed at the sight he imagined and how ungallant the luxuriously appointed pair probably looked at that moment, running for all they were worth.

Just then Nicholas caught up with them.

"I was just telling Thad about the haberdasher who chased us off with a broom because he'd gotten to recognize us."

"Yes," Nick said and spat a curse word.

"Say, Nick!" Nanette gasped and excitedly grasped her twin's arms. "We've just *outfitted* a solution to our problems."

"Sis, you're a genius—and you're right!" He turned to Thad and stuck out his hand again. "If you don't have any-thing better to do than work for a living, Thaddeus Childers, my good man, then agree to work with Nanette and me. You could start by escorting my beautiful sister down

Haberdashers' Row . . . and approaching some goggle-eyed country boy looking for new duds, and taking him to the shop where I just took you."

"We work on a commission basis. Straight ten percent," Nanette said. "It's easy as pie, Thad," she assured. She gave his arm an intimate little squeeze. "Oh, say that you will!" She stood on tiptoe and bussed his cheek again.

Right then Thad would've done anything for her.

"Very well," he agreed.

"Terrific!" Nick said. "Now, where are you staying? Probably some overpriced hotel. We've got to get you into cheaper lodging, where the meals are included in the price. We live at a boardinghouse, Thad. I think that I could talk the landlady into finding a berth for you."

"I'd like that very much," Thad said, realizing that among the things he'd enjoy the most would be a chance to see the beautiful Nanette each and every glorious day.

"We'll go to your hotel and close out your account before they bill you for another day," Nicholas decided. "Then I'll take my ease for a while at the billiard parlor, and you can escort Miss Nanette down past the haberdasheries. Generally, you only need to walk around the block a couple of times before you happen upon a solid 'mark.'"

"I see."

"And at the pawnshop—let Sis deal with the broker," Nick said. "She knows the ropes." He assessed Thad. "You'll find Nanette is quite an interesting and capable girl."

Thad felt his face flush. "I daresay that I consider her, already, the most fascinating woman I've ever been honored to know."

"Has he got potential or what, Sis?" Nick said, winking, chuckling with glee.

"With a line like that, he's a natural," Nanette agreed.

"I wasn't makin' it up," Thad said. "That's how I feel."

"Oh, Thad. You're such a dear," Nanette said. She gave his cheek another buss, then tucked her hand in his. "Your ma must be proud to have a son like you."

"Well . . . I dunno," Thad mumbled, momentarily chastened with the realization of what he was doing, how he was living.

"Where'd you say you hailed from, hon?" Nanette asked as they set off toward the hotel.

"Watson, Illinois."

"Watson. Thaddeus Childers from Watson."

"There'll be no keeping him down on the farm—now that he's seen the big city!" Nick predicted.

"There's no goin' back," Thad agreed.

And somehow the words seemed to have an ugly, ominous sensation, as if they were a dire prediction, even as the world had never seemed more magnificently filled with exciting promises.

chapter
4

Williams, Minnesota

"AIN'T IT A lovely evenin' out?" Lizzie remarked as she boosted herself from the chair positioned beside Brad, who was seated at the head of the large family dining table at the hotel. "It'd be a perfect night for a walk ... strollin' along ... hand in hand ... talkin' ... smilin' ... maybe ever' onct in a while stoppin' to—"

Brad cocked his head as he thoughtfully regarded his wife.

"Is that one of your subtle hints, Liz darlin'?" he murmured, grinning, and started to scrape his chair away from the table as he turned toward his wife, prepared to assist her.

Lizzie stayed solidly where she was and threaded her fingers together beneath her chin.

"It's a hint, yes, but aimed at another, husband dear," she clarified, casting Brad a wink as she gently furrowed a brow, gave an almost imperceptible nod of her head, and tried to convey to Billy LeFave that the moment he'd awaited was at hand. That is, if Lizzie Mathews had anything to do with the matter!

"Ah, to be young," Brad offered, trying to be helpful.

"I figured that mayhap William would like to walk Miss Harmony back to her quarters at Doc Wellingham's residence 'n take the long way 'round so's he can show her the fruit of his handiwork at the church grounds, bein' as she didn't get to mark his progress this noon when nursing duties detained her."

Billy favored Lizzie with a baldly grateful look as he tried to find his voice.

Lizzie encouraged him with a surreptitious, conspiratorial wink. Brad yawned, openly, as if to signal that he was too tired for Miss Harmony to perhaps suggest that they linger over coffee and visit with her folks, whom she didn't always get to see as much these days as she'd have liked.

Billy's heart thudded in his chest.

He pushed his chair away from the table, mentally despising the whining, awkward noise the heavy piece of furniture emanated. For years, he'd considered himself an adult—and a savvy one at that. Now he felt . . . clumsy and coltish in his nervous anticipation.

"I'd be honored—if Miss Harmony is agreeable."

Harmony glanced at the ornate timepiece affixed to the bodice of her frock, an heirloom that had belonged to the late Granny Fanchon Preston, her mother's ma.

She favored her mother and stepfather with a sweet, if reluctant, smile.

"I really do need to return to the hospital," she said, momentarily dashing Billy's hopes that the evening would progress as Lizzie had orchestrated to the best of her ability. "But a walk to the church sounds marvelous. The evening is truly pleasant," she spoke on, causing Billy's spirits and hopes to soar. "And I could use a bit of fresh air."

"The skeeters ain't too bad yet," Lizzie encouraged, "though I reckon they'll be a caution when dusk fully falls."

"I think we can trust William to protect our girl from lumberjacks, wild beasts, and hungry mosquitoes," Brad joshed.

"That you can, sir," Billy promised. "I'll protect her with my life."

He'd meant for the words to be lighthearted bandying, but

he realized that everyone at the table—that is, perhaps, everyone with the exception of Harmony, whom he wanted to realize it the most—understood that his offer was in earnest.

"Fresh air'll do you good, darlin'," Lizzie said. "If you need a wrap to protect you against the night chill, help yourself to whatever's hangin' on the hall tree."

"I don't think there'll be a need," Harmony demurred.

"Returnin' it'd give you an excuse to make a point of comin' callin' again."

"Who needs an excuse?" Harmony said. "Although I'll admit, these past days, I've been cooped up at the hospital almost as much as the infirm who're confined to their sickbeds."

"It may not get any better, either," Lizzie said, glancing pointedly at Rose Grant Ames' grandfather clock, left behind in the hotel. It was a finely crafted masterpiece that not only marked off the days and weeks in steady ticktocks but also tracked the phases of the moon. "Ol' Grandpa Clock's warning that you'll no doubt be right busy. Full moon comin' on."

"Yes, and I remember what you told me long ago about a full moon, Mama," Harmony teased.

"Just as my own mama taught me," Lizzie retorted. "And all of Marc's newfangled medical contraptions or not, there's somethin' about a big ol' full moon that seems to make the wee ones who are destined to enter this life leave their warm confines under their mamas' hearts and come into this world."

"There was an infant born today," Harmony said, "and just as I was preparing to depart to come here to dine, Mr. Mason brought his wife in. She's travailing."

"We won't stay at the church long," Billy quickly made clear, as if fearing that Harmony might change her mind, resulting in a planned opportunity denied.

"Iffen y'all need help and an extra pair o' competent hands

at the birthin', you convince Dr. Marc to let Marissa rest with her new wee one—and I'll hie right on over to assist."

"I'll do that," Harmony agreed.

"Tell Marissa I'll be over to visit in a day or two and take a turn rockin' little Curtis Alton Wellingham a spell so's I get a chance to spoil 'im good and proper myself."

Harmony couldn't help smiling. She enjoyed all of the newborns that had been delivered at the hospital, but she'd been especially smitten by her childhood girlfriend's infant son, and it had reawakened in Harmony a desire to nurture and love a babe of her very own . . . someday. . . .

"I'll do that, Mama. Just think! Before we know it, Molly and Luke's little one will be here, too."

"I reckon Luke's wantin' a son. But it'd be kind o' nice if Molly'd have a daughter. Then the family'd have both a new boy 'n girl to carry on the family line and ways."

"The Mastersons don't seem to have a preference. Just hopes that the babe will be healthy."

"That's been a regular request in my prayers," Lizzie said. "Why, it'll be almost a full-time occupation when I have two sweet little newborns to cuddle and dandle to my heart's content."

Brad winked at Harmony and Billy. "What're we going to do if Lester and Joy make us grandparents within the comin' year, too, Liz?"

"Don't you worry about me, Brad Mathews!" Lizzie warned and gave forth with a good-natured, challenging hoot. "My motherin' abilities were never found in short supply in the past. And my own ma told me that grandmotherin' is a snap 'cause you get to spoil the little ones, and then when they get cranky and fussy and there ain't no pleasin' 'em, that's when you hand 'em back to their ma or pa!"

"As crazy as Joy and Lester are over Marc and Marissa's son, I expect they'll be in the family way before long, Lord willing. I've never seen a couple so daffy over a baby that belongs to others," Harmony said.

Lizzie gave her daughter a penetrating look, then abruptly chuckled and shook her head with amazed amusement.

"You, Harmony Childers, are a fine one to talk about others bein' daffy about babies. You're almost dizzy with delight and glowin' with details each time you and Marc assist a new mama in bringing forth a little gift from heaven."

"That I am." Harmony didn't bother to deny it. "Maybe the babes aren't my own—but I know that each one claims a special little piece of my heart. It's going to be so exciting in coming years to watch them grow up strong and true, and become fine citizens, I hope good Christians, and someday be parents themselves."

"I've been thinkin' the selfsame thing lately. There's been a lot of new citizens added to our town, and not comin' in on the CNR line but arrivin' via Doc Wellingham's infirmary," Lizzie said.

"We've been so busy recently," Harmony agreed.

"Not to rush you, Miss Harmony, or bring an end to this conversation, but if you're sincere about wanting to stroll to the church grounds, we really should depart," Billy reminded.

Harmony touched Billy's forearm in a gesture that bid a moment's more patience from him. "We'll leave in just a moment. I want to give Mama a hug first."

The two women exchanged a warm embrace. As Harmony said good night to her parents, Billy waited quietly, relieved to be going at last. The evening's conversation echoed in his mind.

The first time in all of his twenty-two years that he'd ever nestled an infant in his arms had been only two weeks earlier, when Marissa Wheeler Wellingham had firmly tucked her newborn son, Curtis Alton, in Billy's startled arms and lightly admonished, "Relax, Bill! He won't break!"

Suddenly aware of the tender heft of the precious burden that she'd so naturally entrusted to him, Billy hadn't been so sure, even as his heart swelled beneath the knowledge of the confidence the Wellinghams had in him, the affection they had for him—when he'd entered their domicile drunk and unruly, a vicious heathen and most undeserving of the grace and blessings they'd extended him.

The Wellinghams' baby boy had seemed so . . . fragile. Yet Billy knew that with parents like Marissa and Marc, he'd grow up to be so strong—in stature, yes, for they'd give little Curt the best of care, but with a boldness of faith, too, that would see the little fellow well through life.

Billy had felt a desire to clutch the infant to his chest and protect him with his own strong arms, to assist others in keeping the tiny boy safe. But he hadn't, for he was so afraid that through sheer accident, he'd harm the child by holding him too tightly.

"Relax, I said," Marissa had murmured, patting Billy's shoulder. "Hold him a little snugger," she instructed encouragingly. "That way, Curt will feel more secure."

Billy had done as he was told. With a contented sigh, the chubby-faced infant had cuddled closer, and Billy could feel the gentle baby warmth through his shirt and the baby's gown.

He'd felt suddenly, oddly overcome with love and appreciation. "Little Curt is a world-beater of a baby," he remarked. Then, moved by the strange and heady emotions soaring within him, with a callused forefinger he'd traced the curve of the baby's satiny cheeks.

Curtis had peeped his sleep-heavy eyes open at the contact,

looked into Billy's eyes, and there had been no fear, only trust and acceptance. How strange! Before then, Billy had felt that he'd given Harmony Childers his heart—lock, stock, and barrel. But at that moment it was as if he'd given his heart all over again—but in a different way, to a newborn babe.

Maybe it was as Lizzie once explained, Billy had thought. When you've given your heart to Jesus, the more love you give away, the more love there is to give.

Billy had scarcely known little Curt, but he'd been aware that already he loved the wee mite, and his thoughts had spun ahead to the future and how much he'd relish seeing the boy grow from infancy to mature manhood, Lord willing.

Helplessly Billy had lowered his face. His breath riffled the baby-fine hair, and no one had laughed when he lowered his lips to bestow a soft kiss near the pulsing spot on the baby's crown.

"Oooh," the womenfolk had said, looking at each other as if to say, *Ain't that sweet?* and Billy had beamed as he held the infant and felt so much a part of all of God's creation.

"He seems plumb at home right where he is," Marissa had commented. "Do you mind, Bill? Looks like Curt's about to drop off for a nap. If you'd rather not—"

Billy's arms had tightened almost fiercely. "He's fine right where he is," he'd said. "I've never held a baby before. And this is kind of . . ."

"Well, he's taken to you, that's for sure," Marc had said, grinning. "And you're takin' to handling a baby like you were born for the occupation!"

Everyone had joined together in appreciative laughter and gathered around the rocker where Billy sat as they shared a bit of pleasant conversation.

A long time later Curt had awakened, his arms springing back in startled surprise as his sleepy eyes cracked open to regard the world around him. Tender baby fingers, with nails tiny as little pearls, sought something solid to grasp. They settled around Billy's forefinger—and clung!

Billy had given a rumble of laughter that momentarily startled Curt, whose eyes widened with alarm but then grew peaceful.

"With a grip like this little rascal's got already," Bill had said, "he's going to grow up to be a powerful gent."

"A man as big as my pa, Alton, who he was named for," Marissa had mused. "But with hands deft enough to do the finest of surgery, just like his father."

Billy had felt a sudden, unexpected sting of tears behind his eyes as a strange comparison overshadowed him.

His folks had been killed by a warring band of Sioux in the Dakota territories two decades before. Billy possessed no real memories of them except for the bloated, bloody bodies lying unmoving to bake beneath the searing sun. He also remembered hunger unlike anything he'd experienced before—and hoped never to know again—before the stenchy, grizzled trappers had happened along. They'd pillaged what remained of the burnt Conestoga wagon and roughly grasped Billy, who'd already been so traumatized that he would be robbed of speech for weeks to come, by the nape of the neck and rudely thrust him along with them.

Until the moment he sat with an infant embraced in his arms, he'd never stopped to consider that very likely his own ma and pa had treasured high expectations and bright dreams on his behalf.

He knew that when he was a babe in arms, they'd have surely been appalled and heartbroken had they known what lay ahead of him. First at the brutal, evil hands of others ... then later his life destroyed by his own vicious, ungodly actions.

Suddenly Billy had found himself hugging little Curtis hard in the intensity of his instinctive desire to spare the blessed innocent what he'd suffered in life. The baby let out a sudden squall.

"I said snug, Bill, but not too tight," Marissa had gently reminded, but she made no move to rescue her baby as if he could no longer be trusted to Billy LeFave.

"Something the matter, Bill?" Marc had asked, his physician's sight—so useful in watching for signs of discomfort and pain in helping him to make a diagnosis as he palpated a body—activated.

"No . . . no . . . I was just thinking. Forgot where I was there for a moment," Billy had gruffly explained.

"Such lapses are readily excused," Marissa had said, bestowing an affectionate and understanding pat upon his shoulder. "You've taken to rocking a baby like a natural."

"Maybe . . . someday . . ." Billy's words and thoughts had trailed off when the rush of emotions he felt as he considered holding a child begotten from his own loins was almost more than he could comprehend or deal with.

"Got a hug for me, son?" Lizzie inquired, touching his arm.

Billy was shaken from his reverie. He grinned, pleased. "Why . . . I sure do . . . Ma!" He replied, his tone husky with poignancy and grateful affection.

Before releasing him, Lizzie gave him a secretive extra little hug for courage. "Good luck," she whispered low, her words scarcely more than a breath in his ear. "I'll be prayin' for your intentions, Will."

"Thanks," he murmured in return.

Billy's heart was in his throat as he followed Harmony's graceful exit from the Grant Hotel.

He thrilled to the touch of her soft, smooth, neatly

manicured hand as he assisted her down the front stoop of the solid structure. He was loathe to sacrifice the touch of her fingers against his hand, but the sensations of disappointment and denial fled when Harmony matter-of-factly tucked her slim arm through the loop of his elbow so they could stroll side by side to the church property.

Harmony made small talk, commenting about the area, the residents, and the day's events. But as attentive as Billy tried to be, he was scarcely able to hear what his beloved was saying, his head felt so abuzz with swirling thoughts.

He felt as if there were a committee holding a meeting within his mind, all of the participants arguing and suggesting how he should—or most certainly should not—set about asking Harmony Childers to become his bride. Now, in the Minnesota twilight, feeling the same longings, only more intensified, Billy swatted a mosquito away from Harmony and wet his lips for the words that he prayed would come.

For a moment Harmony's chatter waned. Billy didn't know what to say, but he knew his moment had come, and the sudden silence seemed almost deafening as the breeze whispered through pine boughs overhead. Unnerved, desperate to break the oppressive still, Billy blurted the first thing he could think of.

"Babies! You're sure smitten by those little fellas, aren't you?"

Harmony gave a soft chuckle. "I reckon that I am," she admitted. "They're so innocent, so trusting, so helpless, and when they're bathed and handily cared for, sweet smelling and beautiful. I enjoy looking at each one—seeing every baby as the very handiwork of the Creator. I can't help marveling at the love and care that goes into the knitting of each wee one." For gathering moments Harmony extolled the magnificence of human life contained within a precious, helpless bundle with so much miraculous potential for growth. "I believe that a person would have to have a heart of stone to resist the charm of a newborn babe. Don't you think so?"

Billy had never given the matter much thought.

He hadn't been around innocent young life in his years. His own life had seemed to him to have never even had the veneer of purity. Only corruption—from without, and then soon from within—as he learned the rules of conduct in a treacherous world, cagily so, in order that he might get by and survive.

"The way you love babies, Miss Harmony," Billy said, bringing his thoughts back to the moment as they drew near to the church grounds, "I know that you'd make a wonderful mama."

Harmony didn't bother to blush—even though she could have been flustered at the familiarity of his remark—for she sensed that he meant no untoward intimacies by the observation.

"I've been told that before," she admitted. "Many times."

"No doubt because it's true. I know you're awfully dedicated to your nursing and helping others regain their health. . . ."

"Oh . . . yes! It's become my whole life," Harmony admitted, nodding enthusiastically, but she added no qualifying response that indicated she harbored other goals in life as well.

"I—I was wondering . . . do you think you'll ever . . . want to have your own family? Young'uns?"

Harmony's frown was reflective rather than piqued.

"I . . . don't . . . know. Perhaps someday I will." She gave a light laugh accompanied by a hapless gesture. "I gather that's what normal women eventually want—isn't it?"

Billy shrugged. "Bein' as I'm a fellow, I don't rightly know that I could answer how it is womenfolk commonly think."

"Of course you can't," Harmony said, gently chuckling. "But tell me, Bill, do men of your age ponder the possibility of marrying, settling down, and having a family?"

Billy saw his chance!

"Do I?" He cleared his throat, hoping to dislodge the lump of nervousness that threatened to strangle him until he was robbed of the capacity to speak what he knew might well be the most momentous words of his life. "Anymore, Miss Harmony, it seems that's all I *can* think about. Marrying. Settling down. Building a life. Having children to carry on my line and family name. Raisin' 'em up to know, love, and serve the Lord. . . ."

"Oh," Harmony whispered, her neutral tone conveying a hint of surprise at the depth and fervency of Billy's emotions and how sincerely he expressed them.

Billy halted, faced Harmony, and touched her shoulder, centering her squarely before him. For a moment her eyes widened in startlement when she saw the cast of desperation in his eyes.

"All I can think about, Miss Harmony, is all of those things—and *you*. More'n anything, I want you for the mother of my children. I—I want you for . . . my wife."

There! The words were out!

Billy died a thousand deaths once the syllables had escaped his lips, and it was too late to retract them as he waited for Harmony to give her answer. He wasn't sure it would be a response he'd care to hear.

"Oh, Bill!" Harmony breathed. Surprise but no other reaction was apparent in both her tone and the searching eyes that roved over his features.

His fingertips tightened into the soft, silken flesh of her

upper arm, almost as if he feared—unrealistically so—that she might bolt and flee, that he'd never see her again.

At the idea, his desperation intensified.

"Marry me, Miss Harmony! Oh, please . . . !"

Silence spiraled around them.

Finally Harmony found her voice. She laid her hand over Bill's grasp in a gesture of solace but also as a gentle reminder that he was almost hurting her in the intensity of his desire.

"I—I just don't know what to say," she stammered. "Th—this has rather caught me off guard. . . . And I—"

Billy gave a sickly groan and squeezed his eyes shut, as if he were straining against being overcome by a wave of dizzy nausea.

"If you can't say yes," he blurted wildly, desperately, "then please, at least for the moment . . . don't say no! Let me live on in hope. Tell me that you'll think about it—that you'll at least give me some consideration as your husband."

Harmony seemed to almost wilt with relief. "How understanding and sensitive of you, Bill, to suggest time for me to think. I *do* need to ponder the matter—and pray too."

"I know what *I'll* be praying for!" he whispered.

Harmony squeezed his hand, then touched his cheek. "We must remember not to pray just for what . . . we . . . might desire, Bill, but to ask God that his will be done. He will guide us. He has a special plan for each of us . . . maybe for us to be together . . . or perhaps not."

Suddenly Billy realized that he might not get an answer—any answer—from Harmony Childers as quickly as he had supposed, and he was helpless not to say as much.

"There's no need to be impatient," Harmony reminded, her voice soft and understanding. "The Lord will give us all the time we need for our hearts to listen. And in the meantime, we'll spend time together, talk, share our dreams, learn more about one another ... and discover from godly communication to our spirits if we're actually meant to be together."

"I see," Billy said. How could he but not? He knew that what she spoke was from the surety of her soul. But even so, he was unable not to let a faint timbre of helpless, frustrated disappointment tinge his tone.

"Know this, Bill LeFave, that I'm terribly fond of you. And very attracted to you, too, in a way a woman probably shouldn't even admit to a fellow who's not yet her lawfully wedded husband. But nonetheless ... I am. And I want you to—need you to—know that. I—I've never before felt for another what I feel for you now. But on the other hand—"

"Oh, Harmony, I love you!" Billy breathed as great relief and endless hope burgeoned within him until he feared his mere human body couldn't contain such feeling and remain intact.

When Harmony lifted her lips, an unspoken invitation for Billy to claim her mouth in a kiss, he felt as if he could've died a happy man at that moment, simply in cherishing the joy of what Harmony had willingly granted him. Consideration!

And he knew that he would pray unceasingly that one day, and soon, she would know her mind, heart, and the Lord's will, and that she would offer much, much more ... that they might give themselves to each other in order to more fully present themselves to the Lord and fulfill his purpose.

chapter

5

TWO DAYS HAD passed.

Billy was unusually quiet, Lizzie noticed, and seemed preoccupied. When he wasn't helping around the hotel, donating his time to improving the church property, or assisting people around Williams with his jack-of-all-trades talents, he secreted himself in his room.

Whether he was pondering or praying, Lizzie didn't know, but she suspected that he did both. Although he tried to act normal, Lizzie realized what a burden it was, for a shadowy edge of insecurity clung to him like the humid summer weather.

On the third day, Lizzie could stand it no more!

She was in the kitchen, alone, peeling some Irish Cobbler potatoes, carefully digging out the eyes with the point of her razor-sharp paring knife. She studiously regarded each potato as she worked, but only the better to avoid looking at Will and seeing the aura of dejection that accompanied him everywhere he went.

"Harmony told me that you popped the big question the other evenin'," Lizzie began, not bothering with a preamble of pleasantries before getting straight to the heart of the matter. "And she explained that she wants you to court a while as she makes up her mind."

"That she did," Billy replied. "I find that answer a lot more tolerable than an outright no." He didn't add that he was praying that it wasn't just a genteel way for sweet, ladylike

75

Harmony Childers to "let him down easy," and that no answer *was* an answer in its own way.

With a flick of her wrist, Lizzie flipped a shiny white potato into the vat of salty water to join the other tubers en route to becoming mashed potatoes for the evening meal.

"I have a feelin' it ain't goin' to be a turndown, son. Harmony always has been a girl who wanted to make certain that her head and heart matched up in where they was a-leadin' her."

Billy gave a wan grin.

"A lot like her mama, I've come to observe."

Lizzie cocked her head, then gave a twinkling smile that conveyed she considered being compared to her daughter a lovely compliment.

"I expect you're right, although truth be told, I'm plumb impulsive compared to Harmony."

"I can understand the wisdom in waiting and praying for an answer. But I also know that when ... if ... she accepts ... I'm not going to want to wait very long to take her as my wife."

"I know what ya mean," Lizzie commiserated. "Before we know it, winter will be comin' on. So what are you going to do in the meantime as you wait for an answer and, Lord willing, prepare for a weddin'?"

"Make something of myself," Billy replied. "More than's already here, that is. And optimistically, I'd like to lay a firm foundation for the good life I want and—more than anything—desire to give Harmony and any young'uns we might have."

After finishing with the potatoes and assessing the beef roast planned for supper, Lizzie poured them each a cup of coffee and then sat across the table from Billy.

Impulsively, she laid her work-worn but tender hand over his callused, suntanned grip, squeezing.

"Sounds like you've got a head full o' plans 'n dreams, Will. I always believed iffen you can dream it, likely you can do it!"

"Guess I do have a lot of ideas," he said, taking a sip of coffee and reaching for a golden, crispy, frosted sugar cookie on the plate of home-baked delicacies that Lizzie had solicitously nudged toward him. "Lots of plans and dreams." Lizzie reached for a gingersnap and broke it in half, then daintily dunked it in her coffee, taking a thoughtful bite before she spoke.

"Care to talk about these hoped-for events 'n situations, Will? I'm a chatterbox, I know, but folks seem to think I'm a purty good listener, too. You're welcome to confide, if you're in a notion o' speaking what's on your mind."

Billy cupped the hot coffee mug between his large hands, as if somehow the warmth of the heavy stoneware mug could penetrate his body, which had seemed under siege of a penetrating chill, even though the summer weather had been unusually hot.

"Maybe I would feel more at peace in the matter if I talked about it with a Christian person and tried to sort out my feelings into words. Sometimes it seems that I have so many thoughts swirling through my mind nowadays that my head almost can't contain 'em all. And no sooner am I musing over a wonderful hoped-for eventuality than I find myself snarled in horrible knots of worry."

Lizzie gave a light laugh. "I've been in those straits myself more'n a time or two in my life. I did find that it helped a heap talkin' about it, William."

Billy took a deep breath, then a gulp of coffee, as if the combination could fortify him to begin.

"Well," he began in a voice softly tinged with hope and almost excruciatingly appealing dreams, "I want to give Harmony a secure life. I'm doing all right supporting myself and paying on my bill with Dr. Marc by doing odd jobs around Williams and the hotel. But I want better for Harmony—and myself—than a lifestyle of hard times and a catch-as-catch-can existence."

Lizzie gave Billy an assessing glance, then smiled tenderly as she lifted an eyebrow.

"Now, why does my woman's intuition tell me that you've already got somethin' purty solid on your mind?"

"Because you're among the smartest of women on earth," Billy said, his voice teasing, although they both knew that his regard was genuine.

"And you're intent on marrying a gal that's every bit her ma's equal."

"I am . . . and I have the plans to go along with such a happy outcome in life." He gave a heavy, helpless sigh. "Only drawback is that giving her the life I want to—and know I'm capable of—would mean a bit of uprooting for Harmony. It'd be a peck different from how she's settled in and put down roots here in town. And the way I love her, I don't know if I can even ask it of her—and think it possible, all things considered, that she might still agree to be my wife. Seems I'm asking more'n I am able to offer."

Lizzie's heart clutched at the idea of her baby moving far, far away. With effort, she fought to keep her tone of voice casual and unconcerned.

"What exactly do you mean, Will?"

"I'm not a city fellow. Not even a small-town type. I like the wilderness and feel most at home surrounded by untamed nature and its wild beauty and opportunity."

"Yes?" Lizzie prompted him to go on as she busied herself in the warm, steamy kitchen so she could more handily turn her back to him in order that her features, and the reaction that would undoubtedly flit across them, would be inscrutable.

"When I was sober and went about my business in the northland, I was a good trapper. Among the best, in fact. And that's not a brag, Miss Lizzie. That's a fact."

"I don't doubt that a'tall," she replied.

"When I cut free and went my own way as a mere sapling—after escaping the lecherous old goats who'd taken a helpless tot and turned him into a captive—by working hard, I made . . . and frittered away . . . some big money harvesting fur."

Lizzie gave a hapless, understanding shrug.

"Don't trouble your mind, son. You ain't the first bloke at that impressionable age to follow that bright, beguilin', but oh-so-bitter path. It ain't that uncommon for fellers, even those raised in good and godly homes, to sometimes end up feelin' plumb foolish in their later years for having gotten their values more'n a tad bit moronic and finding that they'd frittered hard-earned jack on bad whiskey, what they thought was good times . . . and loose women."

A suddenly brooding Billy, who seemed in a dark place far distant, took a harsh gulp of the now cooled coffee and winced at the bitter taste of the dregs and the nettlesome thoughts that drew him back to the period of time that Lizzie had somehow sensed and summed up with an apt description.

"You're right. They weren't good times at all," he softly confessed, his voice an echoing ache of bitterness. "They were the *worst* of times. Although I didn't know it at the moment. The women . . . yes, they were . . . loose women . . . but also *laughing* wenches."

Lizzie's breath caught and she coughed quickly to hide her gasp of alarm when she realized the direction in which the conversation was turning. She wasn't sure it was right, had no idea how to counter it, felt in her heart that she shouldn't, and offered a quick prayer for the words of wisdom—and the strength of character and constitution—to hear out whatever William LeFave had to say, without expressing shock, outrage, disgust, or judgment.

"*Laughing wenches,*" he echoed in a dull tone, more to himself than to the woman he hoped would one day be his mama-in-law. "They got me drunk. Pilfered my pockets. Stole my money. Then made me a laughingstock." His voice grew husky with scarcely restrained tears. "They knew all about those old-coot trappers that I'd escaped from. So they had a pretty solid idea of what had . . ."

Billy's voice trailed off. He swallowed hard. But even so, a broken, whimpering, croaky little sob crept out.

Lizzie crossed the kitchen and put her arm around Billy's shoulder as he crushed his face into her waist, which was solidly sheathed in a swaddling apron.

"They knew what had happened to you," Lizzie murmured, her breath faint as the breeze outside the open window.

And suddenly Lizzie too knew what the poor soul had been through.

She strained to keep her riling stomach from revolting over the horrible, degrading, debauching pictures that suddenly filled her mind to overflowing.

"Oh, Will!" she cried in compassion as she realized she could scarcely bear to *think* about what the two reprobates had done to him. And he, scarcely more than a toddler, had been forced to *survive* such an abomination.

Lizzie thought of Scriptures that forbid such unnatural affections. Her mind went no farther than that before she realized that for Billy it hadn't been affection—it had been pure torture.

"No man should be used by another man the way they did me!" Billy blurted the heartbroken words, which were muffled by Lizzie's apron, his tears caught by the faded gingham material.

"Oh ... Billy ... Billy," Lizzie crooned, riffling her fingers through his hair, stroking and comforting him as if in that grown man's body was the tiny, confused little boy who'd lost his innocence when amoral men wise in the ways of the world had evilly stolen it from him.

As Billy cried so wretchedly and Lizzie realized that it was probably the first tears he'd allowed himself to shed over the matter—that he'd locked away all the hurt, pain, shame, and unwarranted guilt for two decades—she felt as if her own heart would fracture under the onslaught of such rending emotions.

"God love you, Will," she sighed, hugged him firmly, and dropped a motherly kiss to the crown of his head.

He looked up at her, his eyes damp with tears, his cheeks shiny from the moisture.

"Sometimes ... when I think ... when I remember ... it makes me doubt my faith. Doubt my salvation—"

"Oh no, Will—," Lizzie started to interrupt.

"I can't help it, Miss Lizzie. If what happened to me had happened to you—you'd have your moments of wonder and doubt, too. I was an innocent little boy, for heaven's sake! How could the Lord have let this happen to me? *Where the hell was God when I was being molested?!*"

Lizzie blanched at the word.

Then she realized there was no way to beautify the ugly, sordid atrocities that Billy LeFave had survived.

"Where was he?" Billy cried out. "What was he doing when they were doing that to me?!"

Silence sizzled between them.

Lizzie knew he expected an answer.

"Oh, Lord," Lizzie groaned, and it was the vocal beginning to an internal prayer begging their Savior for the words that Billy LeFave needed to hear to be healed and made whole.

"Where?" Billy whimpered.

At that moment, Lizzie knew that his faith hung in the balance.

"He was in heaven, Will. And no doubt he was wipin' tears and weepin' in grief over what was bein' done to you. It wasn't his doin'. So don't get yourself all het up and be furious with God. A lot o' folks get plumb irate with their Maker and blame lots o' things on him that actually ain't his doin' at all."

"Hah!" Billy was helpless to contain a muffled explosion of angry doubt, as he was caught in a vortex of returning memories and scalding emotions darkened with the gravest of doubts.

"My mind's just swirlin' with words to say," Lizzie began, suddenly feeling overwhelmed at all the wisdom and wonder that had miraculously filled her, and she realized that the Lord had answered her prayer. She was about to comfort Billy with words that, in the instant between one heartbeat and another, had enriched her own understanding of Scripture and had sharpened to a cutting edge her insights regarding their Creator's purpose and had suddenly made her see the clash between good and evil in a black-and-white manner she'd not quite known before.

After giving Billy a quick hug and pouring them each a fresh cup of coffee, she dropped into the chair across from him.

"I've gotta sit down for this," Lizzie unabashedly excused. "And please hear me out, Will, 'n don't interrupt, because I know what the Lord wants me to tell you for your understandin' as well as my own, so try not to get me sidetracked, or I'll end up wallowin' with a spirit o' confusion instead of godly knowledge."

He gave a silent nod, his eyes grave—but challenging.

Lizzie prayed that his heart would be fertile to hear and digest what she was about to say, even though he was little more than a newborn believer.

"First off, Will, I reckon you feel plumb racked with guilt and shame."

Silently he nodded.

"Well, don't you bother carryin' around those heavy burdens for a moment longer! The sin was theirs, William, not yours."

He stared at her, as if he'd never thought of it in that context before.

Lizzie grabbed a quick breath and rushed on. "Puttin' myself in your place, Will—hard as it is for me to do, for I can only vaguely imagine the horrors that you lived through—I reckon that you hate those two ol' codgers with ever' fiber of your bein'."

"That I do," Billy said, his tone steely. "In fact, if I had them in the room with me right this minute—"

His complexion reddened as suppressed fury infused his being.

"They sinned against you, Will. Their sin was great, because you were an innocent, trusting, helpless, hurtin' little boy—and they took cruel advantage of you in your plight. You've read in Scripture of how Jesus was especially protecting and loving toward little children. He'd have known a righteous anger at what those two adults, who should've known better, did to a child."

At the memory, Billy dropped his strained face into his quavering hands.

"What we've got to stop and remember, even if it's an idea

that at the moment is kind o' hard to humanly . . . choke down . . . is that when our Savior let himself be nailed and left to bleed and die on the cross to redeem us . . . well . . . he took the place of those two men . . . and he took their sins against you and paid their price with the heavenly Father, willin' to pay not only for all the sins you've racked up in life, Will, but payin' the sin-debt o' everyone who's sinned against you. No matter how terrible and serious the sin."

Billy groaned.

"The Lord, Billy, he didn't condone what those men did to you. He hated what they were doin' to you. Hated it! But even as he righteously hated their actions—as only God can—he *loved* those men enough to die to pay for their sins, too. Loved 'em enough to want them in eternity with him iffen they'd only repent, see their need for him, and be willing to accept salvation 'n stop livin' as perverted human bein's 'n let him live within them so they would exist as godly men."

"I have no idea what happened to them," Billy said.

And for the first time that he could recall, he didn't instinctively wish them dead and in hell as they came to mind.

"The Lord's not only our Savior, Will. He's a healer. Why, the Good Book is chock full of miraculous stories of Jesus makin' afflicted folks well. All he has to do is say the word or give you his touch, and you ain't just patched up, *you're healed*. Good as new! In fact, *better than new!* So take it to the Lord in prayer, son. And when you're talkin' with your Creator . . . you might ask him to help you to forgive those who've sinned against you. I know it ain't goin' to be easy, and likely it won't happen in the twinklin' of an eye. But forgiveness 'n healin' will eventually come if you're simply willin' to be willin' to be willin'."

Lizzie suddenly frowned, gave a rueful laugh, and said,

"Does that make any sense to you, Will? What I just said? I ain't even sure I'm makin' sense to myself—let alone gettin' it across to you."

"It's made perfect sense to my head . . . and one day it will to my heart too, I pray. . . . With all of this . . . sin and sordidness . . . in my background, I can't help but question my own worth. I'd never want to shortchange a woman like Harmony by encouraging her to accept and make do with less than such a treasure of a girl deserves."

"That was then—this is now!" Lizzie said, her voice flinty. "You're brand new and very precious in Christ, sharing in his heavenly inheritance, Will. You're valuable to all of us. We cherish you, son, and you've worth to the Savior too. Why, iffen you'd been the only one on earth needin' his redemption, he'd have given his life on the cross just for you! That's how much you mean to Jesus."

Billy thought it over—and smiled.

"You always make me feel better," he admitted.

"Talkin' helps. You've done told me your plans and dreams, so in these comin' few days, I suggest you find the time to do the same with my girl. It's Harmony's right to know—and it'll likely have bearing on the answer she seeks to give."

chapter
6

"So THAT'S WHY you've had a special glow about you these past days, Harmony Childers!" Marissa Wellingham cried as she gave the neighbor girl from Illinois an impulsive embrace, then jigged a few steps in sheer delight. "Huggin' a secret to yourself that Billy LeFave has asked for your hand!"

"Well, yes, he did," Harmony said, and a gentle blush crept to her features at the to-do Marissa was making over the private matter.

"Well, don't keep me in suspense—what'd you tell him?!"

Harmony paused. "I told him that I had to think about it. And had to pray."

Marissa studied the younger woman.

"Yes? And?"

"Those things take time."

"You haven't given him an answer yet?" Marissa gasped. She, as well as anyone in town, knew how smitten poor Billy was with the pretty, smart, and talented nurse.

"No. Not yet."

Marissa gave a theatrical groan, a sound somewhere between sympathy and outright impatience.

"The poor man must be dying the death of a rag doll with every breath he takes. As gaga as he is over you, I don't know how he'll handle it if you tell him no." Marissa cast Harmony a penetrating look. "You're not turning him down, are you?" The question seemed almost a warning not to break the young man's heart and shatter his dream. "Are you? Answer me, Harmony Childers!"

The serene nurse was helpless not to contain a tender smile.

"No . . . I'm not going to turn him down. I'm going to give him my answer tonight when I dine with Bill and the family at the hotel. I'll explain that I do desire to marry him—and explain that certain needs must be met."

Marissa made a face. But then, she knew herself to be the helpless romantic, and Harmony to be the hopeless pragmatic.

"And they might be?"

"Well, one, that I'll need time," Harmony decreed. "After much thought and heartfelt prayer, I have come to know that I want to spend the rest of my life with Bill. I have never felt about another man as I find myself feeling toward him."

"How well I know the feeling," Marissa murmured and gave a fond glance toward the infirmary, where her husband was consulting with a patient. "We've all suspected how you felt about Billy. And there wasn't a doubt in any of our minds as to how he felt about you. He adores you. The entire town does."

"I know," Harmony replied. "And that'll make it that much harder to leave Williams, my family, my friends, the church home."

Marissa's eyebrows flew up in surprise. That news was something she hadn't reckoned on.

"You think you'll have to move? Can't you just—"

"The past few evenings, Bill and I have been having some serious discussions. The Lake of the Woods, traplines, fishing, harvesting wild rice, and other outdoor pursuits for making a living are where his heart and happiness lie. Granted, he's adjusted to living at the hotel. But in reality, he's like a fish out of water. He endures it better only because I'm close by. If I caused him to give up his contentment with his environment to satisfy me ... bitterness might one day set in. I don't want that for him or for me. I love the wilderness, too, now that I've gotten over some of the natural frights I had right after Lester and I moved up here. I like living in town, but I've enjoyed rural life, also. Where Billy goes, there I will go, too, and serve the Lord as he would have me labor."

"I know what you mean," Marissa said. "That's how I felt about Marc when he wanted to set up a practice in an area that needed him. He selected northern Minnesota. But I'd have willingly gone with him to deepest, darkest Africa."

"Before I can leave, I really need Bill to grant me time to put my affairs in order. Marc needs to find a replacement, and I want to ease the transition by remaining here long enough to help him train his new nursing assistant."

"That's very thoughtful, Harmony. Don't worry overly much, though, darling, for I can assist Marc more if necessary," Marissa assured.

Harmony shook her head. "Your son needs your attention, 'Rissa. You just turn your hand to enjoying being little Curt Alton's mama. The bigger your wee one gets, the more demanding he's going to be. Already he's asleep less and less, and awake and active more and more."

"You're right," Marissa agreed. "My helping Marc more wasn't a plausible solution. I guess I didn't want you to alter your plans for our benefit. I want you to be as happy with Billy as I am with Marc. So I didn't want your profession to sidetrack your personal interests."

"I'm sure once word gets around town that my days in Williams are numbered, there will be young women who'll drop by to express an interest in training to become nurses. Or, as well acquainted as Marc's become with families in the area, he might even have some capable individuals in mind, and he could pose offers to them."

"The way his practice is growing, and the way young women have a habit of falling in love and moving away or settling down to raise families, it's likely that Marc will want to instruct a number of nursing assistants so he'll have plenty of help."

"It will all work out," Harmony assured.

"For all of us," Marissa agreed. "You'll have a good life with Billy."

Harmony's features softened further with a tender, optimistic smile that radiated her inner love. "He's a remarkable man."

"He sure is! He reminds me so much of my pa. Billy's downright blossomed. Lizzie keeps comparing it to the change that came over Alton Wheeler when he fell in love with a woman like Sue Ellen Stone."

"Considering that Bill grew up under rough conditions, with no parents, and in dire straits, he's done extremely well for himself. Not many fellows raised under such a set of circumstances and being against such odds would've hungered for knowledge and taught themselves how to read."

"I never really thought of that! It is amazing."

"I thank the Lord for the patient soul Bill met up with each year at the big rendezvous celebration, where trappers, voyageurs, and Indians congregated for a week or two of merriment. That's where he learned the alphabet, rudiments of phonics—he struggled to figure out the rest himself. That paved the way for him now; he's fairly devouring the Good Book."

"He's no slouch at numbers either. One day when we were in Lundsten's Mercantile, Billy was ciphering faster in his head than old Mr. Lundsten did on his paper. There's no question that Billy's a hard worker. Anyone who's hired his services can attest to that. Not to mention all of his donated labor at the church grounds."

"It'll be lovely for our wedding," Harmony mused.

"You can trust Billy to provide a fine cabin in which you'll set up housekeeping."

"It'll take him a while. . . ."

The girls fell into momentary silence, then Marissa gave a wistful sigh.

"All of this talk makes me kind of homesick for the cabin- and barn-raising socials we had back in Illinois when we were young'uns. Weren't they fun times?"

"Oh . . . my, yes!"

Suddenly Marissa had an idea, and she almost blurted it before she managed to censor her tongue and deftly change the topic.

Minutes later Harmony glanced at her heirloom timepiece. "It seems we don't get a chance to visit like this much any- more," she said, touching Marissa's shoulder. "But I'd better check on patients, then freshen up a bit. Billy will be here soon to escort me to the hotel for supper."

Lizzie refilled her coffee mug and Billy's.

"You're makin' a lot o' progress in all that you're doin', Billy. Now, tell me more about these exciting plans you have. . . . It sounds to me like you've already got a time frame in mind."

"I do. I'm not a patient man by nature—I don't think too many of us are," Billy said. "And if Miss Harmony will accept me, then I want for us to be able to be together as soon as possible. That means that I'll need to depart the general area for a while to prepare for us to have a life together. So I'll have to be away for a time. But that's not all bad," he said quickly, as if to convince himself as much as Lizzie. "Being apart by necessity will serve to give her the time she's needing to think and pray. Although, of course, I'd like to think that she'll reach a decision before I leave."

"Where ya headin' for, Billy boy?" Lizzie asked, arising and playfully ruffling his thick hair as she began to do a few tasks around the kitchen in preparation for the evening's dinner hour.

"The islands," he replied.

Billy's eyes glowed as he spoke of the wilderness islands that dotted the gigantic Lake of the Woods, and the wealth of fur-bearing game that could be harvested there. He related how rumor once had it that there was also gold in the area, and adventurous, optimistic men had created a minor gold rush that ended in general disappointment and disillusionment.

"Much as I love the wilderness of the great north woods, I treasure the serenity of the Lake of the Woods even more. When I can be where I can enjoy both the rugged land and the powerful beauty of the sea—well, not to be irreverent, but that's when it's been as if I've known a bit of heaven right here on earth."

"There are those who call this God's country. But I've noticed most men consider the Lord's favorite acres to be wherever 'tis that they've been blessed to make a homestead claim."

"I know that there are men in these forested parts who'd consider me a traitor, but the truth is, I don't like making my living as a lumberjack in the great woods . . . and I feel like I'll never tire of the opportunities afforded upon the shores of such a magnificent lake. There are so many trades to consider. Commercial fishing. Trapping. Maybe even steamboat piloting. I believe I could make a go at any of them."

"Or maybe *all* of them," Lizzie encouraged. "The zest you display, Will, I don't doubt that you can succeed at whatever you turn your hand to."

"I want a life that'll allow both Harmony and me to be happy."

"I've heard it said, 'Do what you love—and the money will follow,'" Lizzie enjoined.

"I'm not terribly concerned about the finances," Billy said. "I've actually got quite a bit of jack to my name—iffen it's still where I buried it and iffen I can find it back and someone else didn't beat me to it."

Lizzie quirked a brow. "Do tell!"

"I've buried more than a few little cache jars of money in my time since I struck out on my own," Billy said. "Traveling alone as I was, I realized I'd make easy prey for a band of marauding Indians or conspiring desperadoes intent on relieving me of my assets. Burying money was one way that if I was ambushed, I knew I wouldn't be left destitute."

"Lord willin', you'll find your caches 'n have a down payment on makin' all your dreams reality."

"If even only a tiny portion of my dreams for making a living and sharing that life with your daughter come true, Miss Lizzie, I'll consider myself a man well blessed, for I'll love where I am . . . what I'm doing . . . and who I'm with."

"We all find our niches in life," Lizzie said, "especially if we're open to new opportunities and allow the Lord to lead us where he would have us live 'n serve. Why, look at me! Seems plumb strange when I dwell on it, but here I am, a middle-aged woman, runnin' a dandy hotel and just as happy as a pig in mud, when for all o' my previous years I'd considered myself as content as you please just bein' a country gal and farmwife. But lo 'n behold if runnin' a town business isn't right agreeable to me 'n mine."

"You're going to hate to return the reins to Rose Ames when she and Homer retire back to these parts," Billy teased.

Lizzie didn't bother to deny it. "I'm a few years older than Rose, so mayhap by then I'll be ready to take it easy. I can't help thinkin', though, of the opportunities iffen this was our family's operation. Lester is really exhibiting a talent for the hotel business. Be nice if one day this could be his. He labors at it as conscientiously as if it was."

"Rose is a hard worker, but chances are, after living the life of a banker's wife in Fargo, she may want to spend her retirement years enjoying leisure with her husband rather than working day and night to care for others. It might be such a thing as she'll someday want to sell—and then Les'll be in a position to buy."

"We're a contented lot, ain't we?" Lizzie pointed out, chuckling. "I'm doin' what I love, Les and Joy are, too, you're about to get set to realize your dreams, and Harmony's been doin' what she adores, in helping Doc Wellingham."

"I've kept that in mind," Billy said. "I'd never set out to find fulfillment of my goals at the expense of Harmony's dreams. But I'm believing that if she'll only agree to be my wife, there'll be no need for compromise in that area. Folks get good medical attention here in town and in the immediate outlying areas. But folks out by the lake are a pretty far piece from a physician or even a midwife. A lot of their injuries and ills could be treated by a nurse with Harmony's capabilities."

Lizzie nodded. "Harmony does feel an obligation to the sick and injured. She'll have a hard time leavin' the infirmary, but if she knows she'll be of the same use up there, it could help her as she reaches her decision. I know she's bound to have reservations about leaving Dr. Wellingham in the lurch. He's been talking about training more nurses. And he really should."

"Harmony and I have a lot of things we'll need to discuss," Billy said, "and I'm hoping to get a chance for us to walk and talk after the evening meal and trusting that she won't feel that I'm pressuring her for an answer."

"How soon are you expecting to depart for your homestead tract?"

"In about a fortnight," Billy replied. "I'll need to erect a nice cabin and make other improvements. Winter comes early to these parts. During the cold months, I'll need my time for running traplines."

"It'll pro'bly be a spring weddin', huh?" Lizzie mused, not really aware she'd spoken her thoughts out loud.

Billy gave an abashed smile. "I wish I could be as confident of Harmony's answer as you seem to be."

Lizzie smiled gently. "Bein' her mama, I've known my girl a lot longer than you have, Will. And I trust that you're going to cherish gettin' to know her even better than I."

The grandfather clock in the Wellingham home had scarcely finished chiming the half hour when there was a discreet rap on the door.

Marissa, who'd just laid Curt Alton down for a nap, went to answer and found Billy all slicked up and waiting to collect Harmony, who appeared immediately.

Scarcely had Billy and Harmony stepped onto the street and she'd secured her arm through his before she looked up with seriousness of intent.

"I have my answer, Bill," she whispered.

Billy felt his heart leap—then lurch—and his pent breath left him momentarily unable to speak words to bid her not to keep him in suspense so much as one unnecessary moment.

"I figured there's no sense making you wait longer."

That was one of the many things that Billy loved about Harmony—her directness. Yet he was helpless not to consider that a prompt answer could go against him.

"And—?" he said, swallowing hard, his blue eyes a swirl of hope shot through with shadows of what would manifest itself as outright despair if her words were not to his liking.

"Yes. My answer is yes."

"You—you'll marry me?" Billy stammered.

Harmony smiled up at him, and her cheeks were appealingly flushed. "With . . . pleasure."

Billy let out a whoop!

Then he impulsively and exuberantly embraced Harmony Childers right where they stood on Main Street, in front of God and an assortment of passing mankind. Unable to restrain himself, Billy captured her sweet lips with his, his pulse going wild at the yielding pliancy of her mouth against his, in a lingering touch so filled with promise.

"You won't regret it," Billy promised as he dared to slip his arm around her lithe waist and give her a happy squeeze. "Lord willing, I'll make you the happiest woman alive."

Harmony raised onto tiptoes and brushed a kiss to Billy's cheek.

"I know you will, Bill. And . . . I think that maybe I already *am*."

chapter
7

St. Louis, Missouri

THE UPSTAIRS QUARTERS where Nanette and Nick shared space suitable for siblings was right above the room Thad had rented from Mrs. Cummings—the rotund and robust landlady, whose figure offered proof of her culinary efforts—and it was beastly hot.

"One more time, Thad," Nanette said, her voice weary, tinged with a fine tone of impatience. "And do pay attention this time!"

"I have been . . . I have been. . . ."

"Now watch me. Pay close attention. So you can do what I do."

Expertly Nanette slapped the deck of cards down before herself, snapped the pack in half, and with beautifully manicured fingers began to shuffle them. Knowing that Thad was watching her, she did a few trick moves, laying the length of the deck up her slim arm, then back down again, shuffling all the way.

She sensed that Thad was mesmerized.

He gave his head a rueful shake.

"Darlin', I'll never be that good."

Nanette shrugged and her bodice, which she'd loosened a bit against the heat, slid to one side, baring the creamy curve of her shoulder. The dark tendrils of her hair, which was piled high, stuck damply, giving her a glamorous, exotic, tousled countenance.

"Maybe not as good, Thad. But at least passable. Here." She dropped the deck in front of him. "You try it."

Gamely Thad set about maneuvering the cards. He was better than he'd have ever dreamed he'd become at handling a deck of cards, but his best was no match for Nanette and Nick at their worst.

"You're getting better," Nanette said.

Idly she reached across to the breast pocket of Thad's lacy shirt and extracted a dark cheroot from the packet that he'd recently begun to carry.

Expertly she bit off the end of the slim cigar, spit, and sent the discarded bit flying across the room. Bracing the cheroot between her beautiful white teeth, she grinned as she lit up, inhaled, and gave Thad a pleased smile through the hazy smoke.

"Look at you!" she giggled. "You still think it's evil for a woman to smoke—though I reckon you've decided it's all right for you menfolk to smoke."

Thad stammered as her words suddenly drove home to him how much his ethics and convictions had changed—bit by bit, moment by moment—as he accepted first one thing, then another, and soon his old life and old ways seemed as if they'd belonged to another.

"Now, Nan, I'm not bein' judgmental," Thad said. "It's just that some things look . . . unsightly. You're so beautiful that it's unseemly to see a cheroot poking from between your lips. It's—"

"It displeases you?" she asked softly and arose, her fingertip stroking the edge of his collar.

"Well . . . yes."

"All right," she said. Nanette removed the cheroot from her own lips and placed it between Thad's. He clamped down and inhaled, no longer choking and coughing over the acrid smoke as he'd done when he first took up the habit. "But I get to stand downwind of you . . . so I can enjoy the scent without smoking it myself, since you think it isn't ladylike."

"Very well," Thad said.

Nanette grinned. "I've got an even better idea."

With a vixen smile, she moved close to Thad, slipped one arm around his neck, removed the cheroot from his mouth with her other hand, and then let her brightly painted lips take its place.

"Ummmm . . . good," Nanette whispered. "I may never smoke again."

Thad grinned, his lips curving against Nanette's. "In that case," he said teasingly, drawing her closer to him in an embrace, "I may never stop smoking."

A moment later the cheroot was dropped, forgotten, to smolder in the glass ashtray as Thad, overcome with emotions for the bright and beautiful creature, captured her in a tight grip in which Nanette was only too willing to be imprisoned.

"Mmmmm . . . nice. . . ." Nanette breathed encouragement as her fingertips sifted through Thad's hair, and he shivered beneath the thrilling unfamiliarity of her touch.

"I love you, Nan." He murmured the words that he'd never spoken to a woman before—words he now found himself saying with some regularity to Nanette, always hoping that she would express similar sentiments in return.

"You're pretty fine yourself," she whispered back. "In fact, I probably love you as much as I've ever liked anyone before."

Nanette's mind went reeling back over the boys and men who'd sought her companionship in their old river town and in the city of St. Louis. Relationships had been like barter for exchange. Her good looks and saucy manner were baubles that beguiled, and men—all men—had seemed helplessly tempted.

In their desire—Nanette found disdain.

But Thad was different. She was unsure why, but he seemed totally honest—captivatingly so—in his genuine affection and admiration, which wasn't merely a gambit to afford him a position on the good side of her nature in order to advance his natural inclinations.

He didn't treat her like a trollop. Sometimes he was a bit disapproving of what he considered tartlike behavior, but she could giggle away his words and attitudes, for his delivery made it clear that even if he wasn't impressed with her actions, she, Nanette Kelly, went unjudged in his eyes and was appreciated for who she was at any given moment in time.

Thad removed his hands from the small of Nanette's back and extricated her arms from around him.

"We'd better stop," he suggested.

Nanette pouted. "You always say that," she complained.

"Only because I care about you and respect you. If I didn't—" He shook his head over what liberties he might then take with her, had he cared not about her well-being but only his own satisfactions.

"You respect me more than I respect myself!" Nanette flared in a sulky tone.

"And that's a pity, my dear Nan. For I wish that you could love and admire yourself even half as much as I do. Then you might care about your future and your—"

She whirled away from him in a flash of lace. Her eyes glinted. "Sometimes I wish you *didn't* love me, Thaddeus Childers! Life might be ever so much easier that way. And,"—she glared at him and tossed her tousled hair away from her lips, which were appealingly puffed from the force of their kiss—"it would be a lot more exciting!"

Thad didn't know what to say to that. And it was words like those that made it hard for him to reconcile himself to the fact that when it came to such matters, Nanette was as experienced as Thad was innocent.

Regardless of where she'd been, what she'd done, or what Nick mercilessly told her she'd become, Thad's eyes saw a charming, appealing innocence that seemed to beg forgiveness for the wrongs she'd impulsively and thoughtlessly committed as the Kelly twins made their way through life in this world.

"I got you a little something," he said, reaching into his pocket.

Nanette's pique departed. "Really?"

"Come get your present, sweetheart."

She took a step toward him. "Give me a kiss," she tempted. "Then the present."

"If you insist," he agreed.

"I do!" she murmured.

Many men had given her trinkets and gifts since she and Nick had come to the Gateway City. They'd meant nothing to her—except what Nick could exchange them for at a pawnbroker's shop. But a gift from Thad—even if it was only a sunny-faced dandelion picked from a crack in a sidewalk and given to her as a sign of affection—she would keep and cherish until her dying day.

He gave her a sweet kiss—pulling away with restraint when Nanette instinctively tried to turn it into an act of deeper passion.

"Now for your gift. Close your eyes and hold out your hand."

Nanette did as she was told.

Thad dropped something small into it.

"You can look now."

Nanette did. She saw a golden locket. It wasn't a bauble purchased at a pawnshop. It was a brand-new item, and engraved too, with the names "THAD & NANETTE" entwined within graceful, curlicuing hearts.

"Oh . . . Thad . . . it's beautiful!" Tears suddenly misted her eyes. "No one's ever given me anything like this before. Everyone else—they're always taking!"

"I wanted you to have it."

With a flick of her polished fingernail, Nanette clicked open the locket. "It's got places for our pictures."

"Uh-huh, but I don't have a photograph of myself. Never had one that little. Reckon I've had only one real picture of myself took. That was one Ma paid for with money she won catchin' a pig at the Watson fair."

"I don't have a picture either," Nanette said. "Oh, well."

"Maybe someday we'll have pictures of us for your locket," Thad said.

"Maybe. 'Til then I'd like to have *something*." Suddenly Nanette seemed to get shy, which was unusual in such a spirited, almost brazenly bold girl. "Thad . . . could I have a lock of your hair? I promise I'll snip it off with my manicure scissors and do the job so that no one can look at you and even tell."

"If you really want to."

"I do."

"Cut away," Thad said and prepared to hold still as Nanette opened her manicure case.

"There!" Nanette said proudly after she'd relieved Thad of a curl of dark, burnished hair. She gently teased it around her finger, then filled the small locket almost to overflowing and closed the hasp again. "Put it on me, Thad?"

"It would be my pleasure."

Nanette turned around and raised her slim arms, then scooped up what raven-black hair had fallen to cascade around her neck and shoulders.

Feeling clumsy, Thad's fingers smoothed the necklace at the base of her throat, then picked at the hook, finally affixing it. A moment before he stood back, he leaned over, his breath warm against the fine, downy hairs at the nape of her neck. Gently he kissed the tender area, which was sweetly scented with expensive perfume.

Almost before Thad knew it, Nanette had pivoted around in his arms and they were locked in an embrace from which there seemed no end. And from which Thad wasn't sure he could remove himself as he always had managed before.

Suddenly the door to the room opened so fast that it cracked against the inner wall of the quarters with an earsplitting bang.

Nanette and Thad leaped apart.

Nick staggered into the room. "Break it up, break it up! We've got things to do!"

"Nick, what—" Then Nanette saw the splashes of blood. "You're bleeding!" she cried.

"Keep your voice down!" Nick said. "I'm bleeding, yeah, but the desperado who pulled a knife on me is lying dead in the sawdust as it soaks up his blood. Enough people know about it already, Sis, without your caterwauling."

"Oh Nick, what are we going to do? You're going to be a wanted man. . . ." Nanette fussed and clucked as she eased away his vest, the slashed shirt, and revealed an arcing slice across his lean rib cage. The tissues were already puffy and inflamed from the force of the trauma.

"What we're going to do is clear out of town. Right now.

Be a good girl, Sis, and pack. Quietly—and quickly. Thad, get me a towel from the washstand, if you would—"

"Nick, I'm sorry—," Thad said, shaken over the turn of events, as he turned to comply.

Nick shrugged away Thad's concerns and the general situation. "It was a case of it being either him or me. I preferred that it be . . . him."

"Where are you going to go?"

"Sis and I will be on the first riverboat leaving St. Louis," Nick said. "Going whatever way it's heading."

"Oh," Thad said, his tone hollow.

Nick seemed to think for a moment. "You're welcome to come along," he finally offered. "If you want to. And if you can keep your mouth shut."

"He can. And he is. And he will!" Nanette decided, settling the matter as she crossed the room and unceremoniously dumped possessions into two valises thrown open across her bed. "I won't go with you and leave Thad behind."

"Really? Why?" Nick asked, seating himself and haggardly pressing a fine linen handkerchief against the wound left by the slashing knife's graze.

"Because, dear brother, he's still a bit naive about life," Nanette said. "Furthermore, as weakened as you are, we can rely on his strength." Then she grinned and entwined her arm around Thad's waist, encouraging him to reciprocate. "We also seem to be falling in love."

At that statement, Nick gave a hearty laugh cut short only when the expansion of his rib cage freshly knifed him with pain. He settled for rudely shaking his head and muttering at Nan that he'd esteemed her as more intelligent than the average woman but it appeared she too had her own weak needs for love.

"If you can tear yourself away from my beautiful, bewitching, and sometimes bawdy sister long enough, Thaddeus old man," Nick said, "you'd better run along to your quarters and pack. We've got a riverboat to catch!"

Watson, Illinois

"Oh, dear Lord, if only you would see fit to spare me a need to do this," Lemont said, his heart feeling as if it were going to break as he retrieved his pen, ink bottle, and the familiar foolscap upon which he wrote to Lizzie and Brad Mathews.

"But your will, not mine."

Lemont Gartner realized that Jesus Christ knew how he felt at that moment: hating to do something, wishing he didn't have to, but aware that it was the Father's will for him to do it. Just as Christ accepted the cross, Lemont knew that writing a letter of heartbreak to Lizzie Mathews was going to be one of the crosses that he would take up in life.

"Lord," Lemont prayed, "I'm trustin' you to give me the words, just as you told ol' Moses not to worry what to say, that you'd give his lips wisdom. And the way you inspired the apostles so that they spoke with the wisdom of God, not from human views. I'm not askin' so much for my sake, Lord, but for Lizzie's. This news is goin' to break her heart. I don't need the manner in which the message is conveyed to make it even worse."

For long moments, Lemont stared at the pad of foolscap.

On Lizzie Mathews' kitchen table, it seemed like his own Calvary. He'd have sooner borne almost any grief upon himself than to have to inflict such a piece of information on a woman as good as Lizzie, a woman who'd known triumph, but a matron who, everyone in the community knew, was all too acquainted with grief too. Even if it was grief that had forged her faith to become the impenetrable armor they all knew it to be.

"Dear Brad and Lizzie," Lemont began, laboriously shaping his letters, meticulously dipping his pen in the ink bottle with dawdling care that even momentarily postponed the awful words that he knew he would have to write.

"Knowing you, Lizzie," he continued,

you've probably noticed a different tone and an infrequency in my letters. It's been because I've had some heavy burdens on my mind and didn't feel up to contacting you about them. I was worried enough, here on the banks of Salt Creek, that I couldn't see much sense in upsetting you at a thousand miles away.

Plus, I guess I was hoping that with all of our combined prayer, the situation would change and there'd be no need to alert you.

Several months ago, Thad became difficult. He's always been the most spirited of your boys, but this was different indeed. Seth noticed it, as did Rory, and they talked to him, as did I. But Thad seemed unwilling to listen to anyone.

As a confirmed bachelor myself, I hadn't really expected him to listen to me. After all, what do I really know? I was always content to work my plot of ground and to neighbor with folks in the community. In all my years, I never seriously went sparking any girls, so I reckoned I didn't know how Thad felt or some of the yens for excitement he had. For me as a young man, a good crop was the most thrilling thing in the world.

Being as Rory and Seth are men who, although somewhat older than Thad, had gone through those same difficult years, I'd confided in them of the difficulties I was having. They chose to speak to Thad. Seth, it turns out, had planned to confront Thad as it was, for his attitude at work, alas, had not been the best.

You know how Thad can be. Mule-headed and hot-tempered. Instead of taking the words as constructive criticism offered by those who love and care about him and want the best in life for him, he got madder than blue blazes and started with some rash talk.

Unfortunately, we didn't pay much mind. We all figured that it was just Thad blowing off steam. But it's proven to be more than that. He was sneaky about it—hung around for about a week—and suddenly he was gone, leaving us waiting for his return. He didn't take anything with him, which fooled us for a few days. By the time Seth and Rory went to Effingham to inquire around, Thad was long gone. St. Louis, we think. Rory wanted to go to St. Louis and look for him, but Seth pointed out that the Mississippi River is a major route of transportation and that Thad, who has always had a hankering for the sea (remember when he'd play pirates as a wee tad?) might take a riverboat or barge to New Orleans or even hie on up to Minneapolis and St. Paul, perhaps en route to Williams.

If Thad arrives in Williams, please telegraph us so that we are aware of his safety and whereabouts, for we're all deeply concerned. And likewise, if we have any word from him or he reappears, we'll extend the kindness of wiring you with the good news.

I'm sorry in letting you down, Lizzie. I know you probably won't see it that way, and bless you for your forgiving nature and understanding heart, but I'm afraid I'm torturing myself wondering what I could've done or what I did that I shouldn't have.

As you can tell, I'm heartsick about this. What comfort I attain comes in knowing that the Lord is watching out for Thad—and all of us—better than we can do for ourselves.

Aside from this, news is scarce. Perhaps I'll feel more like writing in a few days.

I'm thinking of putting my farm up for sale. It's getting to be too much for an old man to handle. But don't you worry about that. You all have enough on your minds with this newest burden.

Katie and Seth assured me that they'd write to you in the coming days. Perhaps Seth will have information that I don't. I regret the circumstances of this letter, and all I can offer for consolation is that we're all praying for Thad on a daily basis.

Love to you all,
Lemont Gartner

Lemont read over what he'd written, decided it was as gentle as he could manage and that it offered hope along with the bad news.

With a heavy heart, he addressed the envelope, found a stamp, then took down a lantern and walked the letter to the mailbox.

And as in recent weeks, he no longer bothered to listen for the sounds of someone progressing up the trail, hoping in his heart that it might be Thad Childers, because he'd realized the overwhelming futility of it all.

chapter
8

SCARCELY ONE HOUR had passed from the time Nick got into the altercation in the saloon, and the trio was standing on the riverfront, waiting to board the *River Queen*, a stern-wheeler that plied the Mississippi River from St. Louis to New Orleans. There were several boats moored at the pier, but the *River Queen* was the next steamboat scheduled to depart the Gateway City.

Nicholas gave Nanette money, and she booked passage for herself, as did Nick, and a short while later Thad segued into the line of persons purchasing a last-minute ticket.

The trio rendezvoused in Nick's economy quarters after the *River Queen* was under way. Nanette breathed a sigh of relief, and Thad felt less as if he were living in a nightmare and more as if it were just a bad dream and true reality was the serenity of the banks of the Mississippi River as the massive boat glided by.

Nicholas was jumpy and short-tempered, growing tense every time there were footsteps on the decking outside the cramped quarters.

"Relax, Nick!" Nanette chided him. "It's not as bad as you think."

He gave his sister a scathing look. "That's what you think!

You'd better be as concerned for yourself as you are for me. If they catch me—where does that leave you?"

At the thought, Nanette's violet eyes shadowed with myriad fears and she swallowed hard. Then a wave of defiance seemed to sweep over her.

"I love you, brother dear, and I care about what happens to you, Nicholas. But I can make my way in the world without you, thank you very much."

Nick gave a scornful laugh. "I'm the brains of this outfit, and you know it."

Nanette sniffed in consternation. "I have my talents, you know."

"Oh, yes. I've heard the gents talk about your 'talents,' and I've seen you in action."

"That was unkind!" Nanette bristled.

"Listen, you two—," Thad said, uncomfortable because of the direction their bickering was going.

"Well, I do have talents," Nanette insisted.

"What, pray tell—other than what's already been noted?" Nick sneered.

She tossed her head and her hair bounced prettily. "I can sing," she retorted. "And although I haven't had any training—I can dance too."

Pain from his wounds had Nick in a foul mood. "You dance with all the grace of a cat covering droppings in a litter box!"

At his crude remark, Nanette let out a very feline yowl and, fingernails bared like claws, leaped across the room, prepared to further wound Nick.

"Listen, you two!" Thad snapped. "That is *enough!* Nan, dear, Nick's in enough trouble without you riling him. And Nick, we're all tense enough without this bickering. United we stand—divided we fall."

"Someone famous said that," Nanette mused.

"Someone more famous than our Thaddeus here."

"You're the one with the infamous reputation at the moment," Nanette retorted. "You're the one who's probably already a fugitive."

A moment later the twins were ready to go for each other's throats again.

"C'mon, Nan. I think we should leave Nick alone so that he can rest. He's not a well man. The best thing for him is that he remain in his quarters so that he'll go undetected."

"You're right," Nick said. "Sorry for my surly temper," he sighed tiredly, as if the weight of the world pressed upon him.

"Your apology is accepted. Nan and I will leave you in peace. We'll get something to eat and make arrangements to bring you something after we've finished dining."

"I'm not hungry," Nick said, slumping back to the cot in his quarters, his face pale. Thad didn't know if it was from blood loss, which had soaked several handkerchiefs and was now being blotted up by a towel furnished by the steamboat for patrons' use.

"You really need to eat," Thad said, thinking of his ma and her nursing skills. "It's important that you keep your strength up."

"I don't have any strength," Nick whispered.

Nanette was across the cramped space with a quick pace. She knelt beside the cot and tenderly touched her twin's forehead.

"That's why it's so important that you eat, Nicky, to keep what strength you still have and regain what's lost."

"I've been thinking," Nick said. "When the steamer docks at Cairo . . . we really need to go ashore and then catch another boat going elsewhere . . . in case they've alerted authorities and they're looking for me."

"We can do that," Thad assured. "We can either go east on the Ohio River or book passage to continue on to New Orleans."

"Memphis, maybe," Nick tiredly stipulated. "Then we should probably switch boats again and lay ashore for a day or two before continuing on."

"Good thinking," Thad said quickly. "Now you rest. Nan and I will go about our business."

Thad gestured for Nan to exit the cabin, and he held the small door open for her to pass through first before quietly securing it after himself.

Suddenly Thad felt confused. In days not that long since passed, when there'd been tragedy or trials it had been so easy for him to seek solace in prayer and turn horrendous situations over to the Lord, knowing that a Creator who had made all could handle any situations that left human beings sorely taxed.

Thad wanted to pray about this matter, but he found himself galvanized with inaction, unable to, for it seemed blasphemous to ask the Lord to protect them from the consequences of evil.

It was a relief when a moment later Nanette looped her arm through his, and her sweet, purring voice detracted him from his own despairing thoughts as they proceeded toward the dining area and were seated.

Nanette excused herself, and when she returned, her amused and delighted mocking eyes were almost the only familiar thing about her. He didn't know just how she had fixed her garments, but suddenly she was looking older than her years, flashy, hard, glamorous—and although she was younger than he, she made Thad feel incompetent. Like a youngster still in knee pants.

Food was plentiful, if conversation was sparse. The strained silence continued afterward as they walked back toward the cabins, carrying a tray for Nick. The quiet seemed to needle Nanette, threatening to puncture her air of buoyancy.

"Did you see the way the gents were staring at me during dinner, Thad?" Nanette said, no longer able to restrain herself from comment. "And the looks their womenfolk delivered in my direction! Stuffy, prissy old cats!"

"You were certainly a sight to behold," Thad said in a voice that was tight with disapproval.

"You don't sound very admiring," Nanette pouted. "What's the matter?"

"What's the matter?" Thad echoed, suddenly feeling a hot wave of jealousy wash over him. "I don't like seeing you revealed like a tart and acting like a tramp. Men were feasting their eyes on you, Nanette!"

She shrugged. "Maybe." She coyly touched the locket containing a snippet of Thad's hair. "But it's your necklace I was wearing where others can look . . . but can't touch. . . . I want only you, Thad." Nan swallowed hard and licked her lower lip. "I got laudanum from the pianist to give to Nicky. He'll be dead to the world, Thad. He'd never know."

Thad felt shaken, torn with confusion, racked with conflicting desires.

"Not tonight, darlin'," he said carefully, keeping his tone lazy. "Now be a good girl and take this food to your brother, then get some rest. We *all* need to keep our strength up and our wits about us."

"Oh . . . Thad!" Nanette protested.

"Your brother's life depends on it," Thad said in a grim tone.

And with that he touched Nanette's arm but did not offer to kiss her good night. Instead, he turned on his heel and quickly entered his cabin, locking the door after himself.

"Men!" he heard Nanette say disgustedly before she turned and strolled away into the dark and humid Missouri night.

Williams, Minnesota

Before Harmony had given Billy her answer, he had known some pleasure in ruminating over heady plans for the future. Now, weeks later, working on the property that he'd set out to homestead on the shores of the Lake of the Woods and looking forward to their marriage, he knew the satisfaction of seeing his dreams becoming reality.

Once a week, Billy left the lakeshore property and traveled to Williams to see Harmony and the folks who'd become his dear friends and would soon be his legal kin.

Billy knew that Harmony was as industrious as he, busy preparing for their wedding and life together. Every time he made the trip into Williams, she showed him more fancywork created by her nimble fingers and with the assistance of Lizzie, Marissa, and Molly.

Billy couldn't help wondering at all that Harmony had managed to accomplish, for he was aware that she'd never been busier at the infirmary. Besides helping to care for the patients there, she was assisting Dr. Wellingham in training several girls, one of whom was Becky Rose Grant.

Knowing that she would soon be leaving him, and aware of Harmony's innate talent for nursing, Marc had seemed determined to teach Harmony all that he was able, even a few procedures generally only undertaken by licensed physicians.

Harmony was not expecting it when one morning, shortly after the train had arrived with freight and mail, Marc had called her into his office and presented her with a stout, leather physician's bag.

"It's yours, Harmony. For you."

"For me?"

"Why, certainly! Open it up!"

She did and saw an assortment of medical paraphernalia and medications and nostrums sufficient to start off the fussiest physician's practice.

"Oh . . . Marc! Thanks!"

"Thank Marissa, Harmony, for it was her idea to start with," he said, slipping his arm around his beaming wife.

"Oh, thank you both!" Harmony cried, impulsively hugging them as tears of joy dampened her eyes.

"You may be leaving our infirmary," Marissa said, "but nursing will never leave you."

"I want you prepared to handle whatever you face," Marc added. "No doubt you'll come across the sick and wounded in your new community at the lake. You'll see folks who don't have the time or the means to come to the infirmary in town. You'll feel better—and so will I—knowing that you can relieve their suffering and deal with them in medical competence, because you're properly supplied."

"Marc and I didn't want to envision you left helplessly wringing your hands in heartfelt prayer over a patient because prayer was all that you were capable of providing due to a lack of medical resources. The good Lord has bestowed blessings on us. We can afford to outfit you, Harmony, so you can better serve mankind in his name."

"I'm so—so touched I don't know what to say," Harmony said, her gentle tone suddenly squeaky with scarcely restrained tears.

"Just promise that you'll continue on as a dedicated nurse, caring for you, yours, and others as you see a need and doing it all the days of your life," Marissa said.

Marc laughed. "We know that'll be the case without

Harmony saying a pledge. She's a born nurse. She couldn't turn away from those in need, even if she wanted to."

"I'll tend to those I encounter as if I was ministering healing care to the Lord," Harmony promised.

"And he'll consider that the case," Marc assured.

Cairo, Illinois

By the time the *River Queen* reached Cairo, located where the Ohio and Mississippi Rivers meet, creating the triangular southern portion of Illinois referred to as Little Egypt, Nick was almost too ill to disembark the paddle wheeler. Thad knew that Nick was too incapacitated to transfer to a different vessel.

"We're going to have to hole up in Cairo," Thad said, taking charge, "so that Nick can get well enough to travel. Iffen the putrefication overtakes him—he could be dead."

"Can we risk taking him to a sawbones?" Nanette asked.

"I don't know if we can without raising suspicion. I don't think he's bad enough to require a physician right now. But if he doesn't get better—yes."

"What are we going to do?"

"First things first," Thad said, his tone grim as suddenly adult responsibilities unlike any he'd ever known had become his to claim and deal with. "We've got to find a place to stay. A hotel—and hang the cost."

"I agree."

"And I don't think Nick's in any shape to disagree, even if he's of a notion to. Once we get settled into decent, quiet quarters, we can look for a pharmacy or mercantile, if no apothecary establishment is available."

"I don't know what to look for," Nanette said. "Sickness makes me feel *ill*."

"I don't know all that much about it, but my ma, she was quite a healin' woman, and I watched her more'n a time or two. I know she made poultices to halt infection. Made me help her every so often. I think I remember how to do it. I'll need some bread ... vinegar ... clean cotton or muslin cloths."

Nanette wrinkled her nose in distaste.

"It's a messy concoction," Thad agreed. "But it works. Ma always said that the acid in the vinegar helped prevent the putrefication from growin' and that the bread somehow or t'other made the wound draw to pull out the infection."

"That's as good an explanation as any," Nanette said. "We'd better be doing something—or all Nicky will require will be pennies to weight his eyelids."

Thad shook his head. "Sometimes, Nanette, you are ... so ghoulish."

"Thank you. I've always fancied that I cut a fine figure of girlish femininity myself!"

"Can't you be serious, Nanette? This is no laughing matter! Your brother's a murderer, we're all on the lam, he has an infection starting—"

Nanette stared hard at Thad. "Would you rather that I cried?" she asked, her voice cracking. "If I hadn't learned how to laugh in the face of misfortune, Thaddeus Childers, I'd have given up on life long, long ago!"

With that Nanette, who tried to be so rawhide tough to live up to her brother's assessment, broke down and wept.

"Nan, I'm sorry. I didn't mean to criticize you. He—he's going to be all right. Tell you what. I'll go round up the supplies I'll need. You stay here with Nicky."

"All right. Wh–what should I do?"

They had nothing with which to do anything.

"Wipe his face with a damp cloth," Thad said helplessly. "And pray. . . ."

"Thad, I've never prayed in my life," Nanette said. "I don't even know how."

There was a forlorn, frightened timbre to her tone, and he knew all too well that her complaint was true.

"Teach me!" she begged, her large eyes made to appear bigger and more luminous with the gathering sheen of tears.

How to pray? It'd been so long since he himself had bothered that Thad scarcely knew where to start. By rote, he fathomed back to his youngest years, when indeed he'd been in knee pants, learning godly truths that gave eternal life to those who believed.

"Our Father," he said. "Say after me, Nan."

"Our Father," she contritely began.

". . . who art in heaven . . ."

". . . who art in heaven . . ."

". . . hallowed be thy name. . . ."

". . . h—hallowed b—be thy name. . . ."

". . . Thy kingdom come. Thy will be done, on earth as it is in heaven."

". . . Thy kingdom come. Thy will be done, on earth as it is in heaven," he heard Nanette trustingly repeat, with the sincereness of an approval- and love-hungry toddler.

What on earth was he doing, Thad wondered. What on earth were they doing? Certainly not living as if their earthly wills were efforts to please their Father in heaven.

"I can't remember all that!" Nanette's voice and demeanor suddenly broke, and the familiar defiance had returned.

"Just wipe Nicky's face off while I'm gone," Thad said wearily. "I'll pray hard enough for both of us."

chapter
9

Williams, Minnesota

"OH, THIS IS goin' to be so much fun!" Lizzie cried as she carried a bundle to one of the wagons donated for the weekend by Mr. Bonney at the livery stable.

Day was scarcely breaking as people, horses, and an assortment of conveyances lined up in the street in front of the Grant Hotel to form a caravan to Billy LeFave's lakeside property.

To Lizzie's thinking, it seemed like a miracle that no one had spilled the beans about what plans were afoot when Billy had been in Williams earlier in the week. Everyone from eight to eighty, so to speak, was in on the delicious secret regarding the cabin raising at the lake.

Folks are folks wherever you are, Lizzie decided. *And people especially like to do a good turn for another when it's a jim-dandy of a surprise and guaranteed to be appreciated.*

Women of the town had outdone themselves preparing foodstuffs now in hampers packed full to brimming.

Children considered the excursion to the lakeshore a wondrous opportunity to swim, fish, skip stones in the lake, and build sandcastles on the beach, along with gorging themselves on food that would taste so much better when eaten outdoors in the fresh air tanged with the scent of open water and seaweed.

Men who'd labored hard through the week viewed the cabin raising as if it were an opportunity to play rather than a day to be spent working to exhaustion for no more pay than the recipient's heartfelt gratitude.

It was a varied assortment of men who lined up by the wagons early Saturday morning. There were brawny loggers, a few fellows from the livery, and several, including Luke Masterson, who worked at the Meloney Brothers Lumber Company office. A large portion of the church's membership were making the trek to the lake, including Pastor Edgerton, who planned to hold sunrise services at the beach, since most of his flock intended to be present for the cabin raising.

Marissa and Molly, with new babes in their arms—Molly's infant a daughter, Susannah—were going to remain at home in Williams, as was Joy Childers, who was going to keep the Grant Hotel running in Lizzie, Brad, and Lester's absence.

Dr. Wellingham was initially a bit reluctant to abandon the small town for even such a short period, but Marissa assured him that she and Becky Rose Grant could tend to patients' simpler needs and that if they were in doubt, they'd hospitalize the individual and await Marc's return.

"They might need you at the lake, Marc. And who knows who might cross your path having long needed an opportunity to consult a physician for care?"

So on Saturday morning, dressed in work clothing instead of his customary suit, Marc Wellingham was present and as eager as everyone else.

Finally the caravan was ready to move out.

"Wagons, ho!" the teamster at the head of the line bawled and gave the reins a smart snap across the draft horses' backs.

Heads bobbing, harnesses jingling, wagons creaking, hooves clip-clopping, passengers laughing, waving, and calling out to others in the procession and those who had to stay behind, the line of wagons methodically surged ahead to progress north along the lonely lake trail.

Near Williams, land was cleared along the trail. Ten miles north it was brushy, swampy in a few places, the trail choked close with cattails. Wagon wheels heaved against the musky mud until the horses hauled the conveyances up a gradual, steep incline and they arrived on a sand ridge. From the top of the ridge and beyond it, they could smell the beach and occasionally catch glimpses of the huge freshwater lake still more than a mile away.

Soon they had an unbroken view of the deep, shimmering azure of the Lake of the Woods, where whitecapped breakers periodically flipped over as waves crested, the drops catching the light and refracting its brilliance to look like diamonds scattered across blue satin.

Seagulls, seeing the caravan, flew out to greet the humans, crying shrilly as they swooped low in search of bits of offal that might prove edible.

Frogs disturbed by the string of wagons passing by on the little-used path issued startled croaks and fled, loudly plopping into the shallow, algae-covered sloughs to hide among the cattails and avoid the jaws of plump bullhead catfish that wallowed in the muddy backwater marshes.

Billy LeFave was outside working on a dock when the wagons' noisy approach drew his attention. Tools in hand, shirtless, he stared, slack-jawed with amazement and totally uncomprehending of what was going on.

"We've come to lend ya a hand, Will!" Lizzie cried out, waving merrily from the first wagon, where Harmony and Brad were also seated. "Many hands make light work, you're aware!"

Grinning, blushing, a bit sheepish, Billy hastily reached for his fading chambray shirt, slid it on, and went to greet his visitors.

The womenfolk instinctively set about their pre-noontime chores while their children scampered off to stretch their legs and play.

The men, adjusting hats to riffle through their hair in order to cool off a bit, hitched their thumbs in belt loops, rocked back on their heels, and unanimously sized up the situation. They grinned with approval when they saw their workday laid out for them. With a minimum of words, the men fell into crews and set about a variety of coordinated tasks.

Billy had already felled trees to create the cabin. A few logs remained to have limbs trimmed, and several jacks, so familiar with axes, made quick work of that task while teamsters guided their horses into place to haul the logs to the building site, where the huge timbers could be notched and levered into position.

The woodsmen, accustomed to backbreaking labors, gave their all. Although it scarcely seemed possible, after breaking from their labors long enough to feast on the noon spread, they redoubled their efforts in the warm, muggy afternoon.

The cabin's walls were completed and the roof half done when the womenfolk took a break from culinary and child-tending duties to unfold tarpaulins, and with the help of several youths who were unable to otherwise help without getting in the men's way, they erected canvas structures as shelter for the night.

After building a large cooking fire, the women set the children to laying smudges and gathering sheaves of long, dry lake grass so that the smoke would discourage mosquitoes from hovering nearby to plague those gathered outside.

As tired as they were, the men labored feverishly, since they were aware that the roof was almost finished. Lusty cheers went up when the last shake shingle was hammered into place. A few lumberjacks shrilly whistled through their teeth, and a couple of them, to the amusement of those gathered, broke into a celebratory jig while others clapped, yelled, and mopped sweat from their brows, grinning over a job well done.

"It'll be a spell before evenin' vittles are ready to serve," Lizzie called out. "But y'all can start washin' up down at the dock, iffen you will."

"Fine idea, Lizzie, my good woman!" Sven Larsen, a Meloney Brothers' lumberjack and a new and staunch member of the church, hooted. He'd been ordered to cut firewood for the church by Luke Masterson as part of his punishment for misdeeds long past, and Luke had long since forgiven Sven his part in cruelly bringing Molly Wheeler to the area as a mail-order bride, part of an elaborate prank that they all now viewed as a major blessing.

Sven's long-legged stride took the Swede across the length of beach. His rough logger's boots thudded on the planks of Billy LeFave's new dock. But when he stepped on the last board—which was merely laid in place, not nailed securely—Sven lost his footing. The plank seesawed, and with his arms pinwheeling Sven toppled into a whitecap—brogans, pants, shirt, hat, and all. A moment later he surfaced, blowing water like a great whale, shaking moisture from his massive beard.

"Last one in's a rotten egg! C'mon in! The water's fine!" he challenged.

Loggers looked at each other, shrugged, and a few stooped to unlace their boots.

"What's takin' you so long!" Sven called.

"Mayhap we don't want to go in boots, hats, 'n all."

"Sissies!" Sven taunted. "I'm just bein' thrifty with my time—takin' a bath and doin' my laundry, too!"

Within seconds there was a great melee. Lumberjacks and townsmen bobbed in the water, splashing and dunking one another as they cooled off following a hot summer day's work.

Sven Larsen, the first worker to take to the water, was the last to wade ashore—sluicing water—if only because some of the town youth, of whom the jack was obviously fond, ganged up on him to give the burly lumberjack a drubbing.

Sven was sneezing water and gasping for breath when the laughing youngsters finally released him after he begged for mercy. But not before his soggy felt hat bobbed off and rode on the crest of a wave.

A seagull squawked, banked sharply, then steeply swooped down and plucked the dripping hat from the water with a triumphant sound.

"Hey!" Sven roared. "Come back with my hat, you confounded silly bird! Drop that hat, I say, or I'll catch you and make a skillet sizzle fine and fancy with your carcass!"

Sven's bellows were echoing across the lake when the bird dropped the hat in a sodden heap on the beach—due to either the vitriol of Sven's threats or the realization that it wasn't a choice tidbit.

"Dinner's served!" Lizzie cried out, clanging on a cowbell for emphasis. "We'll eat hale 'n hearty just as soon as Pastor Edgerton says the blessin' over our food."

An hour later most platters and bowls had been scraped clean. Tired workers took their ease and seemed to draw a second wind. The night was balmy, tinged with smudge smoke. Sparks from a big bonfire illuminated the immediate area.

Someone produced a guitar, another a harmonica, and people began to sing old, beloved, familiar songs and hymns.

Harmony seated herself beside Lizzie.

It was moments before Harmony realized that Lizzie was furtively dabbing at tears.

"Mama—what's wrong?"

"Darlin', I'm so happy. But sudden-like . . . I feel plumb sad too, thinkin' about what has been. Oh, remember the barn raisin's and cabin raisin's we've been part of? Alton 'n Sue Ellen . . . Ma and Pa Preston . . . your pa, Harm . . . Jeremiah . . . and Thad . . ."

"Oh, the way he relished raisings, Thad would have loved this. I wish he could've been here," Harmony said.

"I miss him," Lizzie said. "I wish he'd write more regular than he has, but Thad's young."

"I miss him, too. It'd be so nice if Thad could come to Minnesota for the wedding, and maybe Lemont could travel along, too."

"What a wonderful idea, Harmony!" Lizzie said. "Why, I don't know why I didn't think of it myself. I'm going to go to the depot and send a telegram suggesting that they travel up here, just as soon as we get back to Williams."

"That'll be expensive."

"Hang the cost!" Lizzie said. "You're the only girl o' my very own that I've got to marry off, darlin'."

"And it would be so good to see Thad again," Harmony mused.

"Amen to that," Lizzie agreed.

The Mississippi River, South of Cairo, Illinois

Nick's face was a mottled, reddened mask of fury, the vein at his temple throbbing with rage. At that moment, Thad could no longer recall exactly what had touched off this latest fiery explosion of sibling squabbling.

Ruefully Thad concluded that Nick Kelly after the time spent in Cairo, must be feeling better to have the strength to unleash the volley of invectives that spewed from him.

"There is no room for discussion nor negotiation, Nanette Kelly—you will do as I say!" Nick ordered, his voice like a whiplash.

"You're not my boss!" she flared.

"I'm your brother, and I'm responsible for you—disreputable, irritating, contemptible piece of baggage that you are. I know Thad thinks he loves you." Nick turned to Thad. "If you have a brain in your head, Thaddeus, my fellow, flee from my sister as if she were a carrier of the Black Plague. She'll ruin your life just as sure as we're standing here."

"You beast!" Nanette exploded. Tears sprang to her eyes. "How can you talk about me like that to the one man—the only man—who has ever been kind, decent, and gentlemanly to me? If anyone should flee—we should flee you! *You're* a dark plague!"

"Get out!" Nick ordered, his sharp tone cleaving the area. "Get out of these quarters, you simpering, smart-mouthed snip, before I throw you out on your bustle!"

"With pleasure! Good riddance, Nicholas," Nanette said in a cold tone. "Coming, Thad?"

Not knowing what else to do, Thad followed.

Nanette clenched her hands into furious knots and stomped several paces ahead of Thad, who calmly followed in the wake of ruffling skirts and feminine ire.

"Oh . . . sometimes . . . even though he's my brother . . . I—I hate him!" Nanette said.

"Sometimes those we love are the hardest to love," Thad murmured, reaching out to touch Nan's cheek with a gentle hand.

"You don't know what it's like!" she said, suddenly choking on a sob. Then she burst into a litany of misery: what her ma'd been like, her pa too, and how oppressive the environment had been for her and Nick. "After Pa died, Nick said we could strike out on our own and be free." Nan gave a curdling laugh that was raw with pain. "Nicholas Kelly, who I thought was my liberator, has merely turned out to be another in a long line of captors! I wonder if I'll *ever* be free of him!"

Silence hung in the air.

Thad felt as if a power unrelated to his own strengths filled him.

"It doesn't have to be like this, Nan. We could run away together. Get married. We could start a life somewhere—a decent life. Quite honestly, I—I don't like livin' like this.... The fact is, it goes against all of my raisin' in a godly, Christ-centered home."

Nanette gave another bitter laugh. "You think I do?"

"I don't know.... Do you?"

"I hate it. Oh Thad, you have no idea how I hate it! I hate every day, every moment, of my entire life. It's been horrible. Hideous! Wretched! You have no idea how awful it's been."

"You're right. I really don't think I do," Thad said. "I know from what I've heard you say that it's been a lot different from how I was raised."

"How *were* you raised, Thad? You haven't said all that much about it."

"I guess because I was wantin' to put it behind me. Even though pro'bly a fellow—or a gal—never really can put their upbringing aside."

"So how were you raised compared to Nick and me? Not that I doubt you were raised in another manner, because you're so different. Nice...."

126

"I was raised in a Christian home," Thad said. "And a Christian community."

As Thad and Nanette were seated in a secluded corner of the riverboat's upper deck, with the state of Mississippi to the left and Louisiana to the right, Thad's memories flowed back to the central Illinois land he'd loved—but left—along with the kin who resided there.

Nanette said nothing, simply leaned her head on his shoulder and listened as he talked about the barn raisings, church revivals, town and county fairs, working in the woods, farming, having fun with his family, facing life—be it tragedy or triumph—with unwavering faith and reliance on a loving Creator who had sovereignty over all.

"I've talked long enough," Thad finally said self-consciously.

"I could listen to you forever," Nanette sighed, her fury of a short time before now lost to contentment. "Why'd you ever leave a place like that?"

Thad gave a rueful laugh. "Mayhap 'cause I didn't realize when I was well off. And confused my family's compassion and caring with busybody meddlin'."

"I wish there was folks to care about me like that."

"Oh, sure there are," Thad said, even though he felt haunted, chilled to the marrow, over the loneliness he detected in her tone and demeanor.

"No," Nanette said without self-pity or rancor. "Nicky, in his own way, cares. And I guess you do. Other than that—there's no one who really cares if I live or die."

"That's not true!"

"Isn't it?"

"No!"

"Then please inform me who cares that I seem to have forgotten all about."

127

"Jesus Christ."

Nanette's response to that was an abrupt, explosive laugh, as the idea caught her totally off guard.

"Oh yes, I'm sure that Jesus Christ is really all-fired crazy about *me* . . . and the way *I* live. Sometimes, Thad Childers, you are so naive."

"Maybe it's not all bad—bein' naive and innocent of worldly ways."

"Oh, I didn't mean to poke fault or criticize, Thad, truly I didn't. Maybe it's that naivete and sweet goodness that draws me to you. . . . Now, I can see how God—or Jesus Christ or whoever he is—would like a gent like *you*. As for Nicky and me? Forget it! We're two of a kind. Blighters from the moment of our conception."

"Oh no, Nanette, that's where you're wrong," Thad said, his voice taking on sudden fervency. He reached for Nan's hand, taking it in his to better draw her attention, make contact with her in hopes that it would assist him in convincing her of what he knew in his heart to be true.

"The Lord loves me, yeah, same's he does you—and Nick too. I've been a trouble to the Lord—and my family—since I left home in the heat of anger, left my Good Book and all my raisin' where I'd grew up, and broke more'n just a few of the Lord's commandments. But instead o' him hatin' me for getting away from how he wants me to live, he only wants me to come back to him."

"That pretty talk comes better from you than from street-corner preachers shaking a Bible in your face and talking hell-fire, brimstone, and condemnation. But I have a hard time believing you, Thad, although you're almost convincing in your sincerity."

Suddenly Thad found himself talking about the Good

Shepherd and the lost sheep and the rejoicing when the lamb that had gone astray was found.

"Right now, I feel like the Prodigal Son," Thad said.

"Is that another story like the lost lamb tale?" Nanette asked.

"Yes, but it's not a tale. It's true. Jesus, when he was on earth, used parables and stories to illustrate points of how he was tryin' to teach men to live."

"Tell me about that boy. That Pro—Portugal Son."

"Prodigal Son," Thad corrected. "Well, it goes like this. . . . There was this young fellow, pro'bly about my age. Thought that things at home purty much pinched his fancy, so he asked his father—who was alive and well—if he'd cough up the young fellow's inheritance way ahead of time."

Thad went on to explain how the father provided the headstrong son the money and the boy went away, spent the money too quickly and most unwisely, and found himself impoverished. The boy realized the sinful folly of his ways. He compared his current lifestyle with how slaves lived, and he knew that going back to become his father's slave—he felt unworthy to be his son—was better than what he endured.

"He went back, and not only was he tolerated upon his return home—he was welcomed. The way we who have strayed from our path can trust in forgiveness and acceptance if we return to the truth and seek to walk a Christian journey through the remainder of our days."

Nanette heard him out, then they fell into wistful silence when he finished. Thad, for his part, was suddenly too homesick and choked up to speak. Oh, how he missed his ma, Brad, the girls, Lemont, Seth, Rory, their womenfolk!. . . The more names that flew through his mind, the larger the lump in his throat became.

"Must be nice to have a place to go to," Nanette said. "Family who cares. You're lucky. I've got no one."

"You have me, Nan, and my family," Thad said. "We could return there. You'd love them. And they'd accept and come to love you too, I just know it."

"What about Nicky?"

"If he wants to go with us—he's welcome. I have kinfolk who could find him a job, I'm sure, so that he could make his way in this world."

"You mean *work?*"

"Well . . . yes."

"I don't think Nick would agree to that. But just because he doesn't is no indication that I can't. I'm tired of living like we have been. Having an honest job sounds like a delight to me."

"We can talk about it more," Thad said. "If it's the Lord's will for us to start a new life back in my old home area, then that's where he'll lead us. We can pray it's so."

"You can pray again, darling," Nanette said. "I'm not very adept at it . . . yet."

"You'll catch on," Thad said, reaching for her hand, which he clasped in his own as he prepared to begin.

"Nicky always said I was a quick learner."

"Our Father," Thad began for a second time with Nanette, "who art in heaven, hallowed be thy name. . . ."

Thad's voice softly cleaved the night, and never had the words had more meaning nor given more comfort to him.

"That was beautiful," Nanette said. "But I'll never be able to remember it and learn it by heart like you have. Unless . . . Thad, could you write it down for me?"

"I'd be glad to," Thad said. "I can copy it tonight before I go to bed and give it to you in the morning."

"You're such a sweetheart," Nanette said. "So good to me. I wish Nicholas were better."

With Nanette's face close to Thad's, he only had to move his cheek a fraction of an inch and their lips met. They'd kissed a number of times, but this time it was different, more trusting, more pure, more filled with promise for a good and decent future. A Christian existence, Lord willing.

"You'd better go to your quarters, Nan, and me to mine," Thad murmured.

"I suppose so," she said tiredly.

"Let me walk you to your door."

That night, Thad lay awake a long time before he finally fell asleep. His mind was full to brimming with thoughts, memories, and realizations. He understood now why the Good Book cautioned believers not to yoke themselves with unbelievers, for the way was rocky and difficult when a man and woman weren't of like mind.

He realized he wasn't alone, however, for the men of the Old Testament had, more than a time or two, linked up with women who'd brought them down, and yet there were also stories in Scripture of when, by a beloved's example, an unbelieving individual had come to the Lord. Thad prayed that this would be the outcome for Nanette.

For the first time in weeks, Thad drifted off to sleep in midconversation during a nighttime talk with the Lord. And it felt good. Oh, so good.

chapter
10

LeFave's Landing
The Lake of the Woods, Minnesota

WHEN THERE WAS a lull in the singing, those who'd attended the cabin raising listened to the call of a night bird that drifted in over the still lake. The cry seemed evenly paced.

Upon the fifth cry, Billy LeFave answered in kind.

"We have visitors," he said and arose, walking toward the shoreline. "We need not be afraid. They are my friends, just as you are. I will go meet them."

A buzz of conjecture hummed around the campfire, then became an awe-filled silence as two canoefuls of Chippewa approached, Billy in the lead, and the townspeople heard Billy break into Chippewa.

With Billy translating, the Chippewa band's spokesperson conveyed that they were honored to make the acquaintance of Billy's good friends and that the tribe hoped the people who'd built Billy's dwelling would look on them too in friendship.

Back and forth the cordial conversation went, Billy translating for both sides.

When he had the opportunity, Billy put his arm around Harmony, drew her forward, and made explanations that caused the Chippewa to shyly smile and give enthusiastic nods of approval as they regarded the beautiful blond woman.

With another rapid barrage of Chippewa from Billy, the Indians began to chatter excitedly.

Harmony flushed at the attention she was receiving. "Bill, what on earth are you saying?!" she whispered.

"That you're soon to become my bride. And that you are Nurse Woman. That if ever they are feeling ill—you will make them well. That you have strong medicine to a degree that matches your beauty."

Harmony shook her head, amused. "Bill, you shouldn't exaggerate so. You'll cause them to be entirely too optimistic."

"Better to have them trusting in your miracles than the chants and ritualistic incantations of their own medicine man."

Harmony gave a small shudder. "I suppose you're right."

Lizzie and some of the other women quietly and quickly scuttled off and returned with cookies and confections that had been packed away. Cheerfully Billy invited the Chippewa to partake in the enjoyment of the treats, which they did, readily smacking their lips and giving nods of appreciation.

When the bonfire began to die to embers, mothers herded their children to makeshift tarpaulin lean-tos and tentlike structures to protect them from the night and any unexpected rainfall.

Before the Chippewa could prepare to depart, Billy invited them to set up camp on his property rather than travel on in the dark of the night.

"Son, tell them that they're welcome to break bread with us in the mornin'," Lizzie reminded, and Billy did.

"The chief's brother said that he would be most honored."

Two hours later as the moon lifted high over the Lake of the Woods, creating a silvery path that seemed to lead to infinity, the citizens of Williams and the nomadic Chippewa were settled down for the night.

The only sounds to break the solitude were the relentless lap of waves against the beach, the muted cry of loons, the drone of insects that dared not breech the perimeter of smoke caused by the smudges, and the occasional high yips and long, mournful howls of foxes and timber wolves.

The sun wasn't fully risen but was only tinting the eastern sky a delicate shell pink when Lizzie began to stir for the day. Quietly she poked around in the embers, added kindling to the fire, then put a large graniteware coffeepot on to heat.

Soon she was joined by other matrons, and they worked in companionable silence, peeling potatoes for hashed browns, slicing cured ham to fry, beating eggs to scramble. Minutes later a woman swung a Dutch oven of biscuits on the coals to bake.

Pemmican, smoked fish, and wild comb honey robbed from a bee tree were the Chippewas' contribution to the morning feast.

As the men lingered over coffee, the women attended to dishes with dispatch. Then everyone moved to a sand-ridge bluff overlooking the shoreline, and after they sang an opening hymn, Pastor Edgerton prepared to preach.

The Chippewa, at Billy's invitation, had trailed along and seated themselves expectantly.

The pastor's message was brief, and he spoke slowly, pausing frequently so Billy could more easily convey the wisdom of his sermon and appropriate Scripture and edifying words into the Chippewa dialect.

Within the hour, the Chippewa and townspeople, after exchanging warm good-byes, went their separate ways. Billy LeFave waved them all off, then went into the new cabin that marked the crest of a knoll overlooking the lake.

"I don't know when I've ever been happier," Harmony mused on the drive back to Williams.

"Same here, darlin'," Lizzie replied. "Now, if we telegram your brother and Lem Gartner, when they hie on up here in time for your nuptials, our joy will be complete."

The Mississippi River

First thing in the morning, Thad arose and, recalling Nanette's request, located a pen and plain piece of paper. As neatly as he could, he scripted the entire Lord's Prayer. Then, for good measure, he added the notation *John 3:3* and the assurance, *I'll explain all this to you when we have a chance to talk. Love, Thad.*

It was scarcely past dawn. Many of the late-night revelers on the ship were apparently sleeping in, and Thad enjoyed the still. He wasn't sure when he'd see Nanette, and he wanted her to have the Lord's Prayer, so he went by the Kellys quarters and slipped it under the door, folded in fourths, with the legend *NANETTE* clearly visible on the top side.

Then Thad went about his way.

"How're you doing this fine morning, Thaddeus, old fellow?" Nick called to him from across the teakwood deck.

Thad turned expectantly, then knew disappointment when Nan was not with her brother, who seemed in unusually good spirits.

"Feeling better this morning, Nick?" Thad asked.

"Better than in a long time. I feel almost like my old self."

"That's good."

Nick gave an evil smile and winked. "Is it? I'm not sure!" Then he laughed at his own joke. "It's time to get back to business, though. You and I really need a chance to talk privately, without even Nan hanging around."

"Oh," Thad said, confused.

"We've plans to make before we dock in New Orleans,"

Nick said. "Full summertime now, and with the application of a bit of intelligence, living should be easy."

"I don't know how long I'll be in New Orleans," Thad said.

"Something's come up?" Nick inquired, acting surprised.

"Well, not really. I've just been thinking of returning to the place of my raising."

"Homesick, my man?" Nick teased, warmly clapping Thad on the shoulder. "Well, perhaps I—or my charming sister—can convince you to stay."

"Perhaps."

"We'll talk tonight," Nick assured. "Right now I've got to go see a gent about an interesting prospect."

All day long, Thad wandered about the steamboat, hoping to catch a glimpse of Nan, but she did not appear. Several times he went to their quarters, knocked, but was not bid entrance, and from the stillness, he realized that Nick and Nan were not in their cabin.

The supper hour came and went, and Thad was felt morose that he'd not been able to see Nan and get her response to the Lord's Prayer and explain the additional Scripture to her.

By the time the murky, humid summer evening had grown full dark, Thad was feeling desolate. For what seemed like hours, he'd wandered the ship, then leaned against the railing, waving to the riverbillies and black families who lived along the banks, and watched in amazement when he spotted alligators knifing through the water with more and more regularity.

He sank into his own thoughts, scarcely aware of the revelry on the ship until he realized that it had died down, and then he had a comprehension of how many hours had passed.

"Here you are!" Nick said softly, his voice cheerful. "I've been looking all over for you. It's quiet here—and private—so we can talk."

Thad gave a small sigh. "Go ahead."

Nick drew near to Thad and placed a strong grip on his forearm, as if to prevent him from escaping. Nick dug in his pocket, then produced an ornate cigarette lighter that he'd won in a poker game with a card slid down from where it had been secreted, held in place by a sleeve garter.

He flicked the flint, a flame glared, and he dug in his breast pocket. He withdrew the note folded in quarters, gripped one edge with his fingertips, and with a flick of his wrist snapped it open.

Thad felt sick. At that moment, he realized that Nan hadn't received his note—Nick had intercepted it.

"What's the meaning of *this?!*" Nick asked, fury entering his tone.

"It's the Lord's Prayer," Thad replied. "And a bit of Scripture. Nan requested it."

Furiously Nick balled the note and tossed it to the teak-wood deck in disgust. Then, with a savage flash of his wrist, he backhanded Thad hard across the face, bloodying the startled Illinoisan's lip.

"I won't have you perverting my sister with preachy, pious, do-gooder claptrap. She hasn't been worth a tinker's damn as a shill and pigeon since we've met up with the likes of you! Try to do you a favor, you fool, and teach you the ways of the world! And what do you do in return? Somehow influence my sister in most unsavory ways. Good grief, I'd never have dreamed that the girl could know prickings of the conscience, until you two started making moon eyes at one another—" Nick was sputtering and gasping for breath in his fury. "Well, I won't have it, I tell you! I'll *kill* you before I allow you to ruin my relationship with my sister and turn her into something she's not! I have plans for her in New Orleans. With her looks and figure, the madams will be in competition to have her offer service in their houses!"

"You wouldn't!" Thad gasped, realizing that Nick planned to offer his sister's body for sale. "I won't allow that!"

"Of course I will, and woe be to anyone—including Nanette—who should try to stop me!"

"You'll do that over my dead body!" Thad said, his own temper and sense of righteousness offended.

Nick reached into his pocket. For a split second, Thad thought he was reaching for a cheroot, then Thad realized it was the wrong pocket. A moment later a snub-nosed derringer glinted in the moonlight.

"As you would have it!" Nick said. "I've killed once. It won't bother me to make it twice."

With that Nick squeezed the trigger—but the gun jammed, and only Nick's curse exploded around them.

Adrenaline shot through Thad and his pulse galloped, and he thanked the Lord for the reprieve. Knowing that defiant bravery would be not only foolish but guaranteed fatal, Thad ran along the deck, looking for escape, but there was nowhere to run, nowhere to hide behind cover as Nick thudded along, cursing the pistol he was fumbling with and the man who'd sold it to him.

Suddenly the gun worked and a wild shot rang out, pinging against a wall just above Thad's head. He ducked, running low toward the roar of the paddle wheel that churned up water and propelled the massive riverboat ahead.

Wishing his tight, fancy garments were loose-fitting work clothes that allowed strenuous exertion, Thad scrambled onto a seat near the railing, steadied himself on the rail, poised to leap over the railing, to dive past the paddle wheel chopping to his left so that he could clear its thrashing, dashing blades and swim for shore.

As he tried to steady himself to dive, let his eyes adjust to the darkness, he heard Nick's prowling footfalls, now cautious, stealthy, as he looked for Thad.

"I know you're here somewhere. . . . I'll find you . . . mark my words. . . . I'll find you . . . and then you'll be gator bait!"

Thad's movement as he swung his arms to get momentum for a long, arching dive caught Nick's eyes.

"Aha!" he cried in evil delight.

His arm raised, the derringer flashed flame in the dark, Thad—startled by the report—lurched, and the bullet slammed into his thigh, snapping him forward from the waist, breaking the arch and momentum of his dive. Instead of cleanly slicing out into the water, he toppled—and almost languidly fell right into the chopping, churning blades of the paddle wheel, which battered and beat him as it rained ton upon ton of water down onto him. The force sent him bobbing and swirling into the murky depths, in a hellish torrent that seemed to never end.

Jesus! Save me! Thad cried out in his mind. His body was tortured with pain unlike anything he'd ever known as he was captured in the turning mechanism. Water sluiced around him, and gears roared in his ears.

Then the hammering of the stern-wheeler ended. Kicking hard with his unwounded leg, Thad broke the surface of the Mississippi River, gasping for air, coughing, retching, gagging up river water.

The steamboat progressed downriver. In the gloamy night, Thad could make out Nick's silhouette against the lights on the aft section of the vessel.

As if sensing Thad's presence, Nick raised his arm, the derringer flashed again, and like a demon possessed, madman Nick Kelly cried out his rage and his intent.

"Die, you Christian bastard, *die!*"

At that moment, Thad had never felt so certain that he was about to die. He knew that within moments, with his blood seeping into the river, alligators could swoop upon him, churning up the water in a blood-lust feasting. He prayed that it would not be so. Calling upon the Lord for strength, with every movement pain racked, he began to slowly swim toward shore, hoping that he could reach it fast enough.

Thad's teeth chattered, not only from the chill current of the fast-moving water but from blood loss from the wound to his thigh and the panic that rode high within him.

Thad Childers only made it halfway to shore, awkwardly swimming by force of a primitive instinct lodged somewhere deep within his subconscious memory. Then what energies he had, mental and physical, drained away, and he didn't swim another stroke ... the riverboat rounded a bend and was lost from sight, its merry revelers considering that all was right in their wanton world ... and Thad Childers lost his place in his earthly existence.

Williams, Minnesota

"Wasn't that the most lovely weekend?" Lizzie said as they pulled into the outskirts of Williams, heading back to town from the cabin raising at the lake. "But it's good to be home. No doubt Joy'll be glad to see us return!"

Minutes later the wagon stopped in front of the Grant Hotel. Lizzie, Brad, Lester, and Harmony unloaded their possessions, others gripped their belongings, and amid great cheer and words about what an enjoyable and productive weekend it had been, those who'd taken part went their separate ways.

Joy Childers exited the hotel and went to Lizzie, taking one of the older woman's burdens from her and carrying it herself.

"It's nice to have you return," Joy said.

"Darlin', it's good to be here! Anything unusual go on while we were gone?"

"Everything's been just fine," Joy said. "Better than fine, maybe. I went over to the post office, and Mr. Lundsten gave me the mail. I sorted through it. That letter you've been waiting for from your kinfolk down south has arrived."

"Praise God!" Lizzie said, hurrying her steps. "Joy, mayhap you'll get to meet Lemont 'n your new brother-in-law, Thad. Harmony and I were talkin'—and tomorrow, bright and early, I'm a-going to go to the depot and send off a telegram invitin' 'em to hie on up to the north woods for Harmony and Will's wedding."

"Terrific idea, Liz," Brad said. "I'm surprised that I didn't think of it."

"What a joyous reunion that'll be!" Lester said. "Thad's probably grown to full manhood while we've been gone. He was as tall as I am when I left—and promisin' to grow more."

"It'll be so good to put my arms around my little boy again," Lizzie said.

"And watch him feast on those sugar cookies and gingersnaps that had a way of disappearin' from your cookie jar, right, Mama?" Lester reminded.

"He can stuff himself on cookies now, and I won't grouse at him a'tall," Lizzie promised.

"Here's the letter," Joy said, retrieving it.

"Oh, darlin', let me hobble over to a rockin' chair in the

parlor and kick my shoes off, then I'll open it up and read to you what-all the home folks have to say."

They settled around Lizzie. She kicked her shoes off, wriggled her toes, rubbed her feet together, and slit open the plump envelope from Lemont Gartner.

"Well, here goes, folks!" she said, clearing her throat, unfolding the foolscap, spreading it flat. Lizzie's lips moved briefly as she gazed ahead to get her bearings so that she could read with clarity and accuracy.

Suddenly her eyes widened—then she was unable to stem an anguished cry.

"Mama! What is it?" Lester gasped.

"Liz ... Liz ... whatever's the matter?"

Shaking her head, sobbing, unable to speak, Lizzie hunched forward, her shoulders heaving with misery.

Tenderly, compassionately, his heart thudding wildly, Les firmly removed the sheets of foolscap from his mother's trembling hands. He quickly scanned the letter. His face drained.

"Thad's gone ... run off. . . . They don't know where he went. . . . He's been difficult. . . . Well, you can read the sorry details for yourselves."

Lizzie was in a daze. "Gone. My baby's gone." Then another wave of grief seemed to wash over her. "*GONE!*"

Lester went to his ma, holding her close. "Mama, please, don't take on so. The letter only says that Thad's gone—meanin' he ain't around home right now. It don't mean that he's gone as in *gone*." He swallowed hard. "It don't mean he's dead."

"But he is, Lester. He is dead," Lizzie whimpered. "I know he is. Last night when everyone was enjoyin' the music and fellowship with the Chippewa guests ... a horrible realization went through me. Somethin' awful was happenin' to Thad. I told myself it was just my own imaginin's. But now . . . now . . . I think he's . . . dead."

"Liz—," Brad said helplessly.

"Mama! Please!" Lester implored.

Lizzie turned away from them, her back stiff. Resolute, yet broken, she slowly made her way to her private quarters. Brad started to go after her. Lester restrained him.

"Give her a little while," he said. "I've known her as my ma a heap longer than you've loved her as your wife. Ma's got a special knowledge, Brad. Those of us close to her have always figured that it's a gift of the Spirit. It's for sure she's cautious in testin' the spirits before she speaks or acts. She's very seldom wrong about things like this."

"Lizzie's been troubled for days—weeks," Brad said. "Thad's been on her heart, and worry fillin' her mind. I feel so helpless. Surely there are authorities to contact—but who? And where?"

"It's a big ol' world out there," Les sighed. "Doesn't seem that we can do much other'n pray."

"That's the best action we can take," Joy reminded. "Brad, would you please lead us?" she prompted.

The three joined hands in the parlor and lifted their hearts toward God, asking him to watch over Thad, to preserve Lizzie in her faith, to give them all the strength to endure life come what may and the knowledge that it all served his purpose, and that they might do their part to abide by his will.

"Amen," the three murmured.

Lizzie, at the top of the stairs, her hair smoothed, her dress straightened, only her reddened eyes offering testimony to her recent tears, caused a creak as she descended from the uppermost riser.

The eyes of Lester, Brad, and Joy regarded her.

"I heard what y'all said, and I add my own voice to yours. *Amen!*. . . Bad feelin's aside, until I have more proof than my mayhap foolish, scary insights 'n intuitions, I'm goin' to trust that Thad Childers is alive, well, and one day will be back within the fam'bly fold. I never gave up hope over my brother, so I sure as Scripture ain't giving up over a beloved son."

chapter
11

The Mississippi River, Northern Louisiana

NANETTE KELLY WAS fit to be tied.

And was.

Nicky had trussed her up tight as a Thanksgiving turkey, not only binding her but gagging her for good measure.

The dark-haired beauty was furious—but unable to do one thing to express her rage.

Nick had caught her unawares. Nan had lain awake so long, thinking of a new life with Thad, a decent life, that it had taken what seemed like hours for her to fall asleep. As a result, she'd slept overly long in the morning, even though she'd groggily been aware of Nick stirring around their cabin.

She hadn't been expecting it when she'd been slammed from deep sleep by the force of his attack. He'd been savage in his quick movements.

She was tied up so tightly that she couldn't make a sound, couldn't move at all, was powerless to do anything, even when she heard Thad come to their cabin several times throughout the day, rap gently, and call her name.

She had no idea what was going on.

And when Nick returned to the cabin, which wasn't for long, he avoided her eyes, which she knew were filled with questions and dark accusations that he simply didn't wish to deal with—over actions he didn't feel beholden to explain.

145

After a while, her confused, accusing stares became purposely murderous glares. Nick's only response was to laugh—he was delighted, it seemed, to see a return of the dark side of her.

For a time, Nanette strained against the cords that were binding her, but it soon proved futile and only served to exhaust her further and cause her extremities to ache and her skin to burn beneath the chafing friction of her efforts.

Off and on throughout the day, Nanette—spent, closed up in the stuffy cabin—fell into sweat-drenched, fitful sleep, wondering how long her diabolical brother was going to hold her cruelly captive.

It was well after the midnight hour when Nick slipped into their cabin. Purposely she gave him benign looks devoid of threatening glares, for she realized that it was the fastest way to manipulate him into releasing her.

"Going to behave yourself, Sis?" Nicky asked, forcing head-nodding promises from her three times before he began picking at the knot.

Finally she was free.

Nan's body was so cramped and stiff that when she arose she almost fell over. She grasped at the cot to keep from falling. Then she gestured toward the rumpled bedspread and the bindings coiled on the cot upon which she'd been held captive.

"What was that all about?"

"You'll be happier and healthier not knowing."

Nan gave a disgusted snort. "You owe me an explanation."

Nicky lit a cheroot and blew a stream of smoke in her direction, then took a big gulp from a half-empty, amber whiskey bottle. "I owe you nothing. And you, my dear, owe me plenty. Therefore I merely prevented you from foiling me in a project that I had undertaken."

"Oh. Was Thad in on it?" Nan inquired, realizing that if so, Thad hadn't said anything.

"Thad who?"

"Don't be obtuse."

"I'm not. There's no Thad aboard this steamer."

"Of course not, Nick. We're all traveling under assumed identities . . . to protect *you*."

"Have it your way. No, Thad wasn't in on this. Haven't seen hide nor hair of him."

"You're lying!" Nan said, searching his features for the faint, telltale clues.

"You can't prove it."

Nan felt hysteria rising within her. She had known for days now, maybe even weeks, that Nicky was jealous of Thad, that he didn't like the closeness and trust that had developed between his sister and his protégé. While generally Nick was still nice to Thad's face, Nan was all too aware that at times, in private, his attitude and outlook were nothing short of murderous.

"What did you do to him? Answer me, you blackguard!"

"Threaten me, Nanette," Nick said and stabbed his finger in her face, "and you may meet the exact same fate. If you want it guaranteed that you end up as fodder for the gators, my dear sister, just make inquiries after one Thaddeus Childers around the *Delta Princess!*"

Tears welled in Nan's eyes. "You fought with him? You threw him overboard?" She wilted, then began to sob.

"No . . . actually . . . he jumped. Tried to, anyway," Nick said.

And then he began to emit a low, evil chuckle at the memory and took a couple more swigs of whiskey, darkly laughing like one possessed.

"I hate you, Nicky Kelly! I despise you the way I've never loathed anyone before. One decent person comes into my life— a good man who actually saw something about me to love— and you destroy that too, just like you've destroyed my life!"

"Lying harlot!" Nick raged, his words fast slurring from the effect of the strong liquor.

"Am I?" Nanette coldly asked. "I think not. Although I'd sooner be a harlot and provide for myself than let you spend so much as another copper on my upkeep. I'm striking out on my own, Nicky, just as soon as we dock in New Orleans."

"What're you going to use for funds?" Nick blithely inquired.

Nanette faced him, going nose to nose, toe-to-toe, at that moment not even caring if he killed her for her brashness, so great was her grief over the realization that Thad was dead.

"I'm going to ... use ... the money ... that you rifled ... from Thad's quarters. Money that I know he ... had ... and which I ... knowing you ... am aware that you've stolen. I believe Thad would want me to ... have it ... to help me purchase my freedom from you. . . . And if you don't give it to me ... I'm going to turn you in to the authorities myself!"

Nicky glared at her, realizing he could hardly risk murdering his sister in their cabin or throwing her overboard, with the steamer's late-night revelers still everywhere about.

Reluctantly he reached into an inner vest pocket, took out a wad of cash that had been Thad Childers' acquisition in life, secreted among his belongings in his quarters, and disdainfully threw it at his sister.

"Take it and good riddance."

"Thad wanted to do nice things for me," Nanette said, wiping tears. "Maybe his money can help turn me into the good and genteel lady that I wish to become."

Hastily, unable to bear the idea of spending another moment in Nick's presence, Nanette shoved her belongings into her valise, latched the straps, then struggled out the door with the heavy burden.

They weren't far from New Orleans. The riverboat was scheduled to arrive by morning. She checked her valise with a deck hand on the ship and began to wander around. When she got to the upper deck, the light, humid breeze riffled through her hair, the dampness in the atmosphere making her wavy black hair even more full and curly around her creamy-skinned face.

She sighed deeply, brushed tears, and was about to depart the area to stroll back along the paddle wheel side when a crumpled-up ball of paper caught her eye. Unsure of why she was even doing it, she retrieved the discarded bit of debris and smoothed it out.

She gasped, knowledge flooding over her with brutal reality, when she saw the note that had been meant for her and intercepted by Nicky, with Thad having no idea that her brother had come to despise him as much as Nanette had come to love him.

She read the beauty of the Lord's Prayer, then stared with dismay at the unusual wording *John 3:3* and Thad's written promise that he would explain it all to her when they were together again.

When would that be?

Thanks to Nicky ... never, Nanette thought bleakly.

Brokenhearted but unable to fully face the loss of Thad, and wanting to retain every precious memory of their time together, Nanette smoothed out the note written in Thad's hand, touched by his skin—if later sullied by Nick—and put it in her purse. Then she cupped her hand around the locket Thad had given her that held the sentimental lock of hair . . . and she wept for him . . . wept for herself . . . wept for his family . . . and wept for what might have been . . . if only her evil brother hadn't gotten in the way of what she'd actually started to dare to believe might be God's special plan for her—a new life with Thad unlike anything she'd ever known before.

New Orleans, Louisiana

Nanette hung back, hiding in alcove-like areas, until she was among the last to disembark from the *Delta Princess*. She knew that Nicky would immediately head toward the hotels in New Orleans in order to look for an easy mark to hood-wink with some scam or other or would frequent the saloons in search of a poker game where he could win, if not by luck, then by his craft at cheating.

Nanette decided to stay away from the hotels. When she saw a hansom drawing near, she hailed the driver. When he stopped, she inquired of his knowledge about possible neat, clean, and affordable boardinghouses.

"I know just the residence, miss," the cabbie said, tipping his hat to her as he alighted and helped her into his hired conveyance. "It's a goodly distance, but I'll get you there as quickly as allowed."

"Thank you," Nanette said, sinking back against the plush seat with a sigh, feeling wilted and wounded from all that had happened to her in the past twenty-four hours.

The hansom driver soon deposited her at a boardinghouse, gallantly offering to wait to ensure that there was a vacancy.

Minutes later she returned to collect her luggage, paid him his fare, and added a generous tip that inclined him to help her transport her heavy valise to the three-story home set well back from the street, surrounded by old oak trees draped with Spanish moss.

"Come in, dear girl, and make yourself at home," the plump, white-haired, friendly faced Mrs. Poindexter drawled in a soft, honeyed tone. "For the time being, my home is your home. How long do you believe you'll be staying in our city?"

"Several days. Possibly a week," Nanette said. "Or . . ."

Already she'd decided that she wouldn't remain in New Orleans very long, for she knew that Nick had been captivated by the warm climate and the brawling opportunities, so likely he might choose to settle in New Orleans for a while. The sooner she could put distance between herself and her brother, the safer she would feel.

"You can pay by the day if you like," the boardinghouse owner agreed as Nan settled up for her first two nights' lodging. Nanette knew that she needed to rest, regain her strength, and figure out where she would go, what she would do . . . and maybe even set about learning who she was— aside from Nick Kelly's twin sister and accomplished accomplice in crime.

"Your quarters are on the second floor, corner room. It's nice. Airy and roomy. Bein' as it's a corner room, dear, you'll get a good cross-draft come evenin'. It's cooler there—and we don't have a full house at the moment, so I can offer a corner room."

"I'm much obliged," Nanette said.

"Do you need help to your room?" the elderly lady inquired.

"No. I'm fine," Nan said, smiling quickly.

The older woman seated herself in a cozy reading area near the desk where she transacted business.

"If you need me, I'll be right here," she offered, picking up a heavy book, which Nan correctly judged to be a Bible.

Nan made her way to her room, unpacked, then counted the money that had been Thad's. Then she smoothed out the note that was probably the last writing Thad Childers had done.

She didn't know what John 3:3 meant, and she wasn't sure how to find out, even though she reckoned it was from the Bible. She saw a Bible discreetly placed on a nightstand by her bed. She approached it, picked it up, surprised at the rich heft of the leather-bound book.

She opened it up, wanting to unlock the secret of John 3:3 that Thad had been so eager to share with her. But her gaze soon felt as if it blurred beneath the tiny print, the numbers, the names, and she hadn't the foggiest idea of how to look up a verse in a Bible.

She and Nicky had gone to school as children to escape their parents. She knew they both had fine minds—their teachers had often said so—and she'd learned many things. Scouting her way around references in the Holy Bible was not among them.

Then she thought of Mrs. Poindexter downstairs, so contentedly seated with a Bible open on her lap, as if that was a comfortable and familiar routine in her life.

Emboldened by her need to know, Nanette descended the curving staircase. At the sound of her approach, Mrs. Poindexter glanced up.

"All settled in, dear?"

"Yes, thanks," Nanette replied. "The room is lovely. I know that I'll be very comfortable there. I noticed that there was a Bible on the nightstand."

"Yes, we supply those for the convenience of our guests."

"A friend of mine, a very dear friend, in fact,"—Nanette's voice grew husky as she managed to hold in tears—"wrote me a note. In it he referred to something called John 3:3 and said he wanted to tell me all about it. I'd like to read what he referred to . . . but I don't know how to find it."

"Well, come right here, my dear, and I'll give you a quick lesson in makin' your way through the Good Book. There's the Old Testament, and then there's the New Testament," she began. "John's in the New Testament. Now, see this little number? And this second number also? That refers you to the chapter from a book in the Good Book and then sends you to search out the line of verse. Here's my Bible, Miss Nanette. See if you can find John 3:3 for yourself."

To her surprise and delight, Nanette located the Scripture almost immediately. But when she read it, instead of receiving enlightenment, her confusion only deepened.

"'Unless a man is born again, he cannot see the kingdom of God.' This certainly doesn't clear up the mystery," Nanette murmured, disappointed.

Mrs. Poindexter's eyes twinkled. "Well, I'm sure that your young man will explain it to you beautifully when he gets a chance to tell you exactly what it means."

"I'm afraid that won't happen."

"But my dear—why not?"

"Because he's . . . he's dead . . . now."

Mrs. Poindexter's fingers flew to her throat. Her eyes grew dark with compassion and shared pain. "I'm so sorry, Miss Nanette. What happened?"

"Murdered by . . . a riverboat gambler. . . . I'll never see him again." Then she began to softly weep.

"Not in this world, but 'tis possible in the next," Mrs. Poindexter said, rushing to embrace the crying young girl. "If

SERENITY IN THE STORM

you've got the time, dear, have a seat, I'll get us tea, and then if you're not too tired to listen, I'll explain God's plan for mankind. Your young man can't come back to you . . . but you can choose to go where he's gone. . . . But to do so, you must be born again. Not of the flesh, as you already have been some years ago, but in the spirit, so that you become a newborn babe in Jesus Christ."

For the first time ever, Nanette Kelly knew what it was to feel hope, to savor decency, and to realize that maybe, just maybe, it was as Thad—and now Mrs. Poindexter—said and that a God who created her and cared about her had a special plan for her too. Even for Nicky. But it was up to them to choose to accept what was freely offered to those who would only believe. . . .

chapter
12

NANETTE KELLY HAD planned on staying at Mrs. Poindexter's boardinghouse perhaps forty-eight hours and no longer before she booked northbound passage on a steamer heading up the Mississippi River.

To her surprise, she discovered that each morning, the intent she'd known the night before to depart the area where Nicholas very likely remained had evaporated, and she found herself extending her stay by one day . . . then another . . . followed by an additional day . . . until soon she wasn't thinking in terms of fleeing New Orleans after all.

Thad Childers, Nan realized more than ever, had been a thrifty young man, and by carefully being as thrifty herself, she was able to use his funds to finance what for her was a time of seclusion and healing.

Mrs. Poindexter, who was a Christian woman with strong faith and convictions, was like the mother Nanette had never known, and the woman's presence, love, concern, counsel, and Christian testimony were like a soothing balm to Nanette's soul.

Nanette came to adore the stout, warm-natured, older woman who'd had no children of her own, and she was heartened to understand that Mrs. Poindexter genuinely loved her too. The woman showered her with special kindnesses and concerns that she didn't dispense so readily to other patrons of the boardinghouse. Hungering to spend time with Mrs.

Poindexter and making use of any excuse to do so, Nanette made a point of pitching in and zealously helping the aging woman around the vast three-story structure every chance she got.

Within weeks it seemed that the two were inseparable. Nanette accompanied Margaret Poindexter on marketing trips, to church worship services, and to church women's circles, where Maggie's friends embraced Nanette as readily as her mentor had.

For the first time, Nanette understood what it was to possess Christian fellowship. Maggie was never too busy to explain more fully the meaning of a scriptural passage that Nan had uncovered in her daily reading of the Good Book. A tome that Nanette had once dismissed—unopened—as a boring, ancient document was instead a repository of treasured philosophies and information regarding the earthly life of Jesus Christ, and an unfolding of God's eternal plan for mankind.

The morning following a sleepless night of reading Scripture, when Nanette had thought back about her life in horror over her transgressions and misdeeds, Mrs. Poindexter had sensed that Nan had reached a conviction of sin, and together they prayed for Jesus to enter Nan's heart and become her Lord and Savior. Nanette then knew what it was to be created anew, with the past behind her and a future filled with the glorious promise found in a new and intimate walk with the Lord.

"You were a wonderful singer before you gave your heart to the Lord, honey," Mrs. Poindexter said, "and now listenin' to you lift your voice in praise is like hearin' a heavenly angel sing."

"Thank you," Nanette said. "I've always enjoyed singing. I even did professional entertainment once—although for a very short time—aboard a steamer on the Mississippi River."

"I'm not surprised," Maggie remarked. "You're certainly good enough. And you seem to have a special talent for rememberin' the lyrics to songs. Hear them once—and they stay with you."

"I have been fortunate that way."

"I wouldn't be surprised if singing isn't a special talent the Lord's given you, Nan dear, in order to praise the glory of his name."

"Really?" Nan said, and an unexpected rash of goose bumps rippled over her.

"I love havin' you sit beside me in the pew at worship services," Maggie said, "but I've been thinkin' for some time now that you really *should* be in the choir loft, where you can be of greater service in helping us to lift our voices in praise. Why, you could give our regular soloist relief. Maybe team up and do some moving and inspirational duets."

"That's an interesting thought," Nanette said, feeling awed and humble at the same time.

"You'll consider it?" Maggie said.

"Well, of course. But I wouldn't want to seem to be . . . pushing myself upon people."

"Pushing yourself? Honey, the choir's always in need. If you don't mind, I'll talk to the pastor and the choir director myself if you feel hesitant."

"Well . . ."

"May I? Please?"

Nanette smiled. She could refuse Maggie nothing, especially not when it was something it seemed that her own very soul and spirit cried out to do.

"Of course."

As summer turned to autumn in New Orleans and fall rains began to lash the area, Nanette sang her first solo at worship services. While thunder rumbled outside the house of God that Sunday morn, Nanette Kelly's voice was like a sweet ray of divine light penetrating the threatening darkness, and the girl from the poorest of beginnings shivered as she sensed that indeed the Lord had great and wondrous things in store for her.

Williams, Minnesota

"I'm so glad you suggested a wagon ride out to visit with Harmony—and Will iffen he's at home," Lizzie said, reaching across to warmly pat her husband's hand. "I feel better already."

Brad smiled at her. "I had a feelin' that you could use a day of breakin' routine to help you escape the bleakness that's settled over us for a spell . . . ever since . . ."

Brad bit back the words and fell silent. He didn't even want to mention the letter, for fear that a reminder of its content might pull Lizzie from the sunny mood she was in and drag her back down into the dark depths that she'd struggled through in recent weeks.

"One nice thing," Brad said, changing the subject, "the smoke ain't been so bad. Gettin' kind of used to it, I am. We've had little timber flare-ups and peat bog fires to deal with since July."

"Kind o' puts a tang to the air, to my thinkin'," Lizzie agreed. "Thought that rain back in July was the drought breakin'. But t'warnt, it appears."

"The dry conditions makes for fine travelin', though. It'll be great to see the children," Brad went on. "And I may wet a fishing line while we're at the lake."

"Fresh walleye would be delicious. Harmony's better already at fryin' fish than her mama ever was or will be," Lizzie laughed.

"Practice makes perfect," Brad said.

"Seems that Will's fish trap in the lake is always full. He's been helpin' Harmony salt 'n smoke the catch for the winter months."

Brad reined the horse, and it bobbed its head and turned toward the cabin that so nicely crested the bluff overlooking the lake.

"Yoo-hoo, Harmony! You have visitors!" Lizzie cried out.

A moment later a surprised Harmony flung open the cabin door and recognized them. Clutching at her skirts, she rushed across the space that parted them. Lizzie climbed down off the wagon and threw herself into Harmony's arms.

"Baby, you're lookin' radiant! Marriage certainly agrees with you."

"Yes, Mama, it does! Oh . . . I've never been happier. And I can tell Bill's as content as I."

"We've been so busy at the hotel. And you? How've you been, darlin'?"

"Busier than I've ever been in my life, even at the infirmary. Bless Marc for supplying me with medical needs and for giving me his cast-off doctor books when he purchased new editions."

"You've been puttin' them to good use. He knew you would. We all were aware they'd not be wasted on you, dear."

"The Chippewa trust me," Harmony said. "Thanks to Bill's relationship with them, I know. Plus,"—she shrugged modestly—"I know they're beginning to have regard for me on my own merit." She blushed. "They already think I'm something of a miracle worker, for conditions their medicine man couldn't help. With medical supplies and correct knowledge, praise God, I've been able to help them heal up in short order."

"Ah, they're impressed!"

"It would seem so. They're friendly people. I worried

about being lonely, moving so far from town and everyone that I knew. The Chippewa adore Billy, and they've come to accept me too. I have great affection for the tribe. I'm grateful that they pop in to visit me, even when there's not sickness or someone in need. Although every day or two, it seems that someone's in need of medical treatment, even if it's a minor thing."

"How wonderful. Treatin' a minor condition can handily keep it from becomin' a major complication."

"How right you are," Harmony agreed. The women entered the cabin while Brad opined that he'd set a fishing line right away.

"What a cozy cabin," Lizzie said, taking off her light wrap.

"Coffee, Mama?" Harmony inquired.

"I'd love some, darlin'," she said. "I know Brad will relish a cup, too."

"I'll make plenty."

"It's for certain water's not in short supply at your cabin," Lizzie said. "My, but it's been a hot 'n dry un, ain't it?"

"It certainly has. I'm wondering if the drought will ever break."

"Autumn's here," Lizzie said. "That means fall rains can't be long in comin'."

Harmony put the coffee on, then gave a wee sigh as she seated herself and was helpless to contain a small wince.

"You're lookin' a mite peaked, honey," Lizzie observed, using the comment as a sly opening gambit to pursue her inner suspicions.

Harmony didn't bother to deny it. "It shows?"

"Well, to your own ma, yes it does!"

"I get awfully tired these days."

"That's grand!" Lizzie chuckled. "That's one o' the first signs of a comin' wee one."

Lizzie had just bit into her first sugar cookie, was starting to remark that Harmony's baked goods were as tasty as her own, when there was a commotion outside that drew their attention. Harmony quickly arose to look out the window.

"Oh, it's Way-Say-Com-a-Gouk's canoe," Harmony said. "How nice that she's happened by. You'll get to meet her, Mama. Way-Say-Com-a-Gouk is a few years younger than I. Her father's the chief of the band. I enjoy her so much. It's nice to feel that I have a best girlfriend, just as I did in town."

"Way-Say . . . what all did you say?"

"Way-Say-Com-a-Gouk," Harmony repeated, pronouncing carefully.

Lizzie groaned. "I'll never remember all o' that."

"In Chippewa it means 'Far Away Sky.'"

"Well, ain't that pretty."

"A pretty name for a gorgeous girl," Harmony agreed. "She's so sweet, so friendly, so pleasant . . . so *serene*."

"Well, whatever's goin' on out there, darlin', pardon my sayin' so, but it sounds anything but serene!"

Lizzie hied out of her own chair and was a pace behind Harmony as they went out the door to investigate.

Way-Say-Com-a-Gouk was stolid and calm, but Brad, an ordinarily stoic fellow, was almost hysterical, and the white man braced between them, apparently a trapper, was reduced to wretched, panicky desperation.

"Nurse Woman! Nurse Woman—*need!*" Way-Say-Com-a-Gouk broke her silence to cry out to Harmony in halting English.

Almost as if she were a native-born, Harmony lapsed into slow, careful Chippewa, then listened intently when

Way-Say-Com-a-Gouk burst forth with tumbled chatter that allowed Harmony to only decipher about every fifth word.

But it was enough to give her an understanding of the medical emergency that they faced. And she quailed inwardly at the realization that the man had been so thoroughly and brutally bee stung—and lived. For the first time since her marriage and move to the Lake of the Woods, she sensed that she faced an injury that she was woefully inadequate to tend.

"Oh, Mama," Harmony said, feeling suddenly like a small girl, "I'm so glad you're here! Maybe *you'll* know what to do."

"Lord have mercy if the bloke's *that* bad."

"We'll know in a moment," Harmony said, rushing for her medical bag as Lizzie hurried to her husband and the quiet, unruffled Indian girl who supported the large, pain-racked man between them. He cupped his face with grimy hands, moisture from tears streaking through the dirt that crusted his skin and his clothes from when, Lizzie guessed, he'd writhed on the ground in agony, helplessly crying.

Harmony returned with the bag Marc had given her, and she and Lizzie gently grasped the man's wrists, bringing his hands away from his eyes so that they could assess the wounds.

"Oh, Mama!" Harmony gasped.

The sight almost rocked Lizzie back on her heels. "If that don't beat all!" she breathed in a horror-filled tone.

The man was a pitiful sight to behold.

His face was a puffy mass of inflamed welts. His long hair and full beard had become matted together as he'd wiped away tears and mucus that had formed when the grown man had been reduced to weeping like a terrified, lonely, desperately injured toddler.

But his eye! His eye was the worst!

His facial skin was drawn tight—so tight it looked as

though the skin would offer to split under the pressure as his swollen eyeball bulged out in grotesque proportions.

"We've got to do something—but what?" Harmony cried, as the man was pitifully mewling for relief, someone to ease his terrible misery.

"Oh . . . shoot me! Shoot me 'n end my suffering," the man blubbered. "Please—I'd consider it a favor."

"No—no, not that," Brad said, and his ashen face looked as if he'd be willing to endure a burden of the man's pain himself if only it would ease the man's suffering. "Just hang on, friend," Brad said. "I'm here, and I'm standin' in the gap for you over this."

Surrounded by people eager to help him, the man seemed to quiet down, and his trust allowed him to continue to endure.

"Marc will know what to do," Brad said. "We've gotta get him to town."

"We have no other recourse," Harmony said.

Rapidly Harmony gave directions to Way-Say-Com-a-Gouk, asking her in Chippewa to get blankets, pillows, and clean clothes.

"She can't carry it all," Harmony said, whirling away when Lizzie was able to support the wounded man. Brad went for the horse and wagon.

"Have you got some sterile water in your doctor bag?" Lizzie called after her.

"Yes!"

"Good. Snatch the salt shaker offen the table in the kitchen when you pass through. Oh, hurry ever chanct you get!"

Minutes of flurried activity resulted in the wagon being brought around, a pallet created from comforters and pillows, Harmony's medical bag being opened and the array of antiseptics, ointments, laudanum painkiller, and other nostrums conveniently displayed.

They'd almost forgotten about Way-Say-Com-a-Gouk, who'd said not a word as she deposited the burden of linens and pillows on the straw Brad had hastily spread in the wagon bed. Then she returned with a wooden bucket that sloshed with warm water from the reservoir on the kitchen wood range that was Harmony's pride and joy and a wedding gift from Billy to surprise her.

"Bless your heart, girl!" Lizzie said, gratefully reaching down to take the bucket of water from the stoic Indian girl.

"Ready to go?" Brad asked, poised to snap the reins over the old mare's back.

With a quick gesture and abrupt words, Harmony motioned to Way-Say-Com-a-Gouk to clamber up onto the wagon and join them.

"We may need an extra pair of hands," Harmony said. "She's an intelligent and willing girl. She brings me most of my patients and is always interested in helping me. She seems fascinated—and she's a quick learner."

"We're grateful for her company," Lizzie said and gave the Indian girl with the long, unpronounceable and hard-to-remember name a smile. It was a grin so welcoming that the girl responded with a smile as bright as the sun rising over the horizon come dawn but as soothing as the sunset over the lake following a day well spent.

By the time they were several miles down the road, the man was no longer moaning and twitching with pain. Lizzie and Harmony had long known that they worked well together. Despite the language barrier, Way-Say-Com-a-Gouk neatly fit in, like a well-oiled cog in a healing machine, as the women labored over the wounded man.

"For the life o' me, I can't get that girl's name straight, no matter how many times I hear it rollin' off your tongue, Harmony. But the nature that maiden's got, I think I'm goin' to call her Serenity. 'Sky' might be appropriate, considering the meaning of her name, but somehow it seems too familiar."

For the first time in over an hour, Harmony leaned back, smoothed her hair, and smiled.

She thought a moment, touched Way-Say-Com-a-Gouk's arm, and spoke in halting Chippewa, searching carefully for words to explain the situation to the Indian girl who'd become her best girlfriend.

As Harmony spoke, Way-Say-Com-a-Gouk smiled and humbly ducked her head toward Lizzie, offering a pleased smile. She said a few quick, low words to Harmony but favored Lizzie with another sweet smile.

"I explained that you have a special name you want to call her, Ma, and that it's a true compliment. Way-Say-Com-a-Gouk said that she'd be honored to have you call her Serenity, knowing what it means. She said that the chief named her when she was born but that she's honored to have Nurse Woman's mother credit her with a name, too."

"Ain't that sweet!" Lizzie said.

The man groaned, drawing the women's attention from their moment of camaraderie.

"Whatever do you reckon happened to this bloke?"

"Perhaps Way-Say . . . Serenity will know more," Harmony said and turned to the younger woman to pose the question.

Serenity responded, reminding Lizzie of a dutiful child called upon in the classroom to provide an answer. Harmony listened, nodding, helplessly grimacing as understanding came to her, and she then translated for Lizzie.

"As near as Serenity knows, he must've been beset by

bees—*A-Mo-Ee*—in the woods when he disturbed their bee tree, either on purpose, in a quest for comb honey, or by accident. Little matter," Harmony declared, "because the worker bees, feeling their hive and queen were threatened, attacked the poor fellow."

"We can see that from the welts covering him. 'Tis his eye that concerns me."

"He must've been stung right in the eye," Harmony said.

"Swoll up as it is, that has to be the case. I wonder iffen the stinger's even out? If it ain't, it could start to cause infection. . . . It'll just get worse 'n worse."

"We'd better examine his eye," Harmony said.

"I think the laudanum you've administered has him woozy-like enough that he can stand it."

The area had already been washed and covered with a clean cloth. Harmony whisked it away. The women adjusted their positions to set about the delicate work of examining his eye.

"I hate to waste the time en route, Brad, but could you rein in the horse to a halt for a moment or two whilst we prod around his eye?"

"Sure thing, darlin'," Brad said, seeming to have recaptured his general calm. "Whoa!"

"Lift his eyelid a li'l more, hon," Lizzie breathlessly instructed her daughter. "Oh! There it is! I need tweezers, though."

Harmony's hands were already occupied, and the doctor bag was out of Lizzie's reach. Quietly Harmony instructed Serenity to get the implement and give it to Lizzie, which she did in a deft motion.

With bated breath, the three women leaned over the rough trapper, and Lizzie prayed to God for the surety of hand to pluck the stinger from the man's swollen eye without the sharp tweezer blade grazing the delicate tissues of his eye.

"You did it, Ma!" Harmony cried, relieved, when Lizzie pulled out the black, barbed stinger attached to a yellowish gray venom sac and, holding it between the tweezer tines, triumphantly brought it up to the sunlight.

"Drive on, Pa!" Lizzie cried to her husband before she responded to Harmony. "That I did—but it was delicate tuggin' all the way. I was afeared that the stinger was goin' to break off. His eyeball—it's dryin' out." Lizzie pursed her lips and gestured for the sterile water, then reached into her pocket for the salt shaker she'd secreted there when Harmony had returned from the cabin. "His eye's too swoll for it to tear and bathe the area. His membrane's dryin' out like the white skin inside an eggshell. As big as his eye's gettin', Lord have mercy but we don't want the surface membranes to get crackly and dry and bust."

"It's swelling so markedly that I'm concerned it's going to pop right out of his head, Ma!"

"All we can do is dampen it down with homemade tears. Brine water's the best we can do 'til Marc can attend to him."

"We're makin' good time," said Brad.

"We won't get there soon enough to please me!" Harmony said.

"Well, this ol' drought's provin' to be a blessin' on this day," Lizzie said. "It's the quickest trip I remember us makin' over the trail. Why, even the bog's dry as tinder! Thanks to havin' Serenity along to help us, we'll have the bloke in as good a shape as possible to tender him into Marc's care."

"She's a treasure."

"Mercy! Her fam'bly's going to be plumb sick wit' worry

over her, though, Harmony, for ain't no way we can hie her back to the lake so's she can go home tonight."

"Don't worry, Ma. I left a note on the kitchen table to alert Bill to what had transpired and tell him that Way-Say-Com-a-Gouk is with us. He'll carry word to the chief."

"Good," Lizzie said. "We'll make a point o' gettin' her back to the lake as soon as possible."

Even though they made good time on the trek into Williams, to all of them it seemed like an eternity before Brad drew back on the reins and called, "Whoa!" The tired horse plodded to a halt in front of the Wellingham residence as if it were suddenly too tired to put one hoof in front of the other.

"Marc!" Lizzie cried. "Come help! Oh, please Lord, let 'im be home!"

A moment later the physician appeared at the door. Seeing the commotion, Dr. Wellingham didn't take time to shrug into his suit coat. He rushed toward the knot of kinfolk, and Harmony quickly and concisely sketched in what had happened and what treatment methods they'd administered.

"You all did a fine job," Marc said, as calm and unruffled as the Indian girl. "Brad, if you'll help me, we'll take him into the infirmary."

That done, Lizzie wilted in the kitchen with Marissa, gratefully accepting a hot, strong cup of coffee. Serenity hung back, but Lizzie drew her forward and patted her reassuringly as she explained the situation to Marissa, who smiled warmly, hoping it conveyed what words of English could not. She set a mug of coffee before the Chippewa maiden, gesturing to the cream and sugar.

Brad had gone with Harmony and Marc into the operating area—where Becky Rose Grant joined them—to see if his masculine strengths were needed in addition to their healing ministrations.

Finally Brad joined his wife in the kitchen, gratefully accepting coffee from Marissa, who was dandling Curtis Alton on her lap, having reclaimed him from Lizzie after pouring coffee.

"Your smart thinkin' saved the man's eye—iffen it can be saved," Brad said. "Puttin' that briny water on him prevented further damage. Thought I was goin' to be sick there for a moment when Marc popped that bloke's eyeball right out of his socket and laid it on sterile cloths on the feller's cheek."

"Heavens!" Lizzie cried, swallowing hard herself at the very idea.

"Marc thinks he can save the feller's eye. Says he'll leave it lyin' on his cheek area and continue to drip briny water on the cloths with a medicine dropper. It'll require 'round-the-clock care, but Marc hopes that in a few days the swellin' will go down and then he can pop the gent's eyeball back in where it goes."

Lizzie squirmed. "Kind o' a sickening idea—but interesting. Lord God, I hope it works!"

"Even if the man loses his sight in that eye, havin' an eyeball fillin' the space will be preferable to Mark's removing the eye so he has a saggy pouch of skin in its place."

Finally Marc and Harmony entered the kitchen after leaving the patient in Becky Rose Grant's temporary care.

"You look tired, Harmony," Lizzie observed.

"I am."

"Have you a quick cup o' coffee iffen you want it to rejuvenate yourself, then what do you say we all retire to the hotel? There's a room ready 'n waitin' for you and Serenity, who looks like she could use a rest. Joy and Les'll have everything under control, and when we've all rested up a bit, there'll be a meal fit for a king."

"I'm hungry enough to eat a bear!" Brad said, remarking about their missed meal and the fish that had gone uncaught.

"Mayhap Les will've sent Joy out to hunt down an ol' bear, and you'll be surprised with bear steak for dinner," Lizzie teased, making Brad and Marc laugh.

Serenity looked puzzled. Wishing to let her enjoy the humor, Harmony explained how Joy had saved her brother's life by killing a bear.

"You'll like Joy," Harmony assured.

"Not only will she like her, honey, she'll be able to understand her—and Joy'll be able to translate better what Serenity wants 'n needs to say to us."

"Ready to go to the hotel, Mama?" Brad inquired of Lizzie when they'd all finished their coffee.

"I sure am, Mister Mathews," Lizzie said and gratefully accepted his help up out of the chair. "We set out before dawn for this to be a restful respite. 'Stead it's been a humdinger of an interestin' day."

"We've certainly been busy."

"Busy. And needed. Why, I was kept so occupied that I didn't even have the time or distraction to worry about poor Thad and what's become o' him."

chapter

13

IT WAS SO dark the next morning that Harmony hadn't realized that she'd overslept until Lizzie summoned her.

"You shouldn't have let me sleep so long, Ma!" Harmony protested when she entered the hotel dining room. "Marc and Becky Rose can undoubtedly use a break with the patient."

"Mayhap you think you don't need the rest," Lizzie said, "but I'm thinkin' of a little gal or feller who *does.*"

Harmony's hand instinctively moved to her abdomen. "You're probably right."

"Felt good to sleep, didn't it, darlin'?"

"More so than I thought. Dark as it is, what light came in from behind the window shades, I didn't think it was much more than dawn breakin'."

"It is overcast today. I was hopin' that maybe it was clouds gathering to bless us with a rain—but when I went outside, it seems that it's just smoke thicker'n usual. We've got so used to smellin' the peat smoke for most o' the summer so's that we don't notice an increase in the odor but only have an awareness of the haze."

"Autumn rains will soon put out the fires," Harmony said.

"Be kind o' nice to breathe crisp, clean air come winter, even if it's bitter cold."

The two women said no more about the various smoldering peat fires in the area as Harmony ate a quick breakfast, then departed for the infirmary.

Harmony was being briefed on the condition of the patient, who—thanks to Joy's ability to communicate with Serenity—they'd learned was Jacque Beaufort, and he was indeed a trapper. Becky Rose filled Harmony in that Jacque's condition had stabilized, the eyeball beneath the cloth kept moistened with brine seemed to be relieved of some of its swelling, and Marc was cautiously optimistic.

"Wonderful!" Harmony said. "I'll probably remain in town today and hope that Ma and Brad can see me home tomorrow. Bill and I can likely transport Mr. Beaufort back to the lake when we return to town in a week or so."

The two nurses were chatting when the howling of an approaching Canadian National Railroad train came chugging into town from the west.

"The train whistle sounds funny," Becky Rose said, cocking her head.

"It is strange," Harmony said.

"The engineer's not just pulling the whistle cord at the crossings," Becky Rose said. "He hasn't let up on that horn a'tall."

"Something must be wrong!"

"Oh, heavens — what *now?!*" Becky Rose, who was exhausted, murmured.

At that moment, Marissa came in with a big-eyed, content Curt on her shoulder as she patted his back to encourage him to belch.

"I'll watch the patient," Marissa said, "so you girls can run to the depot and learn what all the commotion is about."

Becky Rose rushed out the door with Harmony a few sedate steps behind her. As they entered Main Street, they saw clusters and knots of people making their way to the depot. Soon the train huffed into sight, then ground to a stop in a clashing grate of steel against steel.

From the hubbub, Harmony and Becky Rose managed to sort out the news.

"Fire's a-comin'!" one of the train's crew bellowed. "She's a big un! Burning like blue blazes several miles to the west, roarin' through the pine forests."

"Oh, heavens!"

"Dear Lord, help us."

"Don't know if the fire'll reach Williams," another crew member bawled, "but you'd better batten down the hatches just in case. Anyone who wants to ride on east and out of danger—hop on board!"

En masse the townspeople turned to stare westward. "I've seen it this bad before," one dismissed.

Another man spit on his finger and held it to the wind. "I think we'll be all right. Breeze ain't quite right."

"Forest fires create their own wind after a while," another gloomily pointed out.

"What're we going to do?" Becky Rose asked, wringing her hands.

"I'm returning to the infirmary. We've patients in our care. We can't leave them."

"There'll be another train comin'," an employee of the railroad said. "If you ain't ready to leave at this moment, you've got time to wait. But don't wait too long!"

Several people clambered aboard, but as many turned toward their homes.

"Just my luck!" Alice Meloney, married to J. H., one of the prime forces behind Meloney Brothers Lumber Company, said, holding up her fingertips, which were stained with red paint. "I just this morning gave a coat of enamel to the porch—and now I'll have to walk back and forth over that wet paint to put canned goods down in the root cellar so that if we're burned out, at least we'll have something to eat this winter!"

"We'd better send some men out west to watch for the fire so's they can ride back and alert folks if we have to flee!" the menfolk of the town concluded.

Harmony and Becky Rose returned to the infirmary. Periodically they or Marissa stepped out into the street and peered to the west to search the sky for increasing smoke or, worse, the licking tongues of orange flames flicking into the sky.

As night fell and the sky darkened, there was a brilliant amber glow that moved to the north of Williams, steadily progressing east, sparing the village.

"Looks like Alice Meloney messed up her newly painted porch for naught," Brad observed.

"She'd have lamented the loss of all that food she 'n her hired girl have preserved for the winter a lot more'n she'll rue slapping down another coat o' paint on them floorboards."

"That's for certain. We're all fortunate. Very fortunate."

Harmony stared to the north from the third-floor landing of the Grant Hotel, where they'd all gathered to view the fire from an elevated perspective.

Helplessly she wrung her hands. "I'm so worried about Bill!"

"Don't fret, darlin'," Lizzie said. "Will's as able to take care of himself under adverse conditions as any man I've known."

"He knows where I'm at, and if he sees fire to the south, he might—"

"No man in his right mind would try to tackle those flames," Lizzie said.

"When it comes to Harmony, Billy ain't in his right mind, Ma."

"You hush your mouth, Lester! Your sister's worried enough as 'tis without you raggin' around and upsettin' her."

"Ma, all I said was—"

"I *know* what you said!" Lizzie took Harmony's hand. "Will's got faith. He'll trust the Lord to protect you, Harmony, when he can't, just the same's I'm countin' on the Lord to watch over Thad wherever he's at."

"Y'all had better get some sleep," Brad said. "I'll stay up awhile . . . and watch."

"When you're tired," Lester said, "come shake me awake, and I'll keep an eye on things."

"I will, son. Now you womenfolk go get some shut eye!"

When Billy LeFave had returned to his property to find it almost ghostly still, fear clutched his heart! Harmony was nowhere in sight and did not answer his call! Dread lashed him as he considered that she could've fallen off the dock and drowned, wandered off looking for berries and become lost . . . or . . .

Hideous possibilities tormented him until he rushed into the cabin and found the neat note left on the round oak table. He almost wilted with relief. He didn't know what he'd do if he ever lost her.

He kept busy around the cabin that night, the better to ignore how lonely he was without his beloved wife present. But Lizzie had warned him that when there was someone in need of Harmony's healing touch, he would have to accept it and be patient.

And he would.

The next day, he went about his business, just as he knew that in town Harmony was occupying herself with her own work.

That evening, though, after the sun went down and the sky

became dark, Billy noticed the disturbing orange glow at the southwestern horizon. At first he'd thought it was perhaps an unusual reflection of the sun against some summer clouds, causing an effect like the northern lights that shone so strangely in the winter sky.

Then he realized that it was a forest fire—and a tremendously big one. It seemed to become more major as he watched it, and he knew that acres and acres of timberland and tinder-dry swamp were burning between the lake and Williams!

What if Williams is burning?! he considered and almost cried out in agony at the thought.

His first instinct was to travel south as fast as he could go, but he knew that no man would stand a chance against such a roaring inferno. Fires like that could pull the very oxygen out of the air until a man would suffocate—if he wasn't burned to death first.

"Oh, Lord," Billy dropped to his knees in the silken beach sand. As fervently as he'd ever prayed, he requested special protection around the people of Williams, especially his wife and her family and friends, whom he'd come to love as his own people.

Billy didn't go to bed that night. Instead he leaned a homemade ladder against the sturdy cabin, climbed up to the peak, sat next to the stone chimney, and stared through the darkness, watching the fire progress, praying all the while.

Come the morning, he trusted that he would know what to do and where to go.

"Williams has been spared," Brad announced when Marissa let him into the Wellingham residence, "but Cedar Spur burned."

"Oh, no!" she cried.

"The fire's ragin' on eastward," Brad said. "Those people are in dire straits. The depot master just said that they've been telegraphin' west, askin' anyone who can help to lend a hand. They're especially crying out for the physicians 'n medical folk, midwives and such."

"I'll go," Marc said. "There'll be menfolk to stay in Williams and see to my property as well as I could myself. I have no patients in critical condition right now. Jacque's doing very well."

"Do you need me to go with you, Dr. Wellingham?" Becky Rose inquired.

"And me?" Harmony added.

Marc sighed heavily. "Let me say that I could no doubt use your services. . . . It's the survivors of the fire who'll desperately need you."

"Then it's settled," Harmony said as Becky Rose Grant nodded agreement.

"What about the patients?" Brad asked.

"I can tend to them," Marissa began.

"You've got little Curt to care for. You can't do it all," Brad said. "I don't expect that the hotel will be doin' a brusque business for a few days. No doubt Liz can spend some time in the infirmary with patients."

"And Serenity too," Harmony added. "I've found her a good assistant when I've helped people from the lake area."

"Joy could hang around to be an extra pair of hands," Brad said, "and to help Liz and Serenity with any language problems."

"It's settled then," Harmony repeated.

"I'll pack my bag with additional supplies," Marc said.

"And in addition, we'll fill up a valise with extra medications and whatever we might need that we can fit in."

At his words, both Harmony and Becky Rose rushed off.

Almost before they had time to fully comprehend what was occurring, it was time to depart.

"Train's coming from the west!" the news rippled through the streets. Very few people got aboard. There were some already on the conveyance who'd been there for a while, and their faces were ashen, their eyes worried, as they traveled eastward toward where their homesteads were, fearful of what they'd find—or not find.

"Oh, isn't that pitiful!" a woman cried as the train progressed several miles east, and everywhere they looked, the ground was charred and blackened. Dwellings at Cedar Spur had burned, collapsing in on themselves to smolder around chimneys that awkwardly jutted skyward. The pole yard at Cedar Spur had caught fire, and the huge mounds of burnt poles glowed orange and shades of blue, so intense was the heat of the piles, which shifted and settled as they burned themselves out.

"My babies!" a woman suddenly shrieked. "Oh, my babies! They're at home—oh, Lord!"

She leaped to her feet, craning out the train windows, her eyes searching—she knew not even for what.

"Graceton's still standing!" she cried, relieved, when she saw the small town come into sight as the train hove around a curve and up an incline. "Praise God—it hasn't burned."

The train lost momentum, slowing to stop at the depot in Graceton.

"I'm getting off here!" the nearly hysterical woman cried, plucking up her belongings.

"Mrs. Bongfelt, you really should stay on board," the conductor said.

"You can't stop me! My babies!" the woman shrieked, wrestling her way off the train.

The fire was to the northeast.

"I've got to go find them! Oh, if only I hadn't decided to go to Warroad to shop. Oooh!"

The train stopped by the depot. The passengers could scarcely hear Mrs. Bongfelt's shrieks and agonized cries, because the engineer of the train leaned on the whistle, constantly blowing the horn. A warning bellowed out over the countryside that a train bound for escape—the last train—was departing the area to outrun the fire, which was now racing parallel to the tracks, and deliver people to the safety of Baudette, the river town, or even Canada across the watery border.

"We've got to go!" the conductor cried, hustling the curiosity seekers back onto the train. Then he and another crew member wrestled a struggling, hysterically crying Mrs. Bongfelt onto the coach.

"If my babies are dead—I don't want to live!" she sobbed. "Please—let me go search for them. It won't take long. Please . . . *puh-leeeeeeeze!*" she begged in a harrowing wail.

"We can't wait, ma'am. The depot agent in Pitt telegraphed back to us. A siding crew arrived in Pitt and said that railroad ties are starting to catch fire. We can't wait any longer—truly we can't—or we might all perish."

Becky Rose and Harmony exchanged wordless glances, then—to the conductor's relief—arose and prepared to take charge of the distraught, irrationally panic-stricken mother.

It was almost more than the two of them could deal with, and Harmony was grateful that Mrs. Bongfelt was a Christian and seemed to calm as they soothingly reminded her of God's promises and protection and that her little children were as dear to their heavenly Father as they were to their earthly parents.

Harmony had been kept so occupied calming Mrs. Bongfelt that they'd passed through the small town of Pitt before she even realized it. A few miles beyond was Baudette, which— except for the hazy smoke hovering to form a cloud cover in the sky—appeared quite normal as the train pulled in.

"*Mama! Oh, Mama!*" a cry went up from beside the depot when a small family caught sight of Mrs. Bongfelt as she prepared to step down from the train, her eyes dazed, her face strained.

She jolted with shock, as if she'd seen an apparition but didn't dare believe her eyes.

"My babies!" she sobbed and threw herself toward her children and her husband, who was wiping tears of relief at the sight of her.

"We were trusting that you'd stay on the train, Mama," he said. "We lit out for safety soon as it got bad. I weathered a fire as a wee tad—and I vowed I'd never put my young'uns through that if possible! We fled before it could catch up with us."

"The fire seems to have died down between Pitt and the burnt-out area around Graceton," the news spread through Baudette.

"Praise God! Maybe it'll start raining and the fire will be stopped for good. Those sod-busters to the east are doing a whale of a job putting out the smaller fires. Maybe the big un will burn itself out."

Harmony, Becky Rose, Dr. Wellingham, and other physicians from the area set up a makeshift medical center, which was divided into units where staff acquainted with one another worked in unison.

"Maybe the worst is over," Marc said come morning, his eyes red from lack of sleep and from the stinging of the smoke.

"I hope so," said Harmony, who was pale and exhausted, her blond hair grimy and her fair skin swarthy from the soot that had settled on her.

But it was not to be.

After a quiet night, the wind picked up again, and the fire that had seemed about to burn itself out between Pitt and Graceton roared forward with new ferocity. Pitt burned to the ground. Refugees from the tiny town, who'd ridden, walked, and run toward Baudette, had grim stories to tell of those who'd stayed behind for whatever reason.

"'Twas awful," a man named John Hooper said, his voice cracking, as he was shaken nearly to tears with the intensity of his remembrances. "I had my team and was intent on escapin' the general area, when all of a sudden I was surrounded by the fire on three sides. I thought I was a goner. Up ahead was the Soley farm, with the fire coming up fast. I whipped the horses on and went to assist them. We turned the livestock loose so they could fend for themselves. Mrs. Soley was at home with only their two hired men. I offered to take them with me—but they declined, saying they'd try to weather the fire in a storm cellar."

"The poor wretches!" another man cried, aghast that they'd turned down a chance to clamber aboard the wagon and rush pell-mell for safety. "Iffen that wasn't a poor choice! Why, I run across a feller in town this morning, a bloke from near Graceton that got burnt out lock, stock, and barrel. He almost lost his life. A neighbor fam'bly of his was intent on waitin' it out in a root cellar. It had two doors in it, and that fire was so fierce that it shot flames clear the length of the cellar. In one door 'n out the other door, from which they sped, runnin' for all they was worth toward the creek. Don't know if they made it or not. The feller was telling me about it, he run hard, and he told me that the wind was so strong that he had to drop to the ground and hang on to bushes so the draft didn't carry him away. He made it to another little creek and pressed up against the bank as the fire destroyed everything in sight. He was red as a tomato and blistered from the heat—but alive. The experience no doubt liked to have scared him out o' ten years of life. While he was lyin' against the creek bank, there was sticks, poles, and big flaming branches flying over his head. The wind was that strong!"

"We'd better pray to be spared!"

People prayed but the fire continued to move steadily east toward Baudette and Spooner. The towns were separated by the Baudette River, which flowed into the Rainy River nearby.

The smoke from the outlying districts had hung over the three towns for days. The village officials, however, contented themselves that there'd be no major difficulty, for they had two volunteer fire departments available, the Rainy River from which to draw ample water, and yet they put an emergency plan into effect: In the event of the fire's imminent arrival, they would sound the fire siren continuously, and it would be a signal for the townspeople to abandon their homes, go to the depot, and the train that was remaining in the area would carry them safely across the river to the Canadian shore.

By evening the air was thick with choking smoke and stinging hot cinders that drifted down from the sky. A vicious wind was howling through town, and soon trees began to fall with loud, thudding crashes that sent plumes of sparks spraying into the night sky, which was gruesome with the billowing clouds of smoke that eerily reflected the amber glow of the fire on the ground.

The fire siren blew, and men ran through the streets crying the alarm, warning everyone to get to the depot.

"Physicians! Nurses! Get aboard so you're waiting on the other side," a crew member called out.

"C'mon!" another one said, giving the women a hand up, helping boost the doctors along. "Get in with the sick! Hurry! We've got to depart for Canada so we can return to get those who remain!"

Within an hour the town was afire, and it looked as if the inferno would reach the oil tanks and the depot before the train could return.

Harmony, Becky Rose, and Marc wedged into a boxcar where there was another physician, his nurse . . . and seven typhoid fever patients!

Harmony touched her abdomen protectively, although there was nothing she could do to guard herself nor protect her unborn child except trust in the Lord.

Anxious people who were left behind, wringing their hands, praying, and waiting for the Canadian National train to switch so that it could return from Canada to rescue them, witnessed a miracle.

The wind suddenly changed direction!

The oil tanks, depot, and a few houses were spared!

It was no miracle to those to the south, who'd thought that they remained safe, when the fire turned back on itself so abruptly that the roar of its retreat was like rolling thunder.

The fire threatened both the Shevlin and Engler sawmills. The mills were saved, but the Shevlin yard fell to the inferno, lighting the town like day as the fire consumed forty million board feet of sawn lumber.

Then the fire jumped the Rainy River to kindle fires on the Canadian soil. Spooner too was burning, and big balls of fire streaked over the boundary water tributary as if they'd been shot from a cannon.

At the Canadian mill, a watchman realized what was happening, and he tied down the mill whistle before he fled for safety. As the steam pressure built, the whistle screamed louder and louder, piercing the night, shrilling until something caved in and the whistle fell silent. The sudden quiet seemed almost deafening.

Come dawn, it was like slowly awakening from a nightmare but looking around to discover that it had been real.

Smoke hovered over the area, but the wind had died. Filthy, sooty, blistered people, hollow-eyed with shock, stood numbly around and regarded the blackened, leveled area where a bustling town had been just the afternoon before.

People still stood in the Rainy River, where they'd waded out the evening before, standing neck-deep in the stream and, when the fire was at its fiercest, regularly dipping their faces and heads into the water to prevent scorched skin and flaming hair.

The area was quiet, and people spoke in low tones.

"Nurse Woman!" The cry, from a canoe proceeding along the Rainy River to the north, which emptied into the Lake of the Woods, shattered the morning still. "Where's Nurse Woman?!"

"I'll be switched!" Marc said, looking up from his patient and easing a kink in his back. "It seems you've a morning caller, Mrs. LeFave. Might I suggest you make yourself presentable?"

Harmony was almost too tired to even manage a weak laugh.

"If I look half as bad as you do, Dr. Wellingham, there's no hope of repair."

Becky Rose looked from Harmony to Marc and back again. "Actually, no offense, Harmony . . . but I think you look even worse!"

"I know a gentleman who'll think that he's never seen you looking more beautiful than he does right this moment." Marc turned away from Harmony and Becky Rose, cupping his hands around his mouth. "Over here, Billy!" he cried out several times, waving his arm high into the air to attract LeFave's attention.

Billy saw Harmony, alive, safe, and he leaped out of the canoe he'd rammed against the bank and scrambled up the steep hill toward her as she hastened into his waiting arms.

"Oh, Bill!" she cried, clinging to him, grateful for his strength when suddenly she felt so weak and woozy with exhaustion.

"My darling," Billy said, covering her grimy cheeks, forehead, nose, and lips with kisses as he held her tightly, as if he'd never again let her go. "I don't know what I'd do if I lost you. It would be more than I could bear."

"I'm fine, Bill. I'm just fine. But I'm oh-so-tired. Take me home. . . . I think they can manage without me now."

"Go on home and Godspeed," Marc agreed, walking with Billy, who carried Harmony to the waiting canoe. "Governor Eberhardt is en route to the area, bringing assistance and encouragement. The Red Cross and state militia are rushing to our aid, too."

"I know these folks in the north woods," Billy said. "As soon as the ashes are cool, the building will begin."

"The militia will be setting up a tent city upon their arrival."

"Good," Billy said. "I can smell rain in the air. And as late in the year as it is, snow can't be far behind. Then the freeze-up."

"If rain's on the way," Marc said, "you'd better paddle up the Rainy and along the southern shoreline for home."

"Tell Mama and the family that I'm all right and that I've gone home," Harmony asked of Marc, her tone almost listless with exhaustion.

"Consider it done," Marc said. "Becky Rose and I will be making our way back to Williams as soon as we can find a way. Someone will see Serenity to the lake shortly, I'm sure."

"I'll explain the situation to the chief," Billy said.

"Tell the chief that his girl has the makings of one very fine nurse."

Billy nodded. "That's what Harmony's been telling me. I'm sure it'll please the chief to have the assessment of an actual physician in addition to Nurse Woman's opinion. Ready to go home, sweetheart?" Billy murmured in Harmony's ear as he helped her into the canoe.

"We're both ready to go home. Your baby and I."

Billy stared at her, thunderstruck, seeming to scarcely believe that it was true.

"You . . . mean . . . you . . ."

Harmony nodded. "Yes!"

"I'm going to be a pa!" he cried. "*I'm going to be a pa!*"

chapter 14

"I SURE DO miss Serenity at times," Joy said. "After having her with us for a week, it seems like there's a void that can't be filled."

"I know what you mean," Lizzie agreed. "At least we get to see her every now and again when we go out to visit Harmony and Will."

"Harmony's doing well," Joy observed.

"That she is," Lizzie said. "I'm grateful that she and Serenity are such close friends. I know that it's going to take a load off Will's mind this winter when Serenity is able to check on Harmony and keep her company while he's out running his traplines."

"She's the kind to pitch in and help, too, and Harmony will allow it."

"Those two girls certainly work well together, whether they're tendin' to housework or their healin' arts."

"It's a good thing Serenity's catching on to nursing so quickly," Joy said. "Bill told Lester that he was going to put a stop to so many people coming to call on Nurse Woman. He knows that they feel they need her."

"Can't say's I blame Will," Lizzie said. "He needs her, too, and that unborn wee one she's carryin'. Iffen he's smart, though, he'll pass the word behind Harmony's back. She'll be fit to be tied if she learns that Will's turning people away."

Joy laughed. "That's exactly what Lester told him, Ma, and Billy thanked Les for the insights."

"Like as not, Will's goin' to have a word with the chief. Thank the Lord that Serenity knows as much as she does. Harmony will no doubt send some nostrums and simple medicines to the camp with Serenity, and she can tend the tribe's needs. As best I can figure, Harmony should be bearin' her wee one about April. Next spring will be nice! It'll be warmer then, easier on a babe. And travel conditions should be such that Will won't have any trouble gettin' her on into the infirmary so that Marc—*and I*—can give her the best o' care."

"It's going to be a long winter," Joy said, suddenly seeming bleak when she considered what the season was always like.

Lizzie put an arm around her daughter-in-law and gave her a quick, affectionate hug.

"Already pinin' for spring, honey, 'n winter ain't even begun! Well, don't you worry, Joy Childers! It's goin' to be a wonderful Yuletide. Even if the weather's bitter cold, we'll be snug as can be in the hotel, warmed by the closeness of fam'bly 'n friends who come to visit. It'll be grand!"

"I wasn't worrying about me, Ma," Joy explained. "I just wish that Harmony and Billy were close by like they used to be. Before . . ."

"There's a time for everything, Joy. Situations change."

"Minnesota winters don't change, Ma. And neither does the lake," Joy said. "I've lived that life. . . . *I know*."

Helplessly Lizzie shivered, and that horrible, awful, eerie, unidentifiable feeling swept over her again. She tried to tell herself that she was just being silly, that it was the fussiness and flightiness of a middle-aged woman.

But when the same sinister sensations plagued her in the dark of the night, she had a terrible foreboding that something bad had happened—or was poised to happen—to a child she loved.

Which child was in jeopardy? Which child needed the prayer power of not only their ma but other concerned Christians that Lizzie could beseech to petition on his or her behalf?

Was it Thad . . . or *Harmony*?

The Big Fire had taken place the first week of October, had destroyed most of Baudette and Spooner on October seventh. A rain began to fall the night of October twelfth and sluiced down for two days. The following week, the first snow came, gently covering the tent city that had been set up by the militia for the homeless survivors of the holocaust.

Life soon returned to a semblance of normal for the residents of Williams and the families that ran the Grant Hotel in Rose Ames' stead.

Harmony and Billy LeFave's life soon returned to a normal routine. Harmony rested up for several days following the fire, and Billy wouldn't even let her cook their meals, so adept was he at preparing foods after years of seeing to his own needs.

"Bill, really, darling, you've got to let me be more active," Harmony protested. "I've got to remain physically fit, not only for my sake but the babe's."

"You need your rest," Billy said. "Surely your ma would agree with me!"

"I agree with you that I shouldn't overdo it, but I've got to do something! Doing nothing's driving me to distraction with the boredom!"

"Perhaps in a day or two I can take you visiting. Or perhaps Serenity will come to call."

"I miss her appearing almost daily," Harmony said. "She's the closest thing to a sister that I've got in these parts now."

"She's a joy to have around."

"And speaking of Joy—didn't she and Serenity hit it off? You could see that for yourself when Lester and Joy transported Serenity and Jacques Beaufort home."

"That they did. I'm so glad that Jacques healed as well as he did. But I sure wish he could've kept the sight in his eye," Bill said. "The loss'll make his trapping a tad more difficult."

"At least he's got partial sight," Harmony said. "And Marc talked as if it might improve over time, though never return to normal. And he'll compensate. People adapt, you know."

"One thing's for sure, you and Ma have a friend forever in Jacques."

"With Jacques fluent in Chippewa, he and Serenity got along well. She opened right up with him."

"Too bad he's much too old for her, hmmmm?" Billy said, smiling teasingly at his wife.

"He's not too old to be a wonderful, trusted friend."

"Serenity learned a lot about nursing from Dr. Marc," Billy said. "Women of the tribe work hard, but the chief's proud of Way-Say-Com-a-Gouk. Her tribe's already calling her Medicine Woman."

"I'm relieved to have her becoming so adept at all that Marc and I've been able to teach her. It puts my mind at ease," Harmony admitted, "now that the winter months are upon us and travel is so difficult. I feel better knowing that the Chippewa have Serenity to offer them care so that they're spared seeking out the services of a shaman who can only chant incantations, leap ferociously into the air in an attempt to scare away evil spirits of disease, and etch tattoos into their skin in an effort to ease their miseries."

"Bless Marc for sending home nostrums, elixirs, and simple medications for Serenity's use. She's the pride of the chief and the tribe. The Chippewa consider Nurse Woman and Medicine Woman angels of healing—as well they should."

"Pray God that there won't be any situations that Serenity and I can't handle," Harmony murmured tiredly.

"I've already figured out how to deal with that," Billy said. "The chief and I talked about it, and I told him that if there was someone seriously ill, they should hitch up the dogs, sled to our cabin, and from there I'd see to it that we got to the infirmary in Williams and a real doctor's care as quickly as possible."

"Bless you, Billy. You take good care of the Chippewa. It's no wonder the chief loves you like a son."

"It's your care that's foremost in my mind, darling," Billy admitted, "although I have a concern for the Chippewa's plight, too. These arrangements seem to serve everyone's interests. And such an agreement will keep you from being overworked—and exposed to sicknesses that very likely you shouldn't be coming into contact with when you're in such a delicate condition."

"You'd wrap me in cotton batting to protect me, wouldn't you, Bill?" Harmony teased, boosting herself from her rocking chair and going to him. He slipped his arms around her, and she riffled her fingers through his thick, dark hair. "You're going to be a wonderful pa."

"And you're going to be the world's best ma. But then, you've had a wonderful example to emulate."

"If I can be half the woman my ma is," Harmony murmured, "I'll die a happy woman."

"She has a strength of faith you don't often see," Billy said.

"Over the years, Bill, you don't know what Mama's endured and stood strong. Her life has been like a modern-day story of Job. That which doesn't kill you seems to make you stronger, she's always said."

191

"She's like a hank of rawhide," Billy said.

"I know. But she's a human, same's you and I, Bill. As Ma gets older and gets tired and the trials and tribulations continue to pile up over the years, there are times when, as her daughter, I wonder just how much more she can withstand."

"Rawhide stretches pretty far," Billy said.

"But it always has a snapping point," Harmony said.

Billy looked at her, his eyes assessing. "You're worried about your ma, aren't you?"

"Well . . . yes . . . I have my moments. But so do Marissa and Molly, who also know Ma's story well. To folks who've only met her in recent years, they can't see the subtle changes where pressures have been brought to bear. Thad's disappearance is riding very heavily on her mind, heart, and spirit. It's her faith that the Lord's protecting him when she can't that keeps her going. I shudder to think of what might happen if something occurred to wrest that conviction from her and leave Mama with nothing solid to hang on to that wasn't a disappointment."

"Pray God that won't happen. Leastways, she's got Lester and Joy, the Wheeler girls and their husbands and families, and us."

"We're all a joy to her," Harmony said, "but I can tell that Ma has her moments of being plumb melancholy. There's things plaguing her mind, bearing down with a heavy burden on her heart."

What she failed to add was that she, Harmony LeFave, who was so much Lizzie Mathews' daughter, was quietly suffering from the selfsame things, of which she'd spoken not so much as a syllable to another human being.

Although new life had sprouted in her body, there were days when Harmony felt as if she waded through a world that was flooded with death, destruction, and the tide was cresting higher, intent on sweeping her away. . . .

Unbidden, her hands dropped to cup her abdomen, as if she could somehow protect her unborn baby in a way that she felt unable to take care of herself, and she knew that she had to simply trust in the Lord and rely on his protection, knowing that nothing would harm her . . . or those she loved . . . *unless he allowed it.*

Night was falling and Harmony had placed a lamp in the window to send a glow into the night to guide Bill home.

She was relieved when she heard the baying howl of the sled dogs that he'd acquired in a mutually beneficial swap with one of the Indians in the nearby Chippewa encampment.

Harmony realized that the sled and dogs made Bill's life a lot easier, for when the weather turned so that it was not convenient to use the old but gentle and agreeable mare he'd purchased right after departing Williams to establish a place for them, he'd been reduced to making his way around on snowshoes. Although Billy was good on snowshoes and could even run while wearing them, the maneuvers required to do so, she knew, couldn't help but be physically exhausting.

Billy unhitched the dogs and tended to their needs before he came into the house. Harmony went to hug him, savoring his embrace, even though his furry parka was icy from the sub-zero temperatures. His cheeks against hers were icy cold, although his kiss was warm.

"Miss me?" he asked, drawing his hand around to gently lie over her abdomen, where their baby grew.

"Mmmmm . . . more than you'll ever know!"

"You're rounding out rather nicely, Mrs. LeFave," Billy

teased. "Your ma seems concerned that maybe you won't be. She sent a little something along for you."

Billy extracted a small, tin, lidded container. Even before she opened it, Harmony detected the faint odor of chocolate walnut fudge.

"My favorite!" she cried. "Oh, I've been craving a sweet treat. These days, I crave *everything*, it seems!"

"Ma's really looking forward to Christmas," Billy said. "She's cooking and baking up a storm."

Harmony smiled. "She must be in her element."

"She is," he chuckled. "I haven't seen her feeling this perky and fine in quite a while."

"That's wonderful."

"And the hotel—wait'll you see it, Harmony. It looks like something off a Christmas card. Pine boughs, ribbons, and candles everywhere. I don't know who's more zealous at the decorating—your ma or Joy."

"It's always especially exciting for a newborn Christian during their first several Christmases, I'm sure."

Billy grinned. "Is that what it is, sweetheart? I knew that somehow this winter seemed different than all the dark and cold seasons of the past. No doubt that's because the Lord has gifted me with not only his Son's sacrifice for me—but everything treasured a man could want in life. A beloved wife . . . a growing infant . . . a big family to love . . . a community ripe with promise."

"We're truly blessed," Harmony said. "What a Christmas it'll be! I'm really looking forward to us going to Williams for a few days, being there to attend Christmas Eve and Christmas Day worship services, and being able to stay at the hotel to be with family and friends."

"It's going to be wonderful," Bill said. "And in the meantime, I'm going to work extra hard around here so we can be away for a few days and return and still feel so caught up that it'll be like we haven't even been away from our labors."

"I really should bake some sugar cookies or something to add to the holiday treats," Harmony said.

"Your ma gave me orders about that, sweetheart," he said. "Your ma told me that I was to impress upon you that we weren't to bring anything along but ourselves and hearty appetites. She told me that the best holiday gift you could give her would be the peace of mind she could savor in knowing that you're takin' an added bit of rest. She was sincere, too, darlin'. She worries about you."

"If that's what Mama wants most of all—then that's an easy request to fill. I have felt tired lately."

"I know you have, Harmony. Thank the Lord we have Serenity to come by and help every couple of days. You always perk up after she's been here to visit."

"I know. She's good for me," Harmony said.

"And you're wonderful for her," Billy said. "She's developing into quite a maiden, isn't she? She'll make some lucky fellow a fine wife someday. And woe be unto him iffen he treats her wrong. He'll have me to answer to!"

Harmony giggled. "You sound just like a big brother, Bill!"

Billy considered the accusation, then laughed. "I guess that's how I feel, and it is how I'm acting, isn't it? Just like Lester when he made clear to me that I wasn't to trifle with his sister or I'd be answering to him!"

"If our Serenity finds someone as good for her as you are for me, Bill, then we'll all rejoice. She's so quiet that you have to directly ask her a question. She doesn't volunteer her feelings easily. I may have to hint around to find out if there's a special young fellow in her life."

195

Billy rumpled Harmony's hair, laughing contentedly. "You, Mrs. LeFave, are certainly your mother's daughter: matchmakers the both of you!"

"Can I help it, Mr. LeFave, if I happen to want everyone to be as happy as I am?"

"I doubt it. Such concern and desire for others seem born right into you."

chapter
15

Watson, Illinois

THIS CHRISTMAS SEASON seemed unusually bleak for Lemont Gartner, even though he knew that there was no real reason for such a feeling of sadness that permeated his days.

He'd received a letter of such understanding and lack of blame from Lizzie and Brad regarding Thad's disappearance that it had brought tears to his eyes. He'd openly wept when Lizzie had penned an additional few lines inviting him to journey up to Minnesota to stay with them at the hotel for a spell to reacquaint himself with the neighborhood children he'd seen grow up, who were now adults with children of their own or babes on the way.

And locally, Katie and Seth had included him, as had Rory and Sylvia, and Brad's daughters kept in regular contact with him.

"Maybe I'm just getting old," he said and helped himself to a fancy cookie that Sylvia Preston had sent over to him with Rory. "Perhaps that's what it is."

Christmas was only two weeks away. Dead grass lay matted and frozen on the hard ground, and the overcast gray skies did nothing to alleviate the oppressive Illinois climate. It didn't look like Christmas outside—and Lem lamented that it didn't feel like the Yuletide season in his heart, either—even though almost every time the rural mail carrier had made his rounds that week, he'd had greeting cards to deposit in the mailbox.

The day the mail was due, Lem watched from the window, and when he saw the approach of the postman's horse and carriage, he shrugged into his coat, went out to collect his mail and pass a few moments and exchange bits of news.

"Here you are, Lemont!" the smiling man said, sorting through the letters, double-checking for accuracy. "I've got to apologize—this un letter for Miss Lizzie was a time in comin', judgin' by the postmark. Must've been a delay somewheres along the line. New Orleans is a long way off but ain't *that* far away that it'd be detained a couple o' months. But mishaps occasionally happen with the mail."

"Right you are," Lemont said, plucking a letter that looked mussy, as if it had accidentally fallen to the floor and been kicked under a counter, desk, cabinet, sorting table, or some kind of machine in a post office along the way.

"Seems mailed a bit early for a Christmas card," the carrier observed.

"Looks more like a letter than a greeting card," Lemont said, studying the envelope.

"I figure it's an old friend of the Preston family. Didn't they hail from Tennessee or Kentucky onct upon a time?" the mailman inquired. "That ain't that far from the Deep South."

"That was my understanding," Lem said. "Kentucky, I think."

"Has to be someone who ain't been in touch with the fam'bly for quite a spell, though," the mailman pointed out.

"How say?" Lemont inquired.

"Look at the address! It's to 'Mrs. Childers.' I knew who 'twas for, of course. But Lizzie ain't been Mrs. Childers in a lot o' years."

"I wouldn't be surprised if it ain't correspondence from a girlhood friend. Someone who, as a girl, knew Lizzie well and now, as a middle-aged woman, has taken a notion to look her up."

The mailman nodded understanding. "As we get older, we tend to really cherish those that we realize were mighty important to us when we were young'uns."

"Must be a decent sort, the kind the Prestons would've had dealings with," Lemont said.

"If you want me to," the mailman offered, "I could forward it up to Williams to Lizzie's current address."

Lemont returned the letter. "Whyn't you do that? With any luck, it'll get there by Christmas, and to hear from an old girlhood friend would brighten Miss Lizzie's day."

"Consider it done, Lem, and if I don't see you beforehand, have a merry Christmas!"

"Same to you 'n yours, friend. Same to you."

LeFave's Landing
The Lake of the Woods, Minnesota

Although weariness dogged every step that Harmony LeFave took, she was enthusiastically looking forward to the trip to Williams. It would be a unique experience for her to travel to town via dogsled. Bill had assured her of her comfort and the quick pace of the part-timber-wolf dogs that would get them to the Grant Hotel in short order.

She wasn't sure when they would leave. A lot depended on when Bill finished running his traplines, skinning out carcasses, fleshing the pelts and then stretching them up to cure, after which they could pack and bathe and prepare to depart.

Bill had promised her that they'd be at the Grant Hotel no later than Christmas Eve afternoon. That was two days away.

Bill had hinted that if the weather held and everything went well, they might very handily even make it to town the day before Christmas Eve in order to have more time with their family and friends over the holidays.

When Harmony heard the yip of the sled dogs coming across the frozen lake, which stretched to the north as far as the eye could see, she assumed it was Bill. But just as teamsters could differentiate one horse's nicker from another's, already Harmony's hearing had adjusted so she could recognize Bill's baying dogs from those belonging to others.

Harmony crossed the cabin and looked out to identify the dog team that was coming closer. To her delight, she realized that it was Way-Say-Com-a-Gouk.

Harmony grabbed her wrap and flung open the door, waving at her friend.

"Come on in, Serenity! What a lovely surprise!" she cried merrily.

She expected the Chippewa girl to return in kind. Instead the stoic Indian girl, who seldom revealed her emotions, was keening in grief and worry.

Harmony's blood ran cold. A chill snaked through her, not so much caused by the bitter winter cold as by a realization of the caliber of trauma required to cause Way-Say-Com-a-Gouk to fall apart emotionally.

The sled dogs, exhausted from their run, fell panting where they'd stopped, and licked at the icy ground to slake their thirst.

"Nurse Woman! Nurse Woman!" Serenity sobbed. She struggled to scramble from the dogsled with a fur-covered burden she clutched protectively in her arms. "Must help me, Nurse Woman! Oh, please!"

Leaning forward as she ran low, Serenity shielded her burden with her torso. She was slipping and sliding on the path where Harmony and Billy's steps had packed the snow hard.

"Must help or die!" Serenity cried.

Serenity rushed in to the familiar cabin, her icy leather moccasins sliding on the warm floorboards.

"What's wrong?" Harmony asked, quickly slamming the door in order to retain what heat was in the cabin. Hastily she stirred up the fire and hefted another log onto the flaring embers.

"Let me see what the problem is," Harmony said, approaching Serenity and the bundle—which Harmony realized was a baby.

"Papoose sick! Afraid die!" Serenity said. She'd been trying to care for the infant, the child of a squaw who was a very close friend of hers. "Way-Say-Com-a-Gouk not work. Need Nurse Woman, even if Nurse Woman's man say she can no longer help Chippewa! Nurse Woman sister to Way-Say-Com-a-Gouk, like mother of papoose sister to Way-Say-Com-a-Gouk."

"What?" a puzzled Harmony asked, confused, even though suddenly it made glaring sense. Billy, attempting to protect her, had asked of the chief that he order the Chippewa not to seek her services but to consult Way-Say-Com-a-Gouk instead. And had probably told them that if Serenity couldn't attend to the problem, they were to seek out Billy LeFave, and he would arrange for the individual to be taken to a real doctor.

"We friends!" Serenity pointed out, gesturing from herself to Harmony. "Hope Billy not get angry you help Way-Say-Com-a-Gouk and friend's papoose!"

"Let me see the baby, Serenity," Harmony said, her calm voice seeming to soothe the distraught Chippewa maiden.

It took scarcely a glance beneath the fur robes and Harmony diagnosed the infant's malady: *diphtheria!*

There was the membranous material in the throat, nose, and mouth. In addition, the baby's breath was fetid. Its tawny skin was cyanotic from its struggle to breathe. Harmony knew that the infant was going to die.

"Can do something, Nurse Woman?" Serenity asked, her tone quietly optimistic.

Harmony met Serenity's eyes, bit her lip to try to stave the tears, and sadly shook her head.

"I can do no more than you've already done, Way-Say-Com-a-Gouk. Even Dr. Marc couldn't help this papoose to live."

"Die?" Serenity asked, her heart and eyes wounded as all hope expired.

Harmony nodded, touching her friend, patting the sickly infant tenderly. "I'm afraid so. I'm sorry, Way-Say-Com-a-Gouk. Very sorry."

"Must go—squaw!" Serenity said, fumbling to rewrap the baby whose life was fast ebbing away. Harmony nodded. Serenity wanted her friend to be able to hold her son even a few more minutes in life before the baby succumbed to death.

"Wait a minute!" Harmony called.

Serenity, intent on her mission, turned back with reluctance.

"You must keep this baby away from the rest of the tribe, or others will get sick and die also. Do you understand?"

Serenity grimly indicated that she did.

"And you must promise me something, Way-Say-Com-a-Gouk."

"For you—I promise anything!"

"Don't let anyone tell Bill that you were here to see me today. He must not find out that you brought the baby to me. Promise me that it will be a secret between us."

"Way-Say-Com-a-Gouk promise," Serenity said, then she stumbled toward the dogsled, threw herself onto the conveyance, and the scarcely rested dogs took off at a dead run across the icy landscape.

Harmony didn't gaze out the window to watch Serenity disappear into the white horizon where it was impossible to distinguish where the frozen lake ended and the overcast sky began.

She looked around her cabin. It was contaminated! Diphtheria was highly contagious! Who knew where flecks of mucus—laden with bacteria—had sprayed when the baby had coughed and choked, struggling to breathe?

Harmony regarded her clothes, her hands, the cabin.

Throwing more logs on the fire, she opened the door, grabbed a towel, and fanned through the air, hoping that as icy fresh air was replenished in the warm confines of the cabin, bacteria were being routed. She threw the towel onto the pile to be washed. Then, on second thought, she tossed it onto the fire, along with the linen tablecloth that had been on the table where they'd laid the sick papoose for Harmony to examine it.

She plunged her hands into the hot water in the reservoir on the wood range, then dripped across to the basin, grabbed a bar of her ma's lye soap and vigorously attacked her hands and arms before filling a wash basin.

She peeled off her clothing, every stitch of it, shivering as she took a hasty but thorough bath, then gingerly plucked up all of her clothing, deposited it in a clean pillow slip, and set it outside to await wash day, hoping the frigid temperatures would kill any contamination.

She felt clean finally, but when she considered Bill falling ill with diphtheria, she looked wretchedly, forlornly, around the cheerful cabin, wondering what she might have missed.

Harmony was reading her Bible and praying fervently when Bill returned home that evening. She felt guilty keeping such a dread secret from him, but she was worried enough for both of them without allowing Bill to carry such a burden as knowing that they'd been exposed to a killer disease like diphtheria!

"I figure we can leave for Williams in the morning if you want, darling," Bill said later that evening after Harmony had prepared their supper.

"We'll see."

Bill looked surprised. "What do you mean? I thought you'd be rarin' to go."

"Oh, I'm looking forward to it . . . but . . . I've felt a bit peaked today. We'll see how I am in the morning. We really shouldn't take chances, you know—"

"You're right. But how I'd hate for us to miss Christmas with your ma and all the family."

"There will be other Christmases if we can't," Harmony assured, as if she was even more eager than Bill to make the trip. "We'll see what tomorrow brings."

That night, Harmony scarcely slept at all. Any time she coughed—she now wondered if it was the onslaught of diphtheria.

"How're you feeling, sweetheart?" Bill asked the next morning.

"Better . . . I think." She paused. "Bill, would you mind terribly if we postponed going to Williams until tomorrow morning? We could still get there in time for Christmas Eve with family and friends at the church."

"Whatever you want, Harmony, is what I want."

"That's what we'll do, then," Harmony said. But she withheld the ominous addition that if she felt worse instead of better, they weren't going anywhere for Christmas. No way was she going to carry diphtheria into Williams.

The next morning, Harmony's throat felt distinctly sore. She gargled with salt water. When Bill was outside taking care of the dogs, she plucked the medical books Marc had given her from the shelf and hastily turned to the section regarding diphtheria.

Her fears multiplied!

It wasn't going to be easy to tell Bill that they couldn't go to Williams, to lay blame on her health and be only half truthful with him. But until she was sure, she—*they*—were not going anywhere!

"We can't go," Harmony said, giving in to the tears she'd somehow managed to hold in since Serenity disappeared with the dying papoose. "I just don't feel up to it, Bill. There will be other Christmases," she promised. "This will always be our first Christmas."

"And we're spending it together," Billy said, kissing her contentedly, while Harmony all but squirmed in his arms, terrified that she might be infecting her beloved with a horrible disease that could choke him of all life.

"I wish there was some way we could send word to Ma and the family," she said.

"They'll be disappointed, that's for certain," Billy said. "But Ma's a smart woman, and she's borne enough young'uns to know how a woman in the motherly condition feels. When we don't show up, they'll figure it out. Like as not, they'll come calling on us before the new year."

By then, Harmony thought, she would *know*.

She knew that until then she had to pray as she'd never prayed before, and she felt a special loneliness in not being able to confide in others and trust them with her concerns so that they could add their petitions to her own.

But she couldn't risk Bill learning that Serenity had innocently exposed them to a most dreaded disease. There was nothing anyone could do, she realized. Her life was in the Lord's hands. And she prayed that it would be long and filled with season after season of happiness, hope, and marital harmony.

Williams, Minnesota

It was the day after Christmas, a sunshiny, blue-skied day, although the temperature was near zero.

Shortly after dawn the small town came alive as people returned to their everyday work routines.

Brad joined Lizzie in the kitchen, feeding the range from the fuel supply in the wood box before he poured himself a cup of coffee and took a seat across from her.

"A penny for your thoughts, Liz," he gently prompted.

She slowly turned, giving him a hazy, distant smile. "I was just thinkin' of old times . . . happier times."

"This wasn't much of a Christmas in some ways, not compared with those we've known in the past."

"It was lonesome-like," Lizzie said, "'thout Thad—wherever he was at celebratin' the Lord's birth—without your girls clustered around the holiday table, without Harmony 'n Will." Lizzie's frown deepened. "Wisht that they'd had time to get word to us that they couldn't come. I hope everything's all right."

"You know how it is for women in the motherly condition, Liz. They can be feeling purty fit one moment and be bedfast with the miseries the next."

"Iffen the weather stays clear and maybe warms up a bit, be

nice if we could hitch the mare to the cutter and travel out to the lake. Maybe spend a night or two with Harmony 'n Will."

"That'd be nice! We'll do that, Liz," Brad assured, agreeable to anything that would return his wife to the sunny nature he'd come to associate her with over the years.

"Maybe we could travel out on New Year's Eve," Lizzie said, "ring in the comin' year with our children."

"Barring bad weather," Brad said, "let's count on it!"

Lizzie cocked her head. "Sounds like the train's comin'," she said.

Brad too listened. "That it is. Well, I reckon that I'll hie on over to the depot 'n meet it when it comes in. Who knows, we might have mail!"

"Mayhap," Lizzie said, but her tone remained unconvinced.

"Don't lose hope," Brad said. "Have faith."

"I try," she said.

"Maybe we'll have word from Rory and Sylvia," Brad said, trying to remind Lizzie of all the years when she'd pined for her brother, Rory, when he'd run off and she had given him up for lost, only to receive a long-delayed letter conveying apologies and desiring to mend the rift that had come between the siblings when in anger, grief, and despair, Rory Preston had rashly walked away from the faith that had been his.

"Anything you're needin' while I step out 'n about the town?"

"You might pick up a few stamps, darlin'," Lizzie said. "With winter settin' on, I'm going to try to mend my ways 'n keep in touch with fam'bly this year. The older I get . . . the more I realize they're all I've got in this world as I wait to be called to the next."

Half an hour later Brad returned, stamping the snow off his boots, shivering against the chill, rubbing his hands together to warm them after slipping off his gloves.

"Anything in the mail, darlin'?" Lizzie called from the kitchen.

"Several things. A letter from Lemont, another from Rosalie, and there's one that's been forwarded up to you from . . . New Orleans."

"Really? I don't recall knowin' anyone in New Orleans," Lizzie said.

"Well, sweetheart," Brad teased, "probably a passle of folks gettin' Christmas cards from us this year said, 'Why, I don't recall knowin' anyone from Williams!'"

"Right you are. I wonder who it's from," Lizzie murmured. "I haven't been Mrs. Childers in years and years."

"Quickest way to solve the mystery is to open it and find out."

"Reckon you're right," Lizzie said, smiling, as she seemed to anticipate a pleasant surprise.

She seated herself at the kitchen worktable, tore open the envelope with her finger, extracted the crisply folded three-page letter from the smudged and smeared envelope that suggested it'd had a difficult time en route from New Orleans to Minnesota, and a small, flat velvet bag dropped out onto the tabletop.

"Ain't that odd!" Lizzie said. She reached for the tiny bag, which was like one a precious, jeweled item would be stored in, and loosened the little crocheted drawstring enough to peer in. "It's a lock o' hair!"

"That makes no sense. What's the letter say, Liz?"

Lizzie unfolded the letter, then moved it back to arm's length to better focus on the writing.

"It says, 'Dear Mrs. Childers, you don't know me, but I feel as if I know you, from all that Thad told me about you when we were together—'"

"Thad!" Brad cried, elated.

"It's about Thad!"

"Read on. Maybe this person knows where he's at!"

Suddenly Lizzie looked at the velvet bag containing the lock of hair—just the color of Thad's the last time she'd seen him. Horror struck to her very heart. She flipped the first page of the letter, then the second.

At that time, Lizzie Mathews began to scream and could not stop.

"Liz! Liz—what is it?!" Brad cried. "Oh my heavens— *Lester! Lester, come quick!* Joy—HELP!"

Lizzie's screams and sobs seemed to rend the Grant Hotel from its foundation to the peak of the roof.

"What is it, Liz?!" Brad questioned, trying to take the letter from her as she crushed it and the velvet bag in her fingers, holding them so tightly her knuckles grew white.

"What's the matter with Ma?" Lester asked, rushing into the room.

"I'm not sure exactly, but it's obviously powerfully bad news—and it has something to do with Thad."

"Mama . . . let me see the letter," Lester coaxed. "Ma, it's Lester. Let me read the letter, Ma."

Like a small child, she calmed with Lester's arms around her, his voice flowing over her. As if she were in a trance, she released the letter to him, but not the velvet bag with the lock of hair.

"It's about Thad, all right," Lester said, frowning as he quickly scanned the letter.

"Thad . . . yes . . . Thad . . . he's dead," Lizzie whispered, her eyes unblinking, her tone as if she were in a hypnotic state.

And then she began to scream again and would not stop, could not stop, until Dr. Wellingham was summoned to the hotel and gave her a sedative, and when it did not work, he administered another and Lizzie sank away to the only kind of peace she would know: a drug-induced torpor.

chapter
16

"WILL YOU BE all right?" Lester inquired.

"Lord willing, we can handle it," Brad somberly replied. "Joy's real good with your mama."

"I know. It'll be a relief when I can bring Harmony back to Williams to be with Ma during this time of mourning. Sis will be like a healing balm for her. Somehow Harmony always knows what to say to comfort Ma in her trials."

"And it's a knack Liz has had in reverse with your sister and my girls, too."

"I wish I were going out to call on Billy and Harmony under better circumstances."

"Me too, son. It can't be helped. Ever since Thad disappeared, I reckon we've all known that it might come to this, instead o' ending in a happy reunion like we all had with Rory."

"It's going to be hard news to break."

"I don't envy you the task, Les. Just make sure that Will's at home with Harmony so that there's the both of you to comfort her. She's in a plumb delicate condition."

"I have an appreciation for that. No one would know it to look at her, but Joy's in the fam'bly way."

"That'll be wonderful news to your mama—when she's ready to hear it. Mayhap it'll ease the pain of her loss a bit if she has another grandchild's arrival to look forward to."

"I'd better go. Assure Ma that Harmony and I—and like

as not, Billy—will be in Williams just as soon as we can get here. I'll be leavin' now," Lester said and snapped the reins across the mare's back. The cutter jolted ahead with a lurch, then sliced cleanly through the snow.

"Godspeed, Les!" Brad called after him. "The Lord be with ya!"

When Harmony had felt unable to go to Williams for the Christmas holidays, Billy assumed that it was due to the miseries and various complaints of a woman whose body was growing heavy with the bulk of an unborn child and who therefore tired easily.

Two days after Christmas, he knew that it was more than that. He didn't understand what it was, but he was wretchedly aware that whatever was wrong with Harmony—it was serious!

He'd noticed that Christmas Day and the following day, she'd gargled with salt water every few minutes but it had done no good, for her voice had grown hoarse and she hesitated speaking.

But anytime Bill suggested taking her to Williams and entrusting her to Dr. Marc's care, she spoke curtly if painfully. "No! I can't go to town. I *won't* go to town. It's not safe for me to leave." But she explained no further.

Then the fever came.

The headaches.

The membranes.

The foul breath.

Nosebleeds.

The constant noisy, rattling struggle to breathe.

"It's settled, Harmony—you *are* going to let me transport you to the infirmary in Williams! I won't risk losing you, and I feel wild with helplessness, being unable to ease your suffering myself. This isn't just a cold or flu—we're going to Williams to see Marc and Ma! They'll know what to do."

"Can't," Harmony weakly breathed. "Mustn't do that to them. . . . I can't go to town."

Billy wrung his hands in frustrated fear. "Maybe you wouldn't make the trip," he thought out loud. "But I can go in and bring Marc right back out. I know he'll come!"

"Can't. . . . People need . . . him."

"*I need you!*" Billy implored, his voice cracking.

"You mustn't go . . . to town. You've . . . been exposed, too. We can't . . . risk the entire . . . town."

"Harmony! What are you talking about? Do you know what's wrong? Tell me! I'm your husband—I have a right to know."

With fevered thoughts, Harmony considered the entire situation. She knew she couldn't shield Billy forever. She had needs, but he did, too, and there was the community to think of.

"Dip—dip—," she began, then was overcome by strangling coughs.

"Diphtheria!" he gasped in horror.

Harmony couldn't speak. She weakly nodded as railing coughs shook her frame.

"How did you get that?! Where did you get it? Who exposed you?" Billy flared to life with questions harsh with fright.

Harmony shrugged. "Somewhere."

"What can I do?" Billy cried. "Who can I get?"

Weak and wan, Harmony simply gave a wilted shake of her head, which was spinning and too heavy with fever to even lift off the pillow. The small gesture said it all: There was nothing he—or anyone—could do for her. Her life was in the Lord's hands.

Near forenoon the following day, Billy heard sled dogs and

looked out to see Serenity approach. Soon she came to the door. He let her in before she had time to knock.

"Come in," he whispered. "Harmony is ill."

Fright and guilt washed over Way-Say-Com-a-Gouk's features, but Billy was too distracted to notice. "Bad sick?" she whispered.

Billy shrugged in confusion. "I think bad sick, yes. I want to take her to Williams to Dr. Wellingham, but she insists that she cannot go. Pray God she's wrong—but she thinks that it's diphtheria."

The stoic Indian girl flinched at the diagnosis.

"I talk to her?" Serenity softly inquired.

Billy was despairing. He raked his fingers through his hair. "Go ahead. And good luck. Perhaps you'll somehow be more persuasive than I."

Quietly Serenity entered the darkened bedroom. She almost gasped when she saw Harmony, who was so blond, fair, and pretty, lying reddened, fevered, and disheveled in the bedclothes that had been tangled from her delirium before Billy had managed to bring her fever down somewhat, knowing it was only a matter of time before it shot back up.

Serenity seated herself by the bed. She touched Harmony's brow. It still felt scorching hot. Harmony cracked her eyes open. They were glassy, hollow, distant.

"You sick," Serenity said. "Must go Dr. Marc."

"Can't . . . too sick . . . quarantine . . . mustn't do this . . . others," Harmony said in a drifting, almost singsongy voice, as if she were too weak to speak.

"Can Way-Say-Com-a-Gouk help Nurse Woman? I do you say!"

"Yes . . . yes, you can help me!" Harmony breathed. "There's something I want you to promise me."

"I do it! Just ask!"

"Take care of Bill for me. . . . Help him to heal."

Serenity looked confused. "He strong! He not ill—"

"Just promise me, Way-Say-Com-a-Gouk . . . promise!" Harmony's hand fumbled for the girl's brown arm, found her fingers, and held tightly. "Promise me!"

"For you . . . I promise," Serenity vowed.

"Thank you. Tired . . . oh, so tired," Harmony panted, out of breath, coughing and choking from the effort of speaking.

"You rest," Serenity said. "Sleep good."

"Yes . . . I want to sleep . . . and sleep . . . and sleep."

A moment later Harmony's eyes fluttered shut. Billy entered the room and regarded his wife. She was still as death except for the noisy rattle from her lungs and the fact that her chest hollowly moved up and down ever so slightly.

The two kept vigil over the sleeping woman for long moments.

Serenity was the first to rouse. She tilted her head. "Someone here?"

"I don't hear anything," Billy said. He crossed the room. "You're right—someone has come calling. I wonder who it is?"

Serenity was a half step behind him. "Les-ter."

"So it is. Maybe *he* can help us to convince Harmony to make the trip to Williams. Or maybe the three of us can simply take her there, with her permission or against her will if we must." Billy opened the cabin door and went out to greet his brother-in-law. "C'mon in, Lester! We're home! What a relief to see that it's you—"

"You may not feel that way for long," Lester said. "I traveled out here on some grim business. It's about Thad." He swallowed hard, then realized there was no way to rid the news of the horror that he felt each time he stated the fact. "He's dead."

"*Dead?!*" Billy gasped, stunned.

"Ma got a letter from some church woman down in New Orleans. Seems she made acquaintance with Thad some time back. She was present when he was killed by a riverboat gambler and thrown overboard into the Mississippi River, down in gator territory."

"Oh my heavens, " Billy groaned, looking as distraught as he knew Lester felt.

"I came out to give Harmony the hideous news."

"She's sick. Bad sick," Billy said, his tone numb with emotion and exhaustion. "That's why we didn't come to Williams for the holidays."

"Joy's in the fam'bly way, too. She ain't been feelin' too sprightly come mornin'," Lester commiserated, misunderstanding.

"It's more than that," Billy said. "I'm afraid if she doesn't get help, she's going to . . . going to . . . ." Suddenly, talking to his brother-in-law, who loved Harmony, too, there was no holding his emotions in check. "I'm terrified she'll die if she doesn't get help—and she refuses to leave the cabin."

"That doesn't sound like Harmony," Lester said. "Maybe if I talk to her?"

"She gets spent easy. But go ahead. Serenity has tried."

"Maybe I'd better wait a spell to tell her about Thad."

"It might be best. Harmony thinks it's diphtheria. But I haven't heard of any outbreaks. I'm praying she's wrong."

Lester had a heavy heart as he let himself into the cabin and nodded at Serenity, who, to occupy her hands and thoughts, was doing up work that Harmony couldn't attend to and that Billy hadn't really noticed needed to be done.

Lester entered the dim bedroom. "Sis? Sis? It's Lester. How are ya?"

Harmony forced her eyes open. "Oh . . . Les," she breathed and then began to gasp and cough.

"You're really sick!"

"I know," she said in a waiflike, wistful tone. "Dip—" She was overcome with choking coughs. "Diphtheria . . ."

"Oh Lord, please, no!" Lester murmured. "Sis, we've got to get you to Marc. He'll know what to do! Mayhap get some vaccine. *Something!*"

"Do nothing . . . contagious . . . medical book . . ."

"Harmony, please!"

"Exposed, Lester. . . . quarantine . . ."

"What are you talking about?"

"Can't carry sickness . . . to town . . ."

It started to penetrate Lester's understanding.

"Medical book . . . bookmark . . . diphtheria . . . read . . . know . . ."

Harmony was overtaken by such a fit of coughing that her fair complexion grew strained, red and mottled from the force of her efforts to simply breathe.

Lester, realizing that his sister was going to die and there wasn't a thing he could do about it, gripped her hand and cried out for Billy, who rushed right in.

Harmony fumbled for his hand, too.

"Lester . . . take care . . . Bill . . . Serenity . . . need you . . . Joy . . ."

"I will, Harmony, I promise."

"Tell Mama . . . love her . . . Brad too . . ."

Tears burned behind Lester's eyes. "I will," he promised, his voice hoarse with tears.

"Bill . . . take care . . . the baby . . . I'm sorry . . . Serenity . . . I love . . . my little sister . . . in Christ . . ."

"I know, darling," Billy said. "She loves you, too."

"Lester . . . ask . . . Ma . . . help Serenity . . . Bill . . . she'll be . . . their mother . . ."

"Sure, sure," Lester promised, even though at the moment, he feared that his mother might come unhinged and be unable to help anyone, even herself, if something didn't snap her out of the state into which she had fallen.

Billy was weeping outright, realizing that moments with Harmony were quickly ebbing away. "About Thad . . ."

Harmony heard him speak. "Ah . . . Thad . . ." An amused smile, a peaceful expression, seemed to envelope her. When she spoke, her words were faint, distant, almost as if she were somewhere between this world and the next.

Lester sensed something eerie. "You know about Thad?" he gently prodded.

Harmony's smile grew even more blissful, and peace swept over her. "Yes . . . I know about Thad," she accepting-ly reassured.

And then she was gone.

With Harmony's departure, Way-Say-Com-a-Gouk began the keening wail of the Chippewa Indians in mourning. Billy wept. Lester was ashen-faced, prayerful, unsure of what to do.

Then he recalled the words that Harmony had spoken to him.

He went to the bookcase that Billy had built for the chunky medical texts. He hunkered down, read the alphabet-ized listings on the leather spines, then plucked a volume from the shelf, noticing that it was a quarter of an inch out of line with the rest of the tomes.

The book fell open—to the appropriate page, because Harmony had inserted a mark there.

Quickly he scanned the long pages of fine print, the etiology, symptoms, prognosis, treatment, and statistical data. Much of it he couldn't comprehend, but he understood enough to realize what Harmony had tried to convey.

"Lord have mercy!" he gasped. "Bill—come quick!"

Stunned, Lester read passages from the textbook.

"You can't leave?" Billy said. "Serenity must stay, too?"

"Yes," Lester said. "We can't risk going out in the world carrying a bacteria as virulent as diphtheria! It could make a ghost town of Williams within a fortnight. . . . We're quarantined. Any one of us could take sick next."

"Les, when you don't return, someone will ride out looking for you," Billy said.

"We'll be watchful," Lester said. "We won't let them enter the house. We can shout to them what the situation is."

"Oh, what are we going to do?" Billy said, seeming on the verge of total collapse, as he was confused, in shock, over his wife's death, the loss of his unborn child. Lester suspected the reality of it really hadn't begun to fully sink in yet.

"We're going to have to . . . bury the dead. We've got to build a box . . . open a grave . . ."

Together the men made quiet plans, as if laying the necessities out in parcels of work would help them hang on to their sanity in a crazy and chaotic world.

The next two days, they slept little, talked seldom, and went through the hours by rote. Both Billy and Lester worked on constructing the burial box. Billy, Lester, and even Serenity worked with shovels, pickaxes, and tined garden forks to break up the frozen soil and dig an acceptably deep grave.

It was wretched work. The men piled firewood and driftwood

219

on a cleared spot on the bluff a ways from the cabin, lit a fire, and let the heat from the flames thaw the frozen earth. When they dug out what dirt could be removed and again hit frozen soil, they repeated the procedure until finally the earth had given way and opened to receive Harmony Childers LeFave's body.

"This is heartbreakin'," Lester said, weeping and wiping tears. "As many folks as knew and loved Harmony, her buryin' should've been marked by people far 'n wide."

Billy could only sob.

Serenity had not stopped her wailing.

The winter wind whisked at the pages of Harmony's Bible, which Lester had chosen to use for her committal services. The wind from the north that blew in off the icy lake stung his skin and caused his tears to freeze even as they clung to his eyelashes.

He read from the Psalms and other appropriate readings.

"Amen," he finally finished.

"Amen," Billy sobbed.

"A-men," Way-Say-Com-a-Gouk keened.

One by one they scooped a shovelful of earth onto the coffin, then the men sent a brokenhearted Serenity to the empty cabin while they faced the grim task of covering Harmony's remains with a blanket of earth that would no doubt soon be hidden beneath a lacy coverlet of new-fallen snow.

Three days after Lester had left for the lakeshore property, Brad was concerned by his failure to return. On the fourth day, Brad, Luke Masterson, and Sven Larsen set out to investigate.

Although none of them spoke their fears, they were unnerved by the prospect of, somewhere along the trail, coming upon Lester Childers injured and frozen to death.

"There's his cutter!" Brad voiced with relief when they could see the clearing around Billy's cabin.

"At least we know he made it this far."

"Yes, because his horse didn't know the way. She wouldn't have been able to arrive here on her own without Les guiding her."

A moment later the cabin door opened and Lester appeared.

"Don't come any closer!" he bellowed.

"What?" Sven cried, chirruping the horse, encouraging it closer, faster.

Lester waved, gesturing them back.

"Come no closer! There's a bad sickness going around in these parts," he said when Sven halted the horse twenty-five yards away. "Diphtheria! We're in quarantine 'til we know it's safe to leave the property."

"God have mercy!" Brad gasped.

He felt a surge of relief when he saw Billy edge in beside Lester and recognized Serenity's shadow as she stood behind the two men.

"Harmony! Where's Harmony?" Brad cried out, his voice anguished.

Lester gestured dully. "Over yonder," he said, pointing toward a charred clearing in the snow that looked like a violent bruise placed on the earth. "We buried her the day before yesterday."

"Oh dear Lord—no!" Brad cried, then began to hoarsely sob, which set off Luke Masterson, who began to weep, too, overcome with sorrow and shock.

"Miss Harmony? *Daid?*" Sven's tone was numb with disbelief, but in his heart he knew, for he didn't even need an answer before he lost control and began to bawl brokenly, like a small child who's just known devastating treatment.

"We can't risk goin' to town and mayhap infectin' people," Lester said. "We've gotta stay put 'til we know if we're goin' to get sick or not." He paused. "So far . . . we're fine."

"Have you got enough supplies, son?" Brad inquired.

"More'n enough."

"We'd better head back to town, then."

"Tell Joy I love her. Remind Ma o' that, too!" Lester said.

"I will," Brad promised, but he feared Liz would not even be in a state of comprehension by the time he returned, so great was her grief, so devastating was her loss. How, oh how, could she be expected to bear up to this too?!

"I don't know what I'm goin' to do," Brad sadly confided in Luke and Sven as they slowly headed back to Williams. "We've all sometimes quietly referred to Liz's entire life as a modern-day story of Job. But 'tis true."

"I know," Luke said. His wife, Molly, had chronicled the triumphs and trials of the people of the Salt Creek community, and Lizzie, in some way, had seemed to be featured heavily in either instance.

"I don't know how much that poor woman can be expected to take without sacrificin' her faculties altogether . . . or, even worse, completely losing—or abandoning—her faith. Why, Job's wife was even pesterin' him to curse God and die, thinkin' that it was logical advice. I can't see how Lizzie's going to come through the knowledge that Harmony's lost to us, when she's still reelin' from learning of Thad's violent end."

"She's made of stern stuff," Luke reminded.

"Miss Lizzie's a strong woman," Sven agreed.

"I know that," Brad said. "But I fear that a body can only take so much before givin' up. Liz has had moments of melancholy long before this. If she chooses to simply give up—there won't be anything we can do about it. For a tough woman, at present she's downright fragile. Iffen the Lord don't put a hedge around her 'n draw some lines over what he's allowin' to happen to poor Liz, I don't know that she can humanly endure. Liz has always been a plucky woman, agreeable to pickin' herself up and going on, but . . ."

"Seems as if lately anytimes she's tried to pick herself up, the rug's been rudely jerked out from under her again," Luke said.

"Life ain't fair. Miss Lizzie doesn't deserve such anguish and misery," Sven said.

"None of us get what we really deserve," Brad said.

"Pray God that no self-righteous individual approaches Liz as Job's friends did, to cast suspicion that she's doin' something to earn the Lord's wrath. . . . Tired as she is, I don't think she could withstand such a cruel accusation."

"Maybe rest would help," Luke said. "Have Marc admit her to the infirmary. He could keep an eye on her, remove some of the responsibilities and burdens from her life, and make sure that she maintains the bodily strength to deal with whatever she must on an emotional and spiritual level."

"That's a good idea," Brad said, "and sounds plumb appealin' to me. Liz has become my life. I don't know what I'd do without her."

"The entire town needs her," Luke said.

"What a way to start the new year," Sven said, his voice sourly sarcastic.

"We can hope for better in the days that follow," Brad said in a tired tone that was all but robbed of faith and conviction.

"We'll do better than that," Luke reminded. "Instead of just hoping, we're going to steadfastly pray for blessings and happiness in the coming year."

chapter
17

THE PROGRESSING WINTER was harsh—and life was, too.

Lizzie's emotional, spiritual, and physical resources seemed to dwindle by the day until Brad soon had no recourse but to turn her over to the care of Marc and the nurses in the infirmary.

Marc suggested that it was in the best interests of his patient that the news of her daughter's passing be withheld until Lizzie had gained sufficient strength to weather another ruthless blow.

Lizzie, who'd always been the one to cajole others to eat in order to regain their strength and health, was now the recipient of such pleading.

She had no appetite nor zest for living. She was even too weak to attend Sunday worship services. The old Lizzie, who'd reveled in hospitality, seemed almost oblivious to callers' presence when friends stopped by to encourage her and try to brighten her days.

Raised by Fanny Preston, even at her lowest ebb Lizzie tried to muster the wherewithal to be mannerly, but even that effort seemed to exhaust her.

Lizzie's condition was so precarious because the first week of January, in addition to her grief, she was stricken by a severe siege of influenza.

The first week or so of her confinement, Lizzie had lain in fevered misery, overwhelmed by influenza's ravaging symptoms. She was too ill to try to think or even really conscious-ly notice who had come to visit her and who had not.

It was the third week into January before anyone men-tioned Harmony in Lizzie's presence, and then it was done by Lizzie herself.

"Now that I'm feeling a mite better, I'm hopin' Will 'n Harmony can venture to town soon. I miss seein' her regularly."

"Yes . . . we all do," Becky Rose Grant quietly agreed, then quickly turned away to blink back her tears.

"I've got to get well," Lizzie said, her voice determined as she stretched and yawned. "Harmony and her comin' babe will need my attendance. Mayhap it'll be a boy child. As close as Harmony was to . . . Thad . . . it might well be that she'll want to name the infant in part after . . . Thad . . . to honor 'n remember him by."

"Well," a flustered Becky Rose murmured, "it's comforting to dwell on happy thoughts . . ." and then she fled the room, for fear further conversation with Lizzie might somehow result in her accidentally blurting the devastating truth.

"How's Lizzie?" Marissa inquired, giving Becky Rose a searching look and recognizing her anxiety.

Becky Rose lowered her voice. "She's talking about Harmony! And wanting to see her!" she hissed.

Marissa had known that moment was coming.

She gave a heavy sigh. "She's going to have to be told."

"I know."

"I'll mention it to Marc. He and the family can confer and figure out how best to break the news to her."

"It shouldn't be postponed much longer."

That night, when Lester and Brad came to the infirmary to see Lizzie while Joy tended to kitchen duties at the hotel, Dr.

225

Wellingham called them into his private study and explained the situation.

"She really must be told about Harmony. She's strong enough now so that I don't worry so much about the combination of shock and influenza and grief literally being the end of her."

"It's not going to get any easier, puttin' it off," Brad said. "It only prolongs our misery in order to spare Liz."

"That's true enough," Lester said. "It's like waitin' for the other shoe to drop."

"It was up to me to break the news to Liz about the passin' of Jeremiah, Maylon, and Alton Wheeler some years back. I guess you could say I have some experience with that kind of thing . . . but I sure don't cotton to the task. It takes somethin' out o' a feller. Though, all else failin' . . . I will." Brad shrugged helplessly. "I—I just ain't as young and . . . strong . . . as I once was."

Lester regarded his aging step-pa with sympathy and understanding. He felt a wave of compassionate responsibility sweep over him when he realized he was now the mature man of the family, in his prime.

"I—I can break it to Mama," Lester softly volunteered. "After all, I was with Sis . . . when she . . . expired . . . died. . . ." He drew a quick breath and swallowed hard, wringing his hands. "But I'd appreciate havin' someone with me when I do it."

Brad and Marc exchanged glances.

"We'll both be with you, Les," Marc assured.

"We'd best be doin' it soon," Brad sighed, "now that we've decided we should."

The grandfather clock outside the hall seemed to punctuate the stretching silence.

"How about right now?" Marc said.

Lester squared his shoulders. "No time like the present. Do it and get it behind me before I lose my resolve."

"Let's go," Marc said and laid a comforting hand on Brad's shoulder when he groaned softly as he boosted from his chair.

Lester paused outside the study and offered a quick prayer that God would grant him the words and the wisdom to do what must be done.

Then he strode down the hall toward Lizzie's sickroom.

"Hello, Ma," he said, entering the cozy corner room.

"Lester!" Lizzie said, managing to smile as she weakly struggled to sit up in bed. Her attempt was cheerful, but her tone was wan. She patted the bed beside her, bidding Lester to come sit close to her.

"You feelin' better, Ma?"

She paused as if to take inventory. "Some, I reckon. Mayhap I'll be up 'n around afore long, feeling like my ol' self again. I sure hope so."

"We're all prayin' for that, darlin'," Brad said, seating himself on the bed opposite Lester.

Marc stood at the foot of the bed.

Brad and Marc, who'd said almost nothing, earned Lizzie's full scrutiny. Her eyes flicked back to Lester, who was suddenly at a loss for words. His lips moved but no sounds came out.

"What's goin' on?" Lizzie demanded to know. "There's somethin' you're not tellin' me. What is it?!"

The three men helplessly looked at each other as Lester's resolve seemed to evaporate. It was not at all progressing as they'd hoped.

"It's bad—ain't it?" Lizzie said, her voice shooting up an octave, becoming shrill and breathy with fear. Her lower lip

227

trembled and tears pooled in her eyes as she stared from one to the other and back again, beseeching them to speak.

Lester dropped his face forward into his cupped hands, strangling on a sob.

"Yes, Mama . . . it is . . ." His voice cracked off, then returned wetly, in a heartbroken, shaky whimper. "Harmony's dead."

"*Dead?!*" Lizzie screamed with a throat-searing sound of confused disbelief wailing off to become a gurgle of raw anger that so cruel a trick would be foisted upon her.

"Yes. Dead . . . diphtheria," Marc softly added. "We're all so sorry. She's gone from us."

"*NO!*"

Then it was as if the wind had been knocked from Lizzie. She couldn't even speak. She could only gasp and clutch at her heart as she looked from Lester to Brad to Marc in mute horror. Her eyes pleaded with them to tell her that it was not true—even as their simultaneously devastated expressions underscored that it was.

"I can't take any more!" Lizzie sobbed, more fearful in her weak and breathy sobs than she'd been in hysterical, screaming grief. Lizzie's coloring grew awful. She seemed about to shatter before their very eyes. Breaths pent, they watched, waiting for her next response.

Like one dying—or wishing to—resolutely Lizzie turned her face to the wall, not even bothering to wipe at the tears that coursed hotly from her eyes, trailed a path down her cheeks, formed a pool in the hollow of her neck, then pattered softly to the linen pillow slip, soaking it and her dark hair, which had fallen from its coils.

Brad held one hand, Lester held the other, but it was as if they were not even present.

"I'm sorry, Ma," Lester whispered. "So close on the heels of the news about Thad, this's been awful for us to try to reconcile to. For my part, I've found that dwellin' on the knowledge that the Lord's sovereign 'n that the Lord gives 'n the Lord takes away helps some."

Lizzie said nothing. The tears just dripped faster.

"We have to accept God's will, darlin'," Brad reminded, squeezing her hand, which was without response.

"Les and Brad are right," Marc affirmed. "It was God's will. We shouldn't question the Lord, for we can't understand his ways. We must focus on the fact that all things work toward good for those who love the Lord."

Lizzie flinched as if she'd been slapped.

Her chin grew steely. Her eyes were pinched shut, stemming the tears. She lay in bed, rigid, her entire body in a state of tremors.

The men observed the change in Lizzie, then—drop-mouthed—searched each other's faces.

Beneath the pressure Lizzie was under, her face reddened, then grew a mottled purple from the effort. Marc reached for her wrist, locating her pulse.

Was it shock? Despair? Anguish? Approaching apoplexy? Anger? Or the coming final destruction of a strong faith that had reached its human limits and been tested to the snapping point? An instant later any confusion in their minds was dispelled as Lizzie shook off Marc's touch so viciously that he pinwheeled away from the bed in amazement.

"SHUT UP!" Lizzie screamed, her voice going hoarse from the forceful onslaught of the words on her vocal cords. "I DON'T WANT TO LISTEN TO SUCH TRIPE!"

Then Lizzie did something they'd never have dreamed would ever occur.

She screamed an oath, a harrowing, baying sound of stark rage.

Then she bellowed another.

"Dear Lord . . . she's comin' unhinged! Marc, do somethin'!"

"Mama! Please!" Lester begged, shaking her arm. She jerked her hand away from his touch and seemed poised to strike him before he ducked out of the way.

Marc moved quickly, leaning over Lizzie, pinning her shoulders to the mattress as she bared her teeth in anguish and whipped her face from side to side, her hair flying wildly.

Marc's calm, dispassionate face was inches from Lizzie's enraged expression.

"Lizzie . . . we've all been in such pain and grief. It's as if our very hearts have been ripped from our chests without benefit of anesthesia, losing Harmony as we did. When the pain's been almost more than we could deal with, as Christians it's helped us to dwell on the knowledge that as much as we all loved and cherished Harmony, the Lord divinely loves her way, way more than we could ever do at our human best."

Lizzie was in no mood to listen.

She wrested her hands up to clamp them over her ears and blot out what had become goading, infuriating words and what suddenly seemed like syrupy platitudes. She'd lived by those philosophies for all the years of her life, but now they seemed like excess, burdensome baggage that she was no longer willing to lug around.

"GET OUT!" Lizzie roared, every bit the match for a young Alton Wheeler at his most obnoxious, brawling best. "LEAVE ME ALONE! GET OUT OR I'LL BODILY THROW Y'ALL OUT ON YOUR EARS! *GET OUT!*"

With Lizzie's enraged orders rending the otherwise quiet infirmary, Marc slunk from his own property, with Brad and Lester a half step behind. They met in the study as Becky Rose Grant stood outside Lizzie's room to monitor her in her grief.

"What are we going to do?" Brad questioned brokenly, slumping into a chair, as if he had no strength with which to go on.

"Leave Lizzie's care to my staff and me," Marc quietly suggested. "We can deal with her wildness and abuse better than untrained immediate family. If we have to restrain her, we'll be aware when it's a necessity. That's hard for family to do."

"Tie her up?" Lester whispered, horrified.

"Only if we must. To keep her from harming herself—or others."

"Dear God," Brad said, his tone sick. "That it should've come to this."

"Pray God we can calm Lizzie and eventually heal her. Or . . . otherwise . . ." Marc's words faded away.

"Or what?" Brad prompted.

Marc swiveled his desk chair so he could stare out the window and avoid witnessing a reaction in Brad's and Lester's eyes.

"Or if somewhere down the line worse comes to even worse, we may have to think in terms of committal to the state mental hospital in Fergus Falls."

"An insane asylum?" Lester cried, aggrieved anew.

Marc quickly whirled his chair around and gestured to shush Lester before Lizzie could overhear the gist of their consultation and react accordingly.

"Pray it *never* comes to that," Marc murmured. "It'd break my heart to have to sign such papers. Even for a brief stay. But it seems our capacity to reach her and reason with her is diminishing. Lord knows how we've all tried."

When a horrible burst of maniacal laughter pealed through the corridors of the infirmary, the three men stiffened in jolted alarm.

"Oh, heavens!"

"Doctor Wellingham!" Becky Rose cried. "Come quick! Hurry! It's Lizzie, and she's—"

Becky Rose let out a thin scream, and the men all but tripped over each other in their haste to go to the corner sickroom.

Calmly Marc sent Becky Rose for some medications. "We'll force them on her if we have to. We must calm her. Pray sedation works. Sometimes when a patient is disturbed, its effectiveness is impaired."

"I'll be right back, Doctor," Becky Rose said.

"Bring restraints!" Marc called after her. His face was ashen as he looked from Brad to Lester.

They nodded, knowing how rough it was for Marc too.

Brad licked his lip. But Lester spoke. "Do whatever you must, Doc. And . . . we'll help ya."

"Thanks. The crazy strength Lizzie suddenly has, it's more than the nurses and I can deal with."

Lizzie, seeming to sense what was afoot, began to struggle.

"Traitors!" Lizzie screamed at Brad and Lester as they held her limbs while canvas and leather restraints were positioned and strapped to the bed frame. "How can you do this to me? I hate you. OH—I HATE ALL OF YOU!"

"Liz!"

"Mama! You don't mean that—"

"Get away from me! Traitors! Leave me *alone!* Get out of my sight!"

"C'mon," Marc said, putting a hand on Brad's shoulder and one on Lester's. "She needs to be alone. Right now the

232

sight of you is only riling her. It's not unusual for those who become this distraught to turn on their families."

"We've got to do something," Brad whispered. "This is terrible!"

Lester's shoulders sagged. "I've lost count of the times Mama's stood in the gap for Christians who were sufferin' the evil oppressions as the Lord was allowin' 'em to be tested by Satan, as he did with Job. It's time for us to stand in the gap for Ma."

"My plans exactly," Brad vowed.

"Folks from church will be falling into line to volunteer to stand in the gap on Lizzie's behalf. Count me in," Marc said.

"I have to have faith that the Lord will put a hedge around Ma and protect her from further tribulations. I can't take much more myself. Losing Thad ... then Harmony ... and being fearful that Ma's goin' to be next."

"Don't expect too much," Billy LeFave concurred with Dr. Wellingham's previous warnings, when the physician had counseled Billy and Serenity in his study before they were shown to Lizzie's sickroom.

"How she?" Serenity asked, her eyes large with pain and concern.

"Devastated," Billy replied. "She's not like the Ma that we've all known."

"I see her," Serenity said firmly, even though her slight form seemed to quail at the prospect, and she chewed her lip, seeming to muster courage.

"Go ahead," Billy sighed. "Try not to rile her."

"Never," Serenity solemnly agreed.

"I'm going to the kitchen to beg a cup of coffee from Marissa," said a shaken Billy LeFave, who'd offered testimony to Lizzie only to have wise words like she'd once offered him for his edification viciously flung back in his face, as if his beloved mother-in-law were a railing heathen.

"Go," Serenity said. She stared after him a moment, then turned, ducked into Lizzie's room, and paused for an instant—hesitantly, reflectively, prayerfully, and trusting the Lord that he would give her the words as he'd inspired and strengthened believers through the centuries.

"Mama Lizzie?" Serenity whispered.

At the sound, Lizzie stiffened as good manners vied with her anger, and she hung suspended as bitter and battling forces churned within her.

A suddenly weeping Serenity moved across the room, flung herself at Lizzie, and clung to the older woman who'd always had a heart of gold overflowing with love, concern, compassion, and caring.

Lizzie tried to maintain her defenses, but Serenity's heartbreak touched a vulnerable part. Lizzie struggled not to respond—not to care—for it hurt too much nowadays to allow herself to feel *anything*. But Serenity was like a tender creature intently burrowing into her arms and heart.

Lizzie was powerless not to eventually clasp the girl to her, returning her hugs. Lizzie's cheeks grew wet, and she knew not if it was from her own tears—which she no longer allowed herself to shed, preferring the choking inner feeling that somehow filled the dark void—or if they were evidence of Serenity's heartbreak.

"Harmony be sad. . . ." Serenity fumbled for words, her lips so close to Lizzie's ear. "She taught me . . . be happy in all things. Know that Lord have his plans. Not all things cause smiles, but sorrow happens to make way for God's joy."

"No," Lizzie tried to deny, but Serenity would not allow it.

234

Her voice grew stronger, and the testimony of a newborn child in Christ speaking wisdom to a mature Christian seemed to dissolve Lizzie's fury.

"The Lord love Harmony. You. Me. All people. Right?"

"Yes." Lizzie was powerless to argue.

"Harmony called home to heaven. Work here done. I miss Harmony. But I rejoice—I see her in Glory when *my* work here done! Then I go home, too!"

Lizzie's hard, stiff, unyielding form—which had been rigid and defensive for so long, as if she could protect herself from added hurts—began to soften.

"You're right. Oh darlin', you're right! And what a work on earth Harmony performed with you, Serenity, and all o' the people she touched. Harmony harvested many, many souls for him! You will, too, healin' the tribe in Harmony's stead, able to do so because she taught you so well that you can tend to the ill without having to seek out others 'cept in exceptional cases."

"You forgive Serenity?" the girl softly inquired.

Lizzie hugged the contrite, confessing girl to her and felt as if one daughter had been taken from her but another young woman had been transplanted into her life to blossom in that corner of her world.

"Exactly as I've been forgiven myself," Lizzie assured.

"You get well?" Serenity asked, then pressed a kiss to Lizzie's cheek.

"I have to," Lizzie said. "Sometimes great wisdom comes out o' the mouth of babes. You may be an infant in Christ, but he uses you well."

"He use you too. Much times."

Lizzie managed a smile—the first bona fide smile in weeks. "Reckon he does at that, and bein' as there's still breath in my body, that means he ain't through putting me to good use some more—iffen I'm willing to do his bidding and serve him."

"Mama Lizzie—Serenity happy!"

"Lizzie's feelin' a mite happier, too, darlin' girl," she whispered, her voice husky with emotion. "I've got to get well, quit feelin' sorry for myself, stop doubtin' the goodness of the Lord, and cease bein' such a piker in matters of faith!"

"You felt . . . abandoned," Serenity said.

"That I did, Serenity," Lizzie admitted. "Until you reminded me that when we're feeling farthest from the Lord is when he's actually hoverin' near, wantin' us to rely on him 'n find a way to give praise and worship in all that we do."

"Yes, Mama Lizzie," Serenity agreed.

"Guess I've learned a heap by wallowin' my way through these dark times. A time or two, I tried to pray before I plumb give up on the effort. It's been even longer since I was able to truly worship," Lizzie mused.

Serenity gave her a confused look.

Lizzie laughed softly. "Among one of the many things clarified in my mind, endurin' all of this chaos and confusion, is that when I pray—it's to tell the Lord what I'm a-wantin' him to do to please my will. But when I worship, Serenity, that's when I accept his will and what he sends my way, without cryin' or complaint."

"We pray?" Serenity suggested, not quite understanding.

"Sure, darlin', but first let's offer some worship."

Spring was finally in the air.

"Sure has been a long, rugged winter," Lester observed when he and Brad took a few moments of ease after helping in the dining room and before they had to turn their hands to midmorning duties.

"I'll say it has been. Be nice to see Billy again. I'm glad he still considers us his family."

"Be nice to see Serenity too. Joy's really looking forward to it."

"Those girls have a lot in common—more, it seems, each time they get together."

"From what Bill said, Serenity's been hankerin' to see Ma."

"Mayhap it'll do Liz a world o' good. The last visit sure helped. Turned Liz's attitude right around. She took a quick likin' to that girl the week o' the Big Fire."

"The fact that Serenity was a close friend to Harmony was good enough for Ma."

"For all of us."

"Billy says that Serenity's been as heartsick and lost without Harmony as he 'n the rest of us."

Brad nodded. "Havin' someone else in the general vicinity to share his sorrow has probably helped him face it 'n heal from it."

"The entire tribe's been more than kind to him."

"He's fam'bly to the Chippewa too."

"Heavens but it'll be good to see 'em again. Joy's been fussin' preparing rooms for their stay."

"I'm hopin' that seein' Billy—and Serenity—will help Liz snap the rest o' the way out of the doldrums she's been in for so long."

"Ma's made a lot of progress."

"Thank the Lord we didn't have to commit her."

"So many willin' to stand in the gap for her made a heap of difference."

"Kind of strange the way she took on, ain't it?"

"Sure was," Lester mused. "Ma's always taken everything in stride—I reckon we expected more of the same from her.

And Billy? Now he's surprised me—diggin' deeper into his faith, grounding himself in the Lord, trustin' God, acceptin' what I'd have swore he'd have found so unacceptable he might have turned to his old ways."

"The Lord works in mysterious ways."

"Mayhap Billy's strength of conviction will help Ma's thinkin' return completely to normal."

"I was afraid Liz was goin' to totally lose her faith there for a while."

"Reckon, truth be told, you've got a mighty powerful faith when you can get angry with God." Lester gave a rueful smile. "He's mighty enough to deal with it and know where Mama's heart was really at nonetheless."

"That he is," Brad agreed.

"I heard it said by Ma more'n a time or two that whatever don't kill you often makes you stronger. Marc was tellin' me once that when you break a bone, it's actually stronger than the limb was before, due to the fact that when the fracture heals, it slaps down extra layers of calcium and strengthens in more'n the bones elsewhere."

"That might be the case with your mama's faith. Sometimes havin' the free will to doubt—and then have those doubts proven wrong—only increases the solidity of faith."

"But it's pure misery when we're a-livin' through it."

"Be a while before we have to start peelin' taters 'n helping Joy with the dinner duties. What do you say we stroll over to the infirmary to greet your ma good morning?"

Quickly Lester arose. "Best idea I've heard today."

"And the mornin's still young!"

Five minutes later Marissa answered the door and let them in.

"What a surprise!" she said upon seeing them. "But . . . but . . ."

238

"But what?" Brad echoed.

"Well . . . your surprise is going to rather ruin our surprise."

"Do tell!" Lester urged.

A moment later there was a commotion down the hall.

Brad and Lester turned, stunned, then broke into grins when they saw Lizzie, dressed in street clothes, her hair neatly coifed, carrying a carpetbag with belongings that had been brought to the infirmary for her convenience.

"Marc's discharging me from his care today," a calm Lizzie said. "Ain't that wonderful?"

"Oh, Liz darlin'! Seems like forever since you've been by my side." Brad crushed her to him while she covered his face with kisses.

"Oh, Les, it's goin' to be heaven to see you 'n Joy anytime I want. I'm goin' to get back in the harness so's that gal can have a rest when she needs it. That's my grandbaby she's carryin'!"

"Let me take your carpetbag, Liz."

Lester crooked his arm into a loop. "Ready to go, Ma? It'll still be a surprise—Joy ain't expectin' this at all."

"Then we'll be *real quiet*," Lizzie said, her eyes sparkling with good humor, "and I'll sneak up behind her 'n go 'BOO!'"

Brad and Lester laughed.

"Naw, I'd better not do that. Not with her in a delicate condition. Just seein' me up 'n about and home to stay will be surprise enough."

"We've got a surprise for you, too," Brad said.

"What?" Lizzie cried.

"You'll have to wait 'til you can see for yourself."

"When?"

"Maybe when we get to the hotel," Brad said, then winked across at Lester.

"Or"—Lester cleared his throat—"maybe not."

"You two!" Lizzie scolded, then gave a hoot of laughter before she slipped one arm through her husband's, keeping her arm through her son's, and let them escort her to the hotel the long way home so that she could greet the good people who'd stood by her and had been standing in the gap.

"Good thing we spent a few extra minutes gettin' here," Brad observed. "Liz, I think your surprise has arrived."

Looking around, then spotting Billy's mare and rickety wagon, she released Brad's and Lester's arms and hurried ahead of them into the hotel. Her pale complexion was high-lighted pink from the exertion. She was thin—thinner than she'd ever been—but she was alive and almost back to being the Lizzie they all knew and loved.

"Will!" Lizzie cried out.

"Ma—you're discharged!" Billy blurted, shocked to find her standing in the parlor of the Grant Hotel.

"Right you are! And just in time to welcome you home, son."

"I brought more company. Serenity's with me. The chief has a favor he'd really like to ask of you, Ma. He'll understand if you have to turn him down. But I promised him that I'd inquire."

"Don't keep me in suspense."

"Way-Say-Com-a-Gouk—you call her Serenity—has no ma and hasn't for a number of years. The women of the tribe have looked after her along with their own. Harmony was educating Serenity, and the chief saw how good it was for her and how helpful it was for her to learn white folks' ways. He'd appreciate it if you could put her to work at the hotel for a while. She's already taught the tribal womenfolk a lot of the healing ways she's learned. Joy'd be a wonderful influence."

"Why, Will LeFave—that sounds more like that chief's doin' me a favor than requestin' one! I'd cotton to such an arrangement, wouldn't I, Brad?"

Brad grinned and shook Billy's hand in greeting. "We both would."

"We all would," Lester spoke up.

"Where is Serenity?" Lizzie asked.

"You have to ask, Ma?" Lester teased. "With Joy, of course."

"They're coming down the staircase now," Brad said when he heard their footsteps overhead.

"Serenity!" Lizzie cried out, opening her arms to the girl.

Shyly Way-Say-Com-a-Gouk smiled, then burrowed into the older woman's embrace.

"Oh, child, it's so good to see you."

"Good be here, Lizzie Ma."

"Looks like we've got ourselves another young'un," Brad surmised, "this one arrivin' purty well full-grown."

Lizzie held her and looked over Serenity's shoulder at her misty-eyed family clustered close.

"Harmony knew what she was askin'," Lester said. "Serenity was remembered in Harmony's dyin' words. She asked Billy to watch out for Serenity, Ma, and for you to watch after both Billy and Serenity, and then she said that she was givin' them both into your care as their mother."

"Oh, how touching," Lizzie said. "Just like Christ on the cross gave his mother to mankind, and his apostle to his mama."

"Poor girl," Brad said. "Undoubtedly Harmony knew what

it'd be for Serenity after her passin'. Hard for an Indian girl 'thout the same background of faith to understand and accept."

"I've been reading chapters from the Book of Job to Serenity," Billy said, "translating into Chippewa as I go along. It seems to help Serenity . . . and me. It hasn't been easy. But we're both accepting it as his will and aware that someday it'll be revealed to us how it's served his purpose. Some fine day when all the tears will be wiped away."

"I need to be reviewing that area of the Good Book myself," Lizzie remarked quietly, goose bumps of delight tingling all over her when she heard Will witnessing from his experience, a true man of God.

"It's helped me to accept what all's happened, the bad along with the good. Serenity couldn't quite get a grip on the concept, and God forgive me if I led her wrong, but onct I explained it to her like the ultimate poker game, with Job anted up in the pot, and likened it to the Lord a-betting on Job's love for him come what may, she caught on real quick."

"A poker game?" Lizzie cried. "Now *that* I've got to hear!"

"Do tell!" Lester said, grinning.

"This should be good!" Brad said.

"Sometime when we've got a spell of unbroken time, I'll explain it. Sure cleared it up for me, for Serenity, and—I gather from what she's said—for the understanding of the entire tribe."

"Praise God!" Lizzie said, chuckling softly. "He does work in mysterious ways, don't he? *Poker rules 'n play!*"

"It's good to be home," Billy mused.

Lizzie looked around the hotel, and it was as if the dwelling had given her a warm, welcoming embrace.

"Amen to that!"

"Better put on your best Sunday-go-to-meetin' dress,

Liz," Brad said. "You've got today off so's you can socialize with those who come to dine over their noon hour."

"What a lovely idea!" Lizzie agreed.

Lester gave his mother a warm hug. "Tomorrow you'll be parin' taters right along with the rest of us."

Lizzie sniffed the air and nodded approvingly over the aroma of succulent baked chicken. "I can hardly wait!"

"Be nice to have Serenity under our roof," Brad mused. "I know she's a hard worker. 'Tween Serenity and Joy, and with Les thrown in for good measure, Mama, we may even slip away more often to spend time with our children."

"Two sons," Lizzie said, touching Will's arm along with Lester's, "and two beautiful daughters," she added, quickly embracing Serenity and Joy. "How lucky can a couple be, Pa?" Lizzie paused. "And a son 'n daughter off 'n away livin' with the Lord . . . in that splendid mansion where there's perfectly prepared rooms awaitin' for all o' us."

Epilogue

"ALL ABOARD!" BRAD Mathews called out theatrically after he'd helped Lizzie—and Serenity, who was dressed in some of Harmony's cast-off clothing, which fit and suited her beautifully—into the carriage.

"This is going to be so much fun!" Lizzie crowed.

Serenity merely nodded and smiled, pleased.

"Got your Chippewa duds, sweetheart, so's you don't give the chief a coronary when you canoe out to the island?"

Serenity grinned and tapped the carpetbag nestled at her feet, which contained her bead-decorated, fringed buckskins.

"I hope the chief won't be displeased," Lizzie fretted.

"We'll find out soon enough," Brad replied.

"Ain't it nice o' the tribe to hold a party for us? Billy says it'll be a regular feast!"

"And of course Liz Mathews is adding to the bounty," Brad commented, nodding toward the hamper brimming with his wife's tastiest culinary efforts.

"Just a few treats made out of items that it ain't easy for the squaw women to acquire."

"I'm really lookin' forward to it myself," Brad said.

"Be nice to spend a few nights at the cabin with Will while Serenity has a holiday with her people, too."

"Everything's workin' out, ain't it?"

"Sure is. There for a while, I wondered if my life would ever feel like it was workin' out again. Wondered if I'd ever know happiness for my own again. I walked a really long, dark valley, Brad."

"I know you did, darlin'."

"It's plumb scary," Lizzie said. "Never would've known what it was to almost lose my faith." She gave a helpless shudder. "I wouldn't wish that experience on anyone."

"Nor would I," Brad said. "But your faith is even stronger these days because of it."

"Reckon it is. Just like you don't miss the water 'til the well goes dry, I 'spect you don't realize how much your faith means to you 'til you live through feelin' like you lost it."

"You had us all purty scared," Brad admitted.

"The Lord 'n I . . . we wasn't on the best o' speakin' terms there for a while," Lizzie ruefully pointed out. "I felt so vulnerable, so forsaken. . . . Started to doubt the Lord. . . . Wondered iffen he even cared. If he'd turned his back on me."

"He never left you, Liz."

"I know that now," she said. "When there was leavin' done, it was me turnin' my back on him, not t'other way around."

"I've never held a hand of poker in my life," Brad said, "but I've been thinkin' about what Billy said about likenin' it to a game of poker. I have some rudimentary ideas o' how the game's dealt out and played . . . and it really set me to thinkin', Liz. I reread the Book of Job myself in recent weeks, and I think I understand what Bill, who used to be a poker playin' bloke in his wild 'n woolly days, meant."

"Do tell!" Lizzie said.

"Mayhap I'll let Billy explain it himself, darlin', but I do have one thing to state, while hopin' my wordin' won't find offense with the Lord. As these past months—in fact, all o' the years of your life—have rolled on, Liz Mathews . . . I know that just as the Lord was believin' in ol' Job, well, sweetheart, the good Lord was bettin' on you too. And in the end—he won!"

Lizzie gave her head a rueful shake and was helpless to

contain a grin when she thought back to Billy LeFave's wild arrival in town and the disturbance that his presence had created when he got injured in a brawl at the Black Diamond Saloon over a dispute in a poker game.

"Life has a funny way of workin' out, don't it? Will's applyin' his ol' misdeeds in the past to his deeper understanding of the Word as a Christian. This really does add a new level of meaning to the wisdom that eventually all things, even the Lord's allowing of evil actions, work toward good for those who love him."

"Even poker?" Brad asked, winking.

"Mayhap. Although it'll remain an untried mystery to me!"

Serenity listened on, smiled, and said nothing, but Brad and Lizzie could sense the aura of eagerness that enveloped her as they neared Billy's lakeside property.

Expecting visitors, Billy had stayed near the cabin, and at the first sounds of the mare's clip-clop on the path, he came to meet them. He gave Serenity a hand down, looking at her with admiring amazement at the changes that two months of town living and Lizzie Mathews' guiding hand—along with Joy Childers' help—had wrought.

He assisted Lizzie from the carriage while Brad set the brake, wrapped the reins, and hopped down himself.

"Will—good to see you!" Lizzie cried, folding him into a hug.

"William. Pleased see again," Serenity said and politely extended her hand, which Billy shook.

"Son! You're lookin' fine!" Brad observed and pumped his son-in-law's hand.

Lizzie's eyes roved the nearby area, then lingered on the settling mound that was Harmony's resting place.

Wordlessly Will offered Lizzie his arm, knowing, without being told, her desired destination.

Serenity, who'd visited the grave so many times, seemed about to rush ahead but then, out of mannerliness, hung back to let "Lizzie Ma" go first.

"It's a peaceful settin', ain't it?" Lizzie said.

Swallowing hard, Billy nodded, blinking a skim of tears from his eyes.

"You've beautified it right nice," Brad said, his own voice thick and husky with emotions.

Serenity was the one who was overcome. Unmindful of the soil, she dropped to her knees, the skirt of her dress scraping across the grass, staining it. Lizzie patted the girl's shoulder and made a mental note to work on the smears of green while Serenity was in her buckskins, visiting the tribe. It'd look fresh as ever by the time Way-Say-Com-a-Gouk was ready to return to Williams.

The girl knelt on Harmony's grave, praying, then wiping tears. When she arose, her eyes were red.

She fell into Lizzie's arms.

"So sorry," she quietly sobbed again and again.

"Shhh . . . don't apologize, darlin'," Lizzie crooned. "Tain't your fault."

"So sorry," Serenity murmured one last time, then she wiped her tears again and hurried toward the cabin to change clothes and prepare for her trip out onto the lake in the canoe that was always left at Billy LeFave's for her use in returning to her people.

Lizzie insisted that Serenity have a quick bite to eat before she left for the island, and Serenity chose to linger over coffee, listening raptly to the conversation, occasionally adding a word or two of her own and smiling with peace and contentment.

"Will, whyn't you walk Serenity to her canoe? Give her a steadyin' hand," Lizzie said, "whilst I do up the dishes."

Brad rubbed his chin and mouth, coughing, as the two exited the cabin.

"Liz Mathews ... iffen I didn't know better ... I'd think you were up to your ol' tricks."

Lizzie gave him an arched look. "Mayhap I just am. And if that be the case—so what? Harmony loved 'em both—I think she'd be smilin' down on their lives if they come to love one another."

"You inveterate matchmakers!" Brad teased.

"This un's goin' to be easy as pie," Lizzie predicted. "Or ain't you noticed?"

"Noticed what?" Brad inquired.

"Men!" Lizzie sniffed. "Why ... it's as plain as the nose on her pretty face that Way-Say-Com-a-Gouk is very attracted to William LeFave. In her own way ... she already loves him. But you mark my words—she's goin' to end up lovin' him a lot more. And he's goin' to one day wise up to the situation 'n respond."

"You think so?"

"I know so!" Lizzie said.

"Will's sittin' down on the dock," Brad said. "I think I'll grab a fishin' pole and go join him. See if I can't hook a lunker while we watch day's end."

Lizzie abruptly reached for a dishtowel. "Think I'll leave the last o' these dishes for seed. Lord knows they'll wait for my return. I ain't watched the glory of a sunset over water in quite a spell. No time like the present to do it."

Hand in hand Lizzie and Brad walked to the dock, where Billy LeFave chewed on a straw of lake grass and mused reflectively.

"A penny for your thoughts, son," Lizzie said, then turned to Brad expectantly as he dug for a copper coin.

She flipped it to Billy, who laughed.

"Wasn't thinking of anything in particular, Ma," he said, then added, "just enjoying the peace of finding moments of ... serenity in the storm."